The

Weight

of

Light

To the Staff of the Washington County Library —

Thanks for Reading!

Sandra Rodriguez

The Weight of Light

A Novel of Redemption

SANDRIA RODRIGUEZ

Washington County Library
201 East Third Street
Plymouth, NC 27962

Copyright © 2011 by Sandria Rodriguez

Langdon Street Press
212 3rd Avenue North, Suite 290
Minneapolis, MN 55401
612.455.2293
www.langdonstreetpress.com

All rights reserved. No part of this publication may be reproduced, stored in a retrieval system, or transmitted, in any form or by any means, electronic, mechanical, photocopying, recording, or otherwise, without the prior written permission of the author.

ISBN-13: 978-1-936782-04-8
LCCN: 2011922873

Distributed by Itasca Books

Cover Design and Typeset by Kristeen Wegner

Printed in the United States of America

In memory of my parents,

Burnett and Rosetta Williams,

and with special thanks to my family

and to Elizabeth "Buffy" Calvert

CONTENTS

PART 1 EMMA (1815-1906)

1   Tucker the Disconsolate 1
2   Silas the Steadfast 18
3   Emma Aloft 33
4   Abraham Laughed 43

PART 2 JUSTICE (1874-1914)

5   Idyll 51
6   Promise Keeping 57
7   Brokenness 65
8   Innocence 77
9   Found 84
10   Lost 87
11   Guidance 91
12   Baptism 98
13   Doubt 105
14   Belief 111

PART 3   BESS (1890-1967)

15	Birth	120
16	Weight	123
17	Courage	134
18	Discord	137
19	Learning	140
20	Emancipation	147
21	Signs	152
22	Murder	155
23	Grief	165
24	Loss	173
25	Deprivation	177
26	Irretrievability	185
27	Poison	191
28	Bequest	196
29	Discovery	202
30	Light	209
31	Revelations	214

PART ONE

EMMA (1815-1906)

I was born a slave on a plantation in Franklin County, Virginia. I am not quite sure of the exact place or exact date of my birth, but at any rate I suspect I must have been born somewhere and at some time.

from *Up From Slavery*, Booker T. Washington, 1901

1

Tucker the Disconsolate

[She] was . . . put to the meanest work that could be found, and although only ten years of age, she was often compelled to perform labour, which, under ordinary circumstances, would have been thought too hard for one much older.

from *Clotel; Or, The President's Daughter,*
William Wells Brown, 1853

THE INDIAN'S EMPTY EYE socket reddened and quivered faintly in unison with his heart. Tucker saw these signs, and his spirit rejoiced. Grimy and stubbled as a fire-scorched patch of wire grass, Tucker's face did not betray his awareness, but his mind, reacting, prodded his body, and he moved. He shifted his weight from one buttock onto both, confident that his aching tailbone could endure the wooden chair until the end. Clouds of abysmal luck that had dogged him for three days seemed to part and float away. The jack, ten, nine, eight, and seven of hearts, splayed fanlike against his narrow chest, assured his battered nerves of victory. He had known all along that when the Indian was thoroughly exhausted, his open socket would twitch with purplish redness like a halved and pitted plum. Every would-be gambler throughout seven contiguous counties knew that much. What Tucker hadn't known was how long it would take to wear the Indian out.

"Why don't you cover your eye hole up when you first start to get tired?" the Indian's son, too young to be a poker player himself, had once asked his father.

"You can't build confidence and trust by changing things during a poker game, specially when you're winning," the Indian had answered. "Doing something crazy as that can get you cut up thinner 'n a hog bladder, faster 'n the eye can blink. Better to lose a hand or two every now and then. Remember that."

"Well, why not cover it up from the beginning?" the boy had persisted.

"Leaving it out's my little gift to human nature. Most folks love a free freak show. Forget to tuck yourself in after taking a leak, and men folks with private parts just like yourn'll climb all over one another tryin' to get a peek. If players didn't want to be unnerved by this here empty hole, I'm sure they wouldn't be. I say, 'Let the gawker beware!' Remember that, too."

Now Tucker read the signs in the Indian's eye socket as clear as daylight.

"I b'lieve he's right upset, the sumbitch!" Tucker thought. "He's holdin' some shit-ass hand, praise be to glory! Ruinin' a man ain't enough for 'im. Got to get mad if he lose one hand! Well, he gon' lose this one, and I hope his lousy carcass rots in hell soon's he does! Ain't nothin' but a stinkin' half-breed no way. Got no business playin' 'gainst white folks so's he can cheat 'em out of what's theirn."

When the game was over, Tucker had won a pregnant slave. But hanging on until the one-eyed Indian lost a hand had proved costly. Now Tucker was left with no choice but to go on home and prepare his wife for the removal of her parents' remaining heirlooms, furniture hauled at great cost from England and carted over land and river to meet its sorry fate. Their money and jewelry, inherited by their daughter, had disappeared soon after her marriage.

Later, their slaves had been split up and sold for ready cash.

"But the baby growin' in the belly of that slave I won gon' be yourn," Tucker anxiously promised his wailing wife who had threatened to "put the law on him" and have him removed from her home since all he ever did was "strive for its total destruction."

"You need somebody to he'p out some 'round here, do anything you want done," Tucker said. "That baby gon' do that, soon's it's growed big enough. Meantime, the mammy, that grown slave, she gon' start right in to make your life easier. That's all I was tryin' to do, to make your life a l'il easier."

So the baby, born in 1815 on a dilapidated homestead near the foothills of Tennessee, became a house slave, named Emma by Mrs. Tucker, and by nine years of age was running the run-down house herself.

* * *

To Mrs. Tucker, Emma was a blessing beyond any since her marriage, miles beneath her station, to the practically illiterate and totally penniless Robert Tom Tucker, a profligate gambler who had cropped up like an overnight toadstool after her mother's death. He had shown up in time to earn fifty cents helping to dig her mother's grave in the rich marrow of earth that had become the family cemetery. This was not a site to invite such stone rubbings as tempted tourists to the Chase family plot at Christ Episcopal Church in Exeter, England. There, Mrs. Tucker's antecedents rested in splendid mausoleums and magnificent sarcophagi under the stony gazes of towering angels. But here, in loamy soil that would someday produce the best tobacco in the hilly region, lay the lonesome grave of Mrs. Tucker's father, Albert Chase. After her ruinous marriage, Mrs. Tucker could only thank God that her mother had not lived the six months between her funeral and her daughter's nuptials, more shameful an example of how-the-mighty-have-fallen than even that envious, controlling, cold-hearted, lipless witch could have borne, tearless, to witness.

That the marriage remained childless came as no surprise to Mrs. Tucker. Her deepest, darkest secrets from her husband were her true age of forty-five when they married and her status, regarding menopause, as completely over that bloody mess. She went so far in perpetuating the myth of her youthfulness as to blame crying jags and mood swings on "that time of the month," not realizing that her husband abhorred children and that his interest in their marriage extended no further than his own material comfort and security. Tucker believed that a child's pathetic helplessness, bottomless pit of a stomach, and wailing insistence on being the center of everyone's attention made parenthood an evil to be avoided at all costs. During times of intimacy with Mrs. Tucker, he was unfailing at pulling out before ejaculating into a lidless fruit jar that he kept, expressly for that purpose, under the bed. To quiet her ardent protestations, Tucker would knowingly invoke the socially sanctioned spirit of Southern womanhood.

"My poor dead mama drew her last breath while birthin' me, and I just can't let my manly wants and desires be the cause of you leavin' this green earth," he would tell his wife while patting her shoulder. "Sure, it's a right big sacrifice I'm makin,' but I'm willin' to make it. You the purest, prettiest, saintliest, sweetest thing ever happened to me, and I ain't never gon' let nothin' hurt you. I ruther bear this here hurt myself."

To a few men of coarse character with whom he drank and caroused, Tucker contended that "ballin'" his wife, instead of the whore they shared when they had the money, would be more to his liking if he could keep the state flag, a banner that he loved and respected, over her long, muley face the whole time he was "up on top of her hard-ass sawhorse of a body." In truth, not a sprig of patriotism for Tennessee existed in Tucker's breast. He did not hail from that fair state and could not have identified her flag if it had been draped around his thickened waist, post-coitus, to hide his shrinking prong.

Inveterate liar though he was, and though he seldom harbored an honest wish to tell his wife the truth, Tucker's selfish prediction about Emma's future usefulness to her mistress proved prophetic. The burden that Mrs. Tucker bore as guardian of the family's hearth and health was lightened commensurately by Emma's increasing age and aptitude for housewifery. As a young girl, Emma quickly absorbed all that Mrs. Tucker could teach from her store of "knowledge befitting a slave." And as the mistress began to disappear more and more often beneath the tunnel of her sunbonnet to avoid aggravating her severe erythema, and later behind the wide front portal to the house, Emma became indispensable as her only dependable link to the outside world. Mrs. Tucker's social standing seemed to have evaporated after her marriage, and while a few folks charitably defended her unfortunate choice of a husband by pointing out her ignorance, at the time, of Tucker's true nature, they failed to convince anyone, including themselves, that she had not stepped into a shit pile with her eyes and nose wide open, cowardly accepting the first proposal of marriage that she had ever received rather than risk facing the remainder of her unhappy life alone. In truth, after merciful death had claimed her harridan of a mother, Mrs. Tucker fully expected an additional gift from God, reasoning that she deserved greater recompense for having suffered so long under her mother's iron fist. As an answer to her prayers, Tucker's appearance had been God's twisted joke, since Tucker was more daunting a trial than Old Lady Albert Chase had ever been. God's true blessing to Mrs. Tucker was Emma, who took on all the shopping for the family, as well as all errands and business concerning money. After all, Mr. Tucker could not be trusted, in his wife's

English vernacular, "to take his arse within horseback riding distance of a whorehouse or card table with a fucking penny!"

* * *

During her early adolescence, Emma attained her full adult stature of five feet eight inches—shorter than some women at the time, but taller than most. She was wide shouldered and expansive of breasts and buttocks, so perhaps it was Tucker's greedy eyes that conceived, planted, germinated, and nourished his scheme to breed slaves for sale on the open market with Emma as mare and himself as stud.

"Who else I'm gon' use for sirin' niggers?" he asked himself. "Bad luck's done taken every slave buck off of the place, and the po'-white sharecropper men folks we usin' to farm, well, who in their right mind would let somethin' that sorry father slaves 'spected to work, and work hard, too? White trash couldn't be trusted to keep their mouth shut 'bout my business no how." Then Tucker remembered a saying that condoned his planned actions: "God don't he'p nobody 'ceptin' the ones try to he'p theyself. Why's he gon' he'p somebody too triflin' to lift a finger for their own good? He won't do it. Says so in the Bible."

* * *

At 11:05 on a sultry June night, Tucker slipped out of bed, confident that the rhythm of snorts and starts from his wife meant deep sleep. He was reasonably confident, too, of the time, for day after day, several times a day, he had counted off seconds and minutes after the cast-iron mantle clock had clanged its single peal to announce the hour. These exercises in judging the length of five minutes were conducted during daylight hours, allowing Tucker to stroll nonchalantly past the clock to check his accuracy, when his mental calculations indicated that five minutes had passed. Tucker was not a meticulous man, but the necessity of correctly identifying a time of night when his wife was submerged in deep sleep was paramount to the success of his life's grandest scheme.

Mrs. Tucker had an irritating habit of waking around midnight and prowling through the house for a solid hour like an inconsiderate ghost. She would light candles in the bedroom and fall asleep reading in a creaking rocking chair. As often as not, she would nod off and drop her book on the floor, its thud startling Tucker awake and plunging him into paroxysms of certainty that he had been shot. Often she was hungry at night and would clomp around the kitchen, helping herself to leftovers from supper, clanging her flatware against her plate like a demented woodpecker. Sometimes she would sit at her father's desk writing and sobbing intermittently. Tucker did not know that she was filling pages and pages with raving remonstrances against her father, Albert Chase, for dying and leaving her defenseless, epistles that she would later bury in shallow, hastily dug holes at the head of his grave. Had Tucker known, he would not have cared unless caring could have somehow helped to preserve his sleep.

When Tucker slipped out of bed at approximately 11:05 p.m., he had silently counted off his estimation of five minutes following the mantle clock's clang. He put on the soft leather slippers that had belonged to Mrs. Tucker's dead father and that were a million sizes too large for Tucker's smallish feet, shorter by at least two inches than his wife's man-like paddles. He had once tried on a pair of her everyday button tops, simply because they looked so huge, while she was safely ensconced in her bath, only to find that his toes and heels were practically lost in the roomy expanses. Yet, Mrs. Tucker had complained bitterly and often that the shoes were "trying to rub every bit of soft skin off my poor feet."

"These here slippers of your papa's mighty comfortable," Tucker had offered helpfully. "Maybe you oughta try 'em."

"Why on earth do you think a lady such as I would wear a man's shoes?" Mrs. Tucker had retorted in her most exasperated voice. She herself had kept the slippers soft by rubbing them with a tallow-saturated cloth, a job that she had undertaken during her father's long illness and had cherished ever since. Keeping the slippers soft, even after her father was too ill to rise from his bed and put them on, had imbued her with a consoling pretext of control over uncontrollable circumstances. After her father's death, the smell and texture of tallow still seemed to comfort her. Periods of stress often found her fleeing to the area of the washhouse where the lengthening fingers of candles were dipped and hung, dipped and hung.

"Wanta see how I'm gon' add some dried mint leaf to one batch of tallow, some dried rose petal to another, Missus?" Emma asked Mrs. Tucker, whose errant husband had come home without her father's watch suspended from the gold chain and fob that no longer hung from the pocket of his vest. "I done ground up the mint and roses and made a little batch of green powder and a little batch of red. They gon' make a mighty pretty smell when the candles burnin'."

Guiltily, Mrs. Tucker busied herself by helping Emma with the candle-making, work, she believed, that was meant for black hands, not her own white ones, now as brown and speckled by age and rough tasks as the Dominique hen eggs that she so coveted for breakfast.

Around 11:05 p.m. when Tucker slipped out of bed, he did not bother to don his late father-in-law's often-darned dressing gown, shortened many years ago to fit him, both in sleeve and in hem, by Emma's mother who had been sold five years after the marriage to pay a gambling debt. Tucker wore a nightshirt, an article of clothing as foreign to his experience before his marriage as was the dressing gown now folded neatly across the back of a chair. He made his way cautiously out of the room and down the stairs of the two-story house, out a side door, and around to the back of the wraparound veranda. Tucker was happy.

He paused on the steps leading to the backyard and contemplated the world around him. The inky sky, pierced by infinite stars, hung just above the treetops lining the nearby hills. This world, this unlikely Eden that he had been allowed to inhabit for a while, seemed intimate and finite, contained in a tight circumference between earth and sky, with him at its center. The moist night air rested softly upon his skin, and he thought of his imaginary mother, not of his natural mother, May, who had borne him from the seed of her own father, delivering him during the noon hour when she had left the field to boil cabbage, potatoes, and dumplings for the family's dinner. Her water had broken in the woodshed, and she had staggered backwards under the cleaving pains of labor and the weight of the stove wood that she carried. Dropping the armload of wood, she had squatted in the powdery dirt and reached beneath her open thighs to catch the life that was her third son. She had severed the umbilical cord with a hatchet used for splitting kindling, suctioned into her mouth the mucous blocking the baby's nose and throat, and rinsed him at the pump like a freshly plucked chicken, removing the paste and blood clinging to his skin. Then she had wrapped him in a clean flour sack and placed him in a small, cloth-lined wooden box with a cover made from chicken wire. She had thrown a piece of clean cheesecloth over the box and hastened to hide it in the teeming green jungle of the cornfield.

"Whar you a-goin' to in sich a hurry?" her father asked four days later, on Sunday afternoon, when dinner had been cooked and eaten and the kitchen cleaned. She had exited the house and begun to walk slowly in the direction of the cornfield.

"Goin' to relieve myself in the field," she responded. "Too hot and sticky in the outhouse today. Seem like the smell in there would near 'bout turn my stomach and make me lose my dinner."

"You ain't et much of nothin'. Can't live 'thout somethin' t'eat, and you eatin' for two."

That evening, he came in for supper carrying the box and its four-day-old cargo. "Looky here what I done found, young 'uns," he said to May's towheaded sisters and brothers while looking straight at her. "May here can take care of 'im 'til I git a chance to find 'im a good home. He a right pert li'l feller. Been fed good. Clothes clean as a whistle."

When six weeks had passed, May's father placed the boy in his little wood and chicken-wire box on the floor of the cart, settled himself on the buckboard, grabbed the mule's reins, and disappeared into the distance just as he had done twice before. Also as he had previously done, he returned from his journey the following day and resumed his almost nightly visits to May's corn husk mattress.

Tucker did not think of May, his biological mother, of whom he knew little, but of the imaginary mother that his mind had first created and summoned when he was a lonely, unloved child. Always rich in kindness and beauty, she was unerringly bereft of sound example or advice, and now she morphed, as she had done since his adolescence, into soft and suckable parts of womanness. Recently, conjuring up his imaginary mother had drawn his mind to the child Emma's breasts that seemed to him to stand at attention and salute his mouth and tongue whenever she was nearby. He allowed his hand to move underneath his tent-like nightshirt and to encircle his manhood, a mere bump like the knobby fetlock on the back of a horse's leg. "Come on, boy," he told it encouragingly, appreciatively, manipulating it with consummate skill. Still stimulating himself with his right hand, he stepped off the veranda and stole upon the windowless room attached to the summer kitchen where Emma slept.

For a moment Tucker was taken aback to find Emma fully awake, sitting cross-legged on her straw tick completing intricate embroidery of a large white peacock on an ecru linen tablecloth. Working by the dim light of a single candle, Emma's head was bent over her work, and she did not hear Tucker's few steps from the veranda across the dew-muffled grass. She had stripped to her under skirt and had propped the door to the room half open to enjoy the stirring night breeze. In the shifting candlelight, Tucker perceived that the universe was on his side.

Instead of finding Emma asleep and having to awaken her, she could see and appreciate him, and he her, throughout their first time together, Tucker thought. He stepped into the room, cleared his throat, and raised in both hands the hem of his nightshirt. His manhood fully erect from his solitary foreplay on the way to Emma's room, he thrust his pelvis out three times in rapid succession, and Emma screamed in fright at the lunatic now parading in front of her, his flapping inner thighs discolored from fat-on-fat friction, his pubic hair stringy and thin, his scrotum like dried apples used as mummy heads on All Hallows' Eve. Emma screamed before Tucker could try to calm her or clamp his hand over her mouth. "But who can hear her?" he asked himself, and relaxed. The sharecroppers would have to be sitting up waiting for a scream in order to hear Emma all the way to their hovels, he reasoned, and even if they did hear, why would they care?

"Come on and give it to me," he said to Emma. "You know you been wantin' me to get it a real long time."

He leaped upon her, but by then she was sitting straight up on her knees like a sentinel prairie dog checking the terrain, saw his leap coming, and with a wide arc of her right fist, hit him on the side of his mouth and removed his left incisor, which dangled by a string of bloody gum. Tucker was shocked. He had heard that nigger women were mules, but it had never crossed his mind that a thirteen-year-old girl could beat him in hand-to-hand combat. Strangely, he was aroused in a new and breathtaking way. He took the dislodged tooth from his torn mouth, grabbed the front of Emma's shift, and tore it from her body. He pushed her against the wall, ramming himself inside her. Immediately his semen spewed out, but his verbal gibberish of carnal satisfaction became a tortured howl that cut through the star-studded darkness. Tucker reached for his buttock, and what he knew he would find was the handle of an ice pick, plunged into the meatiest part of his stringy flesh, up to the hilt. His hand, in blind agony, did not encounter a hilt, per se, at the locus of searing pain. Rather, it detected what felt like, and indeed was, a trail of coarse thread. He did not puzzle over this strange state of events because a pair of iron fireplace tongs, wielded from behind him, smashed into his head. The sky's brilliant stars went unaffected by this, as by all other earthly violence of the night, but Tucker's lights dimmed, and flickered, and then they went out.

* * *

"Is he dead?" asked Mrs. Tucker.

Emma crawled over to Tucker's prostrate body, his bloody face on the edge of her bedding. She placed her index and middle fingers on his carotid artery.

"No'm. He breathin'," she said. "Bleedin' a lot, though. Head bleedin', mouth and nose bleedin', and he bleedin' a little down there. Ears ain't bleedin', though."

"What is that exactly?" asked Mrs. Tucker, squinting at her husband's pallid backside from which flowed a length of thick white thread and two tiny rivulets of blood.

"Pea sack needle in there," answered Emma, who was still naked and bleeding herself. Blood mixed with semen dripped down her thighs. Her right fist was beginning to swell, but cushioned perhaps by Tucker's fleshy jowl, her skin had not been broken when her knuckles collided with his face. "Them needles used for sewing up tow sacks when you got 'em full of shelled peanuts ready to go to market. They real thick and they kinda curved, make it easier to sew nice and snug and keep the peanuts from spillin' out. I uses 'em for embroiderin' when I'm thickenin' the biggest tail feathers on turkeys and peacocks and such. Makes the feathers kinda rise up from the cloth. Needle might of broke off in there." Emma inclined her head slightly toward Tucker's behind.

"Long as he isn't dead," said Mrs. Tucker, "but if he ever bothers you again, he will be dead because I'll kill him, so help me God." In her voluminous white nightgown, she knelt by her husband's body and tugged smartly at the embroidery thread, hoping to dislodge the large needle. The thread snapped, but the needle did not move, and Mrs. Tucker considered the shame, the utter degradation of having an expensive doctor or any other halfway decent person witness the scene that lay before her. She wished to run and hide among the candles in the washhouse. As if to signal that this was no time for such self-indulgence, Tucker began to moan.

"Maybe you better clean yourself up and put your clothes on and help me get him out of here. . . . Now, how are we going to do that?" Mrs. Tucker looked around as if expecting the walls to answer her.

"Roll 'im onto a sheet or quilt and drag it to the house, I reckon. Least, that's the only way I can see." Emma wrapped as much of her body as she could in her torn underskirt, grabbed her clothes, and went to the well where she sluiced herself in cold water. Then she wadded the ruined shift between her legs and dressed herself.

"Think you can get that needle out?" asked Mrs. Tucker the moment Emma was back in the kitchen. Again, Emma crouched beside the body of her attacker. She pressed hard with both hands around the periphery of the needle hole, but Tucker's grainy sinew did not release its hold.

"Need to cut it a li'l bit, make crosscuts to get to the eye, then string a piece of wire or doubled twine through it, and yank the needle out."

In addition to moaning, Tucker now began weakly to thrash about.

"Light another candle so you can see, and do the cutting right now before he fully wakes up. No way I can hold him down once he does. Got what you need over on the kitchen side?"

"Got plenty sharp knives and wire for trussin' poultry. Got nice clean rags to bandage and catch the blood. Lord willin', it'll be out well fore he completely woke, lessen the needle break off and part of it won't come out. Could let it stay in and fester 'til the pus push it out. Could get Doc Stevens to cut it all the way open and take it out."

"No doctor," said Mrs. Tucker.

"Think you can hold one of the candles up a li'l bit so I can see better, please, ma'am?" As Emma quickly made her preparations, it struck Mrs. Tucker that her father and this thirteen-year-old nigger, this special pet, maybe not even fully human, were the only beings that she had ever loved. Emma swiftly made the two small incisions, pressed on the flesh with her left hand to part it and reveal the eye of the needle, threaded it with truss wire with her right hand, stood straddling Tucker for leverage, and yanked the needle out. During the short time that it took Emma to perform the operation, Tucker was steadily screaming. Mrs. Tucker placed the candle that she had been holding on the floor and bent so low over Tucker's face that her mouth was almost touching his ear.

"You can hush up all that hollering this very minute," she hissed, "or I'm going to lay those fireplace tongs to the other side of your evil, empty head and send you straight to hell! I bet you'll be quiet then!"

Perhaps Tucker heard the passion in her voice cracking with strength derived from desperation. Perhaps he saw the fierceness in her eyes glowing gold and bottomless in their hawk-like stare. But the splotchy red face that Tucker beheld floating just above his own, its nostrils and mouth pinched by leanness of flesh and by nerves sprung to their coilless limits, lived in his mind as Satan in all his scarlet scaliness, come to collect his dues. Tucker shut his eyes and his mouth. Five minutes later, leaning upon the shoulders of his wife and the child that he had just raped, Tucker hobbled silently across the grass to the big house, up the stairs, and, under his wife's direction, into the tiny bedroom that had been used by Mrs. Tucker's childhood nursemaid.

"Throw a sheet on the bed!" Mrs. Tucker ordered Emma. Thus began Tucker's life as pariah under what he had long ago come to regard as his own roof.

* * *

"Why, I b'lieve that there's Old Man Albert Chase's daughter in that carriage. I know that's her nigger gal drivin' the hoss. She come into town 'bout twicet a month, for groceries and sich, but it's been years since I seen Old Man Chase's daughter." The speaker, Caleb Watson, seventy-five years old and hard of hearing, sat on the front porch of Conway's General and Dry Goods Store. He was alone and spoke loudly to the dusty air for his own benefit.

"Can't be sure that's Old Man Chase's daughter lessen I catch a glimpse of her face. Seem like she all covered up in a veil, hot as it is!"

Indeed, Mrs. Tucker wore a straw-colored hat with a dense veil pouring from its brim, breaking its fall at the top of her collarbone. Dreamed up and refashioned by Emma from an old gown the day before, her dress was pale green, and a strip of its material circled the crown of her hat. She carried a parasol woven of what seemed, erroneously, to be of the same flax-like material that comprised her hat.

"Her shoes just as shiny as a coal-black, sweatin' nigger runnin' a race," Caleb Watson thought as he watched her descend the carriage steps before he could lift his old bones and walk them across the street to help her down. And the "nigger gal," busy tying the old horse to the hitching post, outraged Caleb by not doing a thing to assist the lady. By the time Caleb had risen and crossed the dusty street, Albert Chase's daughter had disappeared inside the Slocum Family Bank with her nigger right behind her. The urge to know her business was strong in Caleb's heart, but how could a dirt-poor old man like himself boldly tree a "'ristocrat's" daughter when his clear intent was to turn her private financial concerns into public knowledge? Thinking better of pursuing Albert Chase's daughter into the bank, Caleb contemplated the old horse and carriage with great curiosity, but the horse was wearing blinders and evinced no more interest in Caleb's prying presence than did the ancient carriage. The old man trudged back across the street and resumed his chosen stance as gossip-monger to any passersby with the time and inclination to listen.

In exactly one hour, judging by the chimes from St. Mark's Episcopal Church, an edifice that served the well-to-do and that Caleb had never entered, he saw Albert Chase's daughter exit the bank and stroll leisurely to her carriage, her nigger gal in tow. Caleb did not rise to hurry across the street and help the lady to her perch, not even to glean juicy tidbits of what her business had been. Regarding the former, Caleb saw that his assistance was not needed since Charley Slocum, president and owner of the Slocum Family Bank, had escorted the lady to her carriage and had given her his arm until she was safely seated. Regarding the latter, it occurred to Caleb that despite his being a white man, just as white as Charley Slocum, in a setting of "big dogs" he had no voice; he was as invisible as and far less valuable than a nigger, male or female.

* * *

When Emma gave birth at fourteen to a sickly baby who grew into a runt of a child, Tucker was secretly disappointed, thinking that his masculinity was impugned. As far as he knew, this was the only fruit of his loins, and the puny nigger nitwit disgusted him. But Emma doted on the boy, holding him totally innocent of the circumstances under which he was conceived. When he was four years old, Mrs. Tucker died suddenly from a one-day battle with appendicitis, and her husband, incredulous at his inability to access one red cent against the Chase house and land, sold Emma and Sammy the Runt to a breeder from South Carolina. Billed as a smart two-year-old, Sammy brought a respectable price. Billed as a docile and prolific bearer of strong slave babies, Emma filled Tucker's palms with gold. In spite of this windfall, Tucker was incensed that the "thievin' bitch" he had married and devoted years of his life to had connived with Slocum, "the biggest crook in the county," to cheat him out of his rightful inheritance and had kept him in the dark about her dirty deal until she was dead. "If she wasn't already dead and buried," he told himself, "I'd kill her and feed her ugly, cut-up carcass to the hogs! And who's to say I can't do it now?" he asked rhetorically. "Any man got a shovel can dig! Any man got a axe can chop bones same as wood!"

2

Silas the Steadfast

One day, when we had a smooth sea and moderate wind, two of my wearied countrymen who were chained together, preferring death to such a life of misery, somehow made through the netting and jumped into the sea.

from *The Interesting Narrative of the Life of Olaudah Equiano, or Gustavus Vassa, the African, Written by Himself,*
Olaudah Equiano, 1789

EMMA'S FIRST PREGNANCY as a breed mare in South Carolina produced twin boys born in 1832. In a flash of generosity prompted by greed, Emma's master promised that if she continued to be a prolific bearer of healthy children, he would never separate her from Sammy by selling the boy, even though he was feeble-minded. Emma gave birth to a second set of twin boys eighteen months later, and a son ten months after that. Her only daughter came the following year. All of Emma's children born in South Carolina were sired by the same massive slave, and when the first set of twins reached five years of age, they were sold as seven-year-olds who were almost ready for all-day field labor. Even though slave traders routinely assessed the teeth of slaves—like those of mules and horses—in order to verify their age and soundness, in corroborating the age of Emma's children, the intactness of all their milk teeth seemed not to register. Perhaps the traders knew the truth of the twins' approximate age but were willing to overlook the seller's dishonesty. And why should they have equivocated over such a pristine issue as honesty, having already committed their numbered days on earth to the heinous purpose of trafficking in human flesh and having planned, in turn, to resell the twins as seven-year-olds? In 1838, when Emma had not become pregnant twelve months after the sale of her first set of twins, in a flash of power devoid of mercy, her master snatched Sammy the Runt from her side and sold him along with his four-year-old twin brothers.

"I'm gon' leave or I'm gon' die," Emma said to herself. "This here heart, this mind, this here body, they ain't no use for nothin' good I can make out, and they sho ain't no use for me or my churren. I'm 'bout the lowest thing there is, lower'n the mules and hogs and dogs. Lower'n the cats and chickens. Everything fed better'n me. Hogs and chickens killed for eatin', true, but look like they can be happy sometime—scratchin' grain, guzzlin' slop—and their life worth somethin' to them 'fore they die. Dogs and cats can't keep all their litters, true, some even drownded, but I can't keep none of mine. Why I'm a person? Ruther be a snake. Ruther be dead than to bring more churren into this life of sorrow. Can't read and write nothin.' Don't know nothin.' They say the scripture say God got a better place for all his churren. He better get it ready. I'm goin' under the water. Goin' soon."

"Got two places," came a response. "One of 'em's on earth. You come to the father when it's time. It ain't time yet. Meantime, I come to you."

* * *

After four weeks of biding her time during the darkest nights of the month when the moon was new, Emma bound her year-old daughter to her chest and put on an old coat of the master's, his mud-caked brogans, and a gray felt hat of his that she had stolen. She could not hope to carry her two-year-old son, for he remained on a neighboring farm where he had been placed with a wet nurse soon after Emma's daughter was born and her surprisingly thin milk was inadequate to support two children. Armed with hard tack, corn pone, smoked beef hoarded over time, and a resolve to keep on going, Emma set out on a Saturday night to find her way to freedom.

Her companion was a sturdy lance for leaning upon when she was tired, or for beating the bushes to warn poisonous snakes and night creatures of her advance. Her companions were the trees, bushes, and grasses, the nuts, roots, leaves, persimmons, and tart apples that would witness her passing and would hide, shelter, and sustain her. They were the leafy greens that she would steal from late gardens and eat raw, the hen's eggs that she would pilfer, the milk from swollen teats, the white and sweet potatoes from straw-covered banks. Her companion was her daughter, whose little head emerged like a bird's from the folds of the coat as she rode on her mother's chest. Her wide eyes gaping or sleeping, she rode at peace with the world, ignorant of her place within it. Emma's companions were the rivers whose banks she paralleled, the stars that pointed her northward, and the voice and vision of the Son of God.

"Go the night 'fore the Sabbath," the voice had told her. "Can't put you on the posters 'til Monday. Give you two nights and a whole day. Wear the mar'sar's clothes and shoes. Th'ow the dogs off a little, keep 'em runnin' back to him. Food on your back, baby on your chest. Carry the crushed poppy, case the baby need quietin'." And when she felt hesitant: "Go 'head. God ain't never forgot nobody."

* * *

She set out following the Pee Dee River, hiding days and traveling nights. Time after time, she was helped on her way by brave and compassionate slaves who envied her courage and prophesied to themselves and to Emma that one day someone like her would help them to "leab dis ole lan'" and follow the drinking gourd to freedom. She walked for weeks from the Pee Dee River to the Waccamaw to the brackish swamps of the Cape Fear where a free black man, rowing her across the river, was hailed by white men who appeared like dim spirits in the sheet of fog covering the river bank that they had just left. "Save my baby, please suh, and God bless you, suh, and keep y'all safe," she whispered from underneath his fishing nets lying on the boat's floor. Leaving her daughter behind, Emma slipped quietly overboard and felt the cold, muddy water swallow her whole.

She saw him in the river, his hand cupping her mouth and nose, allowing her to breathe in and out large gasps of air. His long, dark hair flowed with the current. His sad eyes were kind and weary, and his robe, phosphorescently white in the dirty water, seemed oddly unaffected by the river's flow. He led her to the shore and ministered unto her, emptying her shoes of muddy water and seaweed, spreading her coat and dress upon a bush, drying her clothes, provisions, and body in the fire of his countenance.

"Is that you, Lord?" she murmured.

"Them that know me need not ask," he said. "Go east and serve my peoples, for how else you gon' serve me?"

* * *

Reynolds Sutton from Chatham County in eastern North

Carolina had hired out fifty of his slaves to work near Mount Bevel during cotton picking and corn gathering season, and he had come to collect his property and his rent and to see the country at the same time. In the early morning hours, as the fog began to lift and the sun to pierce the day's gray shroud, one of his slaves, Silas, came upon Emma sleeping under the low hanging branches of an elderberry tree. Silas was on his way to the gristmill, a bulging tow sack of corn upon his back, to have the corn ground for porridge, hoecake, and pone on their journey home. Perhaps he would not have detected Emma, obscured as she was by the leafy branches and the eerie light, had her right hand not reached from beneath the foliage, as if it had been dismembered and left upon the ground. Silas walked over to the tree and, keeping his sack of corn in place upon his back, bent down for closer inspection. He saw that the hand was that of a Negro—a youngster or a woman—and it extended from the sleeve of an old coat.

"Hey dere!" Silas said softly, nudging the hand with his foot. Emma, fully awake, neither moved nor spoke.

"Nobody here but Silas," Silas announced reassuringly, suspecting a runaway slave or else the remains of one, in which case reassurances would be wasted. "Come on out if you ain't dead. If you ain't dead, I make sho' you get a good breakfast. Come on out."

Silas took the hand that had not moved, and, tugging it gently, he felt its resistance as Emma parted the overhanging branches and crawled out to face her future.

"I'm 'mong the livin' still," said Emma. "I'm travelin' through to up north. Need some food, place to rest durin' the day. Can you he'p me, suh?"

"Come 'long with me to the grist mill," Silas answered. "We talk on the way. Folks seein' us think you one of us. We not from 'round here. Been here hired out, and now the corn and cotton is in, we leavin' for to go back home today."

"Where y'all from? Y'all goin' north?"

"We b'longs to Mar'sar Reynolds Sutton from Chatham County, northeast of here on the Albemarle Sound. We leavin' today, but we can hide you in the wagons, give you food and shelter, let you rest and sleep. I 'magine you mighty tired."

"You say y'all goin' east?"

"Northeast. If you go 'long with us, we try to keep you safe. How long you been runnin'? You hurt any?"

"Not hurt, 'ceptin' my spirit, like so many other folkses. Just tired and hongry. Done lost all my churren. Someday I see 'em round the heavenly throne. Left my last chile when I jumped in that river. Ruther to pick my own death in the muddy water than to let 'em take me back, or to kill me, or to kill the po' innocent man he'pin' me, or my baby girl. Ruther drown, but I won't let to drown. Christ done saved me for to serve him. Drug me all the way 'cross the river and out of the water 'cause Lord knows I can't swim. Dried me off so I wouldn't die of cold and sent you to find me, 'stead of white folks. . . . Won't you 'feared I was dead? Ain't you scared of haints?"

"Thought you might be dead. Glad you ain't. But I ain't scared of no haints. Haints ain't never done nothin' to nobody I ever known of," Silas said, smiling. "All the harm I for sho' known of ever come to me or anybody else, none of it come from no haints. It's the livin' that's done the harm every time."

"What day is it, suh?"

"Name's Silas, and it's Sat'day, day 'fore the Sabbath. . . . What might your name be?"

"Emma. . . . Please to meet you, Silas."

"Please to meet you, Emma."

"I should of asked what month it is. I been runnin' a right long time."

"It's November, Emma. End of the second week. We be home way 'fore Chris'mas."

* * *

During the forty minutes that it took Emma and Silas to walk from the grist mill to the woods by the plantation where Silas had worked for three months, Silas concocted a plan to incorporate Emma as a free black into the Reynolds Sutton caravan. Lacking complexity or flair, the plan simply required that Emma hide in Silas's wagon until the second morning of the journey when he would "'scover" her "in the bushes" and then convince the master to pay her a monthly wage to work for him.

"If I'm free, I'm gon' need papers to prove it," Emma said. "I ain't got no papers."

"You lost 'em when you fell in the river yestiddy. You been hidin' ever since 'cause you know you need free papers to keep from gettin' claimed or sold by any white person with a mind to claim or sell you. If you with us, nobody can claim you 'cause Mar'sar Reynolds vouch for you."

"Why he not gon' claim me or sell me hisself?" Emma asked. "Why he not gon' breed me to bear churrens so he can sell 'em off? I don't never 'tend to lose another chile!"

"None of the Suttons is breeders. I hearn of them breedin' farms. None of us been hired out for breedin'. I'm big and strong, but I ain't never *had* to do no matin'. Course I done it, but I ain't never had to, and I ain't never done it just to own churrens. So why he gon' make you do it?"

"Maybe he sell me into slav'ry. All this runnin', why I'm gon' run right back into slav'ry?"

"Mar'sar Reynolds done give my granny her freedom when she cured his pappy of the pneumonia near 'bout two years ago. It so happened that ole Doc Ward horse had th'owed 'im, and he broke his hip and couldn't get 'round for quite a while to take care of Ole

Man Reynolds or any of his other patients. Granny nurse Doc Ward and Ole Man Reynolds, too. Doc Ward say she can doctor for him any time she got a notion, say she the onliest reason he can walk today, and say she save Ole Man Reynold's life 'cause that pneumonia sho could of killed 'im. Mar'sar Reynolds give Granny her freedom, he so happy for what she done for his pappy and for Doc Ward, too. If he givin' 'way freedom, why he gon' go and steal yourn?"

"I ain't never saved his pappy. And if he so unnerstandin', why I need to hide from 'im for a whole day and night? If you 'scover me in the bushes tomorrow, and I lost my free papers when I fell in the river yestiddy, how I got so far from the river already, 'lessen y'all followin' the river? If he so unnerstandin', why we don't just 'proach 'im now? And why he gon' pay me to work for him when he got plenty slaves workin' for free?"

"Let's just say you fell in the river a few days ago," said Silas patiently. And we can't 'proach 'im now 'cause if anybody been lookin' for you 'round here last night or this mornin', he might of hearn 'bout it, and he might turn you in if he know you here. If you 'scovered over a day's travel east of here sometime tomorrow, he can b'lieve you ain't the runaway slave he might of hearn 'bout 'cause how you gon' get that far that fast 'thout a horse, lessen you can fly? And why you runnin' east 'stead of north, when north's where freedom lie? And he gon' hire you for salary if you can do somethin' he need right bad. We gon' decide later on what that gon' be.

"Now, keep out of sight here. We be 'long in 'bout a hour or so. They's loadin' the wagons now. Mine gon' be the last wagon, and I'm gon' stop here a minute to check the mules, and a few folks gon' go in the bushes to relieve theyselves, and you slip out 'mongst 'em. We hide you when we camp, feed you after. I have you your breakfast when I come back."

"I'm much obliged, Silas," said Emma. "You a good man. The Lord sent you to me, and I'm gon' thank 'im while I tarry here 'til you return."

* * *

Travel by day, sleep by night. Travel on the road by mule or horse and wagon, not by wading through swamps, wet all the time. Nice wide tarpaulin for shelter against cold dewy nights and sharp November rains. Ample food to fill the belly. No gnawing hunger except the hunger of heartbreak. Laughing, joking, singing, and evenings when they stop and set up camp, dancing to the staccato bleating of jug, the thrum of knuckles on scrub board, and the cascading wail of juice harp. And sleep. Tragedies that had reigned in Emma's life gave way in her dreams to her children playing, to their bringing her gifts of colored leaves and wild flowers, and to the joy in their faces when she would still the bees and steal their honey. Instead of trying to close her heart against love for children born only to be ripped from her arms and sold, Emma had embraced the fiercest adoration of her offspring. From the time of knowing that she was with child, she would send soft words and songs and gladness inward to the embryonic mass. "I'm gon' have you near 'bout thirty years," she would tell them, "'cause every year I'm gon' love you 'nough for five years' time, plus the nine months I'm carryin' you round. You a wanted chile, and you a loved chile!"

Four days into the journey, a band of three horsemen were suddenly upon Reynolds Sutton's caravan. Galloping over the damp clay road, the horses raised no dust that would have warned of their steady advance. They proceeded to the lead wagon, where Reynolds Sutton rode mid-road, astride a sorrel mare, and talked with his overseer, who was driving the wagon.

"Hi' y'all doin?" said the obvious leader of the band. He was wearing a tin sheriff's badge fastened to his sweat-stained brown work shirt. All three men looked old, far older than Reynolds Sutton, who was fifty if he was a day. Teeth were scarce among the newcomers, and excepting the leader, whose potbelly protruded up and over the horn of his saddle, they were pitiably thin. Their pant cuffs were muddy and tattered, and the stench from their long unwashed bodies hinted of rotting meat.

"Very well, thank you," Sutton responded. "Mighty fine day for traveling. Godspeed you all!"

"Thankee," the newcomer said, and Sutton smiled and returned to his conversation with his overseer, expecting the derelict band to ride on.

"We got business with a Reynolds Sutton, and we think you the one," the sheriff said to Sutton's back.

"What kind of business do you have with Reynolds Sutton?" Again Sutton gave the man his attention.

"We lookin' for a runaway nigger gal carryin' a pickaninny 'bout a year old. Could of reached the Cape Fear area a few days ago. All these here niggers b'longs to you?"

"I didn't catch your name or the names of your posse," Sutton said. He slowed his horse and told his overseer to signal the wagons to halt.

"Ain't mentioned no names." The sheriff spat a wallop of dark brown tobacco juice on the sweet-potato-orange clay road and seemed to wait for its integration into the earth before resuming his speech. "I'm a legally deputized sheriff out here to keep scallywags from stealin' other folkses property. Ain't got to tell you my name or nothin' else if you a nigger stealer. Taken us two days of hard ridin' to catch up with y'all. All three of us just got deputized, and b'lieve you me we got plenty other things to do. But that runaway gal got a hundred fifty dollar price tag on her head, extra thirty for the pickaninny, long as they alive and ain't hurt up too bad when they delivered back to the rightful owner. We intend to get that money and split it up square and equal 'tween me and the boys here." He clambered from his horse. "Get down," he said to his men, and they dismounted, too.

"Seems to me you all ought to find the woman you're looking for before you go counting your money," Sutton said.

"We fixin' to find her right now or my name ain't Robert Tom Tucker," the sheriff retorted. "We know she and that pickaninny of hern in one of these here wagons, and we gon' find 'em if it's the last thing we do on this here green earth."

Sutton slid off his saddle and stood facing the men on the road. "See here, now," he said, spreading his arms and palms in openness to the interlopers. "Why don't we just deal with this like civilized human beings? These are my folks. I rented them out, and now I'm taking them back home. The runaway you seek is not among them, and I advise you to accept my word on the matter. I don't want my people upset by you all disturbing them and searching through what we're carrying. They're tired, been traveling four days after working hard for months. Why don't you gentlemen just get back on your steeds and look for your escapee somewhere straight north? A runaway slave woman with a hundred fifty dollar bounty on her head is too smart to run east rather than north. Seems to me smart lawmen like you ought to know that."

"There's other hunters gone north lookin' for her," the sheriff said. "This here route won't covered, and we think it's the right one, what with y'all leavin' Mount Bevel just a few days ago."

"What does this runaway look like?" Sutton asked. "Do you have a picture of her? In case we run across her and her baby, maybe we can notify you, providing you let us know where we can send word."

"Naw, we ain't got no picture," snarled Tucker. "Who gon' make a picture of a nigger brood sow no matter how much she worth? But we seen a slave bill on her. 'Bout twenty-three or -four but younger lookin'. Tall, broad, fit for havin' churren. Right pretty for a nigger. Answers to Emma."

"Jesse," Sutton called out to a man in the second wagon, "will you get Emma-Maisie, ask her to step down here with me and our company?" Jesse went to the fourth wagon where Emma-Maisie was riding, and she did as she was bid. Her eyes were wide with trepidation, her lips taut, her body shaking with fear and incredulity, for how could she, born on the Sutton plantation where she had lived all her life, be handed over to this poor white trash in place of some runaway slave woman that she had never seen? She could not bear to be separated from her mother, father, sister, and brothers or from the handsome slave on Crawford's plantation who had asked her to jump the broomstick come Christmas. Silent tears coursed over her broad cheeks and the edges of her mouth and wet the thick homespun covering her ample bosom.

"She the one!" Bob Tucker shouted as Emma-Maisie approached the spot where the four men stood. She stopped in front of Sutton. "Yassuh?" she asked, her face averted to show her submission but also to hide her tears.

Still holding his horse's reins in his left hand, with his right hand Tucker drew his pistol and held it between Emma-Maisie's eyes. Then Emma, riding in the last wagon, struggled to rise from her seated position, but Silas placed a viselike hold on her left knee, a hold that would leave a bruise for three months, and she could not stand.

"He don't know and don't care who he lookin' for, long as he can get a chance at that reward money," Silas whispered to Emma. "Anybody name Emma good 'nough for him."

"Get up on this here hoss," Tucker ordered Emma-Maisie. "I'm gon' get that pickaninny of yourn, and y'all goin' with us!"

The yellowish scrim of the weak afternoon sun was rent by a pistol's crack, and both of Emma-Maisie's arms flew up, shrugging off the sheriff who was shorter than she, and except for his protruding stomach, smaller than she. Her palms covered her forehead to stanch the flow of her innocent blood. But she saw almost instantaneously her own clean hands and the sheriff's horse, its legs bent as if in mid canter, as it folded to the ground. Then Emma-Maisie saw the horse roll to its side, bleeding from mouth and ears as the hole between its eyes spewed viscous red against its grayish face.

"Go back to your wagon, Emma-Maisie," said Sutton, "and you three throw down your guns." The men saw the well-oiled rifle barrels aiming at them from every wagon, and they hastily complied. Then Sutton raised his pistol and fired it a second time in the direction of Tucker's right ear, missing it by a hair. And he fired two shots at the sheriff's muddy boot tops, grazing the cracked leather on each.

"You'd have a long walk back to where you came from," Sutton told Tucker, "if you were going anywhere. Now, you and your posse get busy digging a grave for that dead horse. From the looks of it, you didn't take care of her while she was living, but you're going to bury her nice and deep, leaving room for something extra."

The sheriff's water burst forth in a tepid, sticky cascade that spread upon the front and legs of his pants.

"Have somebody bring down three spades!" Sutton yelled to Silas, who was pointing a rifle from the last wagon.

"Now, you all had better dig fast," said Sutton when the shovels appeared. "We don't have all day to deal with the likes of you."

The men began their digging in the earth beyond the roadside ditch. There the soil was somewhat softer than the clayey surface of the road. "Get their guns," Sutton told Jesse, who retrieved them from the road where they still lay.

"You all think you're digging a grave for a pig?" Sutton asked the men.

"I ain't never buried no hoss 'fore now," one of the heretofore silent sidekicks answered.

Sutton took the man's shovel and backed up several paces.

"Start back here," Sutton directed. "You!" he addressed the other silent partner. "Start here in the middle, and dig out to here on this side." He took the man's shovel and made a few notches in the dirt to mark his instructions. "You dig out to here on the other side," he said to Tucker. The men saw that Sutton had equally divided the large rectangle that was their digging area.

"This is going to take a while," Sutton said to his slaves. "Most of you can follow Jesse to our appointed place to spend the night, but Silas, you wait for me and the shovels."

"Glad to, suh," said Silas, but Jesse, thinking that there was safety in sticking with Sutton, interjected that none of them would mind the wait and that if the digging dragged on too long, a few men could simply jump off the wagons and help.

The afternoon, seemingly so quiet, was filled with birdsong, the ka-chug of bullfrogs, the caws from crows circling overhead. The shovels striking against the ground seemed to suck at the earth, sluicing out rocks and tree roots. A buzzard flapped its wings from a dead tree across the road, and the posse—hearing one of the slaves wonder aloud how buzzards seem to know immediately when something, especially something large, lies dead and unburied—was greatly afraid.

They slowed perceptibly in their digging as they neared the point of finishing the grave.

"No need of slacking off now," Sutton said into the funereal silence of the afternoon. "Not finishing in a reasonable time could get you killed earlier than you otherwise would. So get to it."

The sweating men, their heads like mangy cats escaping a washtub, got to it.

When the grave was finally dug, Sutton directed Tucker and his men to rope the dead horse to their two nags and to drag it into the grave.

"Now, stand on this side of the grave, facing the woods,"

Sutton ordered. The slaves looked away as Sutton fired three shots in swift succession. Looking back, they saw that only one of the men had fallen into a heap atop the horse. A foul odor permeated the still air as if the other two, left standing, had emptied their bowels.

"Drag your partner out of there," Sutton said. "I didn't shoot him any more than I shot you. Hurry it up, or he gets buried alive!" The two men scrambled to pull Tucker to safety before covering the nag with layers and layers of dirt.

"The buzzards won't get that horse, but they might get you, as bad as you smell," said Sutton. "Now, get out of here, and you won't ever come near me or my people again if you know what's good for you. If I ever see ary one of you again, I'll kill you on sight."

"Thankee, suh! Thankee, suh! You a real gen'eman!" they chorused as they quickly mounted the two horses. The gaunter of the animals carried the extra load. The stronger horse had taken off, spurred by the whip of its rider, before Tucker had been able to climb up onto its back.

3

Emma Aloft

"Now just what is this here Victory?"
"It what we get when we fight for it."
"Ought to be Freedom, God do know that!"

from "Conversation on V," Owen Dodson, 1946

ON SUTTON'S LAND, living in freedom among his people, the twenty-four year old Emma would rise from her bed at night, taking care not to awaken Silas's granny with whom she boarded. She would steal outside to stand beneath the roof of the world, embracing the frigid darkness to prove that she was awake, alive, real, and in her right mind. For a period of seven weeks, she kept up the nightly ritual of feeling the earth beneath her bare feet, feeling the air on her upturned face and bare arms, and when the jolt of God would enter her body through the center of her palms, she would weep tears of gladness and thanksgiving. She kept a sharp stick under the steps to the cabin door, and it was her trowel for digging beneath the crust of the yard to find a clean morsel of God's earth that she could eat and make a part of her body. Someday her body would return to dust, and the earth that she absorbed now would remain a part of her flesh and would ward off any semblance of strangeness, of separateness from the earth, her home and true mother, after her death. In rain, she cupped her hands to catch and drink of heaven's bounty poured down in cleansing consecration.

Then the night came when Granny said, as soon as Emma had banked the fire, blown out the candle, and risen from her bedtime prayers, "Don't go out there no more, baby. You already livin' your thanks to the Lord God. He done hearn you, and he pleased, and he want you to get your rest. Don't break your rest no more, and don't go out there no more, half naked, 'fore you catch your death of cold. He ain't got no use for you dead."

* * *

Emma had come to Chatham County intent upon giving such gifts as she could find to give, but Silas had taken her to his granny, who had surprised both him and Emma with her own gift.

"Been waitin' for you," she had said, taking Emma's wrists and turning her hands, palms upward, then using her own thumbs to straighten Emma's curled fingers. "Yeah, Lord!" Granny had murmured. She had taken Emma's chin in her right hand, tipped Emma's head slightly back, and peered upwards into her eyes.

"I been waitin' and hopin' for you," Granny had repeated, "for some time now. You the one to carry on for our peoples." She had given Emma a sudden, dazzling smile, revealing a mouth full of nubby, caramel-colored teeth. "The right one come mostly from outside, not from us. That's his promise to our peoples in our tribulations down here. He gon' keep on sendin' a comforter 'til the las' comforter come. Mighty glad you here, chile. . . . Thank'ee, Silas," she'd said, turning to her grandson. "You done found the perfeck, son, and I thank'ee."

Silas had not been aware that he had been looking for anyone, let alone a comforter for the people. Neither he nor Emma had the vaguest idea of how she could fulfill Granny's shocking expectation.

* * *

In addition to cooking for Reynolds Sutton, for which she was paid, Emma became Granny's apprentice. The woods, fields, pastures, roadsides, and gardens were Granny's vast pharmacopoeia, and the inhabitants of the plantation, both human and animal, were subjects in her hands-on laboratory. Emma learned the skills of midwifery, bone setting, fever breaking, boil and abscess lancing, tooth extraction, and respiratory relief, as well as relief from headache, backache, earache, toothache, indigestion, rheumatism, arthritis, edema, menarche, and a host of other complaints. She learned to stitch wounds, to treat bloody flux, thrush mouth, and painful elimination. She learned to channel the restorative mysteries of blood, bones, feathers, rocks, wood, water, fire, air, and earth in healing. She learned the power of prayer, faith, concentration, touch, incantation, exaltation, hope, charity, humility, compassion, and love. She taught the ways and benefits of sanitation to those who subsisted under unsanitary conditions. She was an accomplished healer, confidante, psychiatrist, absolver, listener, and inspirer. To the people that she served, Emma provided balm for the mind and for the body; but as for her own needs, she appeared to most to be sufficient unto herself.

"I ain't never been so full up, Lord," she said in one of her solitary addresses. "Every day is a blessin'. Every day my soul is just full up, even at the worst times. But there's times sometime, Lord, I don't know what to do or say, and I open my mouth and maybe you speak for me, and then there's times you don't. That po' l'il chile et all that lye, and when I got there his lips and chin looked all gnawed, and his tongue all swole and blackish and pushin' out of his mouth, and he 'bout dead and I can't save 'im and wouldn't if I could 'cause he got to be in such pain in his th'oat and in his po' stomach that I can't hardly stand it. I can't save 'im, and I ain't got no comfort for his mama and papa. I ain't got no comfort for the l'il chile spose to be 'tendin' to 'im. My tongue feel thick and swole like hisn, and I can't speak. Don't no words come to me, and I feels like I'm under deep water. And I handed that chile, who had just died in my arms, I handed 'im to his po mamma, and then I just make myself say somethin' 'cause I can't do nothin'. And I say, 'This was a good baby, a happy baby. He done brought happiness to this here family. He done made this family to laugh and sing after they work hard all day. He done hug and kiss the other churren with love. Everybody gon' 'member that. Everybody gon' carry that sweet l'il chile in their heart and mind. Everybody gon' take a l'il bitty piece of that chile joy and gon' give it to everybody they see. That child gon' keep on makin' folkses feel a l'il bit better every day, long as they 'member him, even though he gone.'

"Problem is, maybe what I said ain't true. If I speak wrong, Lord, please forgive me. Don't let what I say hurt folkses, Lord. Take my words and turn 'em 'round and turn 'em into somethin' for your service, Lord. Do I give a l'il piece of my baby girl to the peoples, her l'il head peepin' out, ridin' on my chest? She never was a bit of trouble, just brung me joy, just a l'il angel. Do I give a l'il bit of my twins, fine, big boys, sangin' and dancin'? My l'il son took from me when he no more'n a year old, do I give a l'il piece of him? My l'il Sammy, Lord? I don't want to do evil by speakin' lies. Just stop my tongue, Lord, from speakin' evil."

And Jesus answered her: "You ain't lied. You speak from your heart, and your heart know sorrow. You touch the peoples and lifts 'em up. Can't do no evil when your heart's 'umble and you 'tendin' to do good.

"You ain't no ways evil. Judas not even evil. He was weak, true, but he had a job to do for to fulfill the word of my father and for to lay out the way of salvation for all my father's churren. You know I had to die, don't you? How else was I gon lan' on that cross and show the way to everlastin' life?"

* * *

The impact upon Emma of realizing that she was free, of serving no master but God, of seeing the world through the eyes of a woman, not a slave, of having proprietorship over her own body, of receiving recompense for her work, was profoundly, if cautiously, exhilarating on the one hand and sobering in its awesome responsibility on the other. As Emma saw it, her purpose in life was to lessen the suffering set loose upon the world. She became a beacon for slaves who were running to freedom—nursing the ill and injured, feeding the hungry, heartening the discouraged, and setting them on their way. In the twelfth year of her marriage to Silas, on a night when bad dreams revealed all of her children, dressed in rags and barefoot in deep snow, paraded in front of her by an overseer with a bloody, leather whip, she was awakened in horror and confusion by a rattling at the door. She arose hastily and flung open the door, expecting to see her children suffering from the harsh and unrelenting forces of man and nature. But standing before her was only a waif of a child, a boy who looked to be around seven or eight years old. In the moonlight, Emma could see that the lower portion of the child's body was caked in dried mud.

"What's the matter, chile?" she asked, drawing him out of the moonlight and into the dark room where Silas lay silent in their bed.

"We hongry," said the child, "and Mama sick and Papa got his leg caught in a trap. We seen your light when darkness come on. Papa sent me 'cause he and Mama can't come."

"Where they at? And how many?" Emma put her dress and apron on over her night clothes, put on her shoes, and tied a dark band of cloth over her hair as the child talked.

"Down a piece to the swamp where we hidin'. Been hidin' waist deep in mud and swamp water seem like a long time. There's four of us. Papa, Mama, me, and Lizbess. Papa can't run no more, and Mama sick. Bad stomachache. We come out the swamp and we been restin' 'neath the trees on the edge of the land."

Silas had slipped into his pants and had gathered the corn bread left over from their supper and smeared a chunk with butter, and the child was hungrily devouring it. Silas spread half the cake of butter over the remaining corn bread, took the bowl of leftover collards and white potatoes from the cupboard, and placed them on the table. Then he stepped out to the well to draw up the jar of buttermilk cooling there. When he was back and Emma had packed the provisions, Silas said to her, "This time I'm goin' with you, Emma."

"No," said Emma. "Sposin' we ain't back 'fore time for you to get to work? The wrong folkses might be askin' questions. You stay here, and I be home soon's I can." She carried the milk and the bowl of food in a straw basket, her medicines in a sack. She and the boy walked—almost ran—down to the swamp and into the trees.

Sitting on the ground, his legs stretched out in front of him, his elbows reaching behind him perched on a log, was a man in agony. His head was thrown back, his teeth clenched, his cheeks wet with silent tears. Emma lit her lantern. The man's foot and ankle had been mangled in the steel claws of a trap set for a large coon or a bear or a man. The trap was muddy. Mud and blood mingled on the man's leg and foot, bloated and already rancid with pus. The stench seemed palpable. Flies and maggots fed. The mother lay a few paces aside, clearly pregnant, holding another waif, a girl, much younger than the boy. The girl ate greedily of the food that Emma had brought. The mother and father, clearly exhausted, professed no appetite. The father was feverish and near despair.

"Lord, don't make me have to chop off no leg," Emma

prayed silently. She thought of having to use the hatchet, its lighter blade and shorter handle easier than the axe to wield with accuracy.

"I got to go back," she said aloud. "Gon' get some he'p. But first I got somethin' to calm y'all, take the pain away for a while, let y'all rest. The boy can watch over the l'il chile. He big, almos' a man." She drugged the parents and left the boy and his sister to fall asleep for once in a long while with their stomachs full.

* * *

In the end, the unborn child was lost, but they were lucky with the father's leg. It was saved, first by the blacksmith, a slave who belonged to Reynolds Sutton and whose powerful arms commanded the plantation's bellows and hammered and shaped its iron like supple reeds. He conjured the metal maw from the mangled ankle, disturbing the blanket of flies and writhing larvae. Then the leg was saved by Emma, who used laudanum to still the father's agony over nights and days while wild honey, pungent smoke, extract of arnica, jimson weed, and the salicylate skin between the outer bark and marrow of the medicine tree waged war against the decay that claimed his flesh. Daily massages, hot compresses when they could be managed, a healthful diet, rest, exercise, prayers, hopeful predictions for the broken man and his family's future, and an unceasing commitment to their well being—these were the gifts, the antidotes to death of the body and of the spirit, that Emma, Silas, and their accomplices from the slave community provided, and when five weeks had passed, the family resumed their night journey to the north, the man hobbling on a crutch that Silas's father had made years before. He carried a store of raw fruits and vegetables, hoecake, and dried meat in a sack on his back. The sack hung from a harness that Silas had fashioned by tying rope around the man's torso and adding straps to fit over each shoulder. Emma had encased the shoulder straps in cloth lined with tufts of cotton. "Every last thing they got gon' be on his back," Emma had told Silas. "Lord knows they ain't got much, but the weight of their food gon' pull on them shoulder straps. He already weak and painin' enough without gettin' sores rubbed onto his shoulders. That rope right strong and it might cut into his flesh after so much time if we don't pad them straps with tickin'."

"You sho 'nough God's chile," answered Silas, "down here doin' his work, lookin' out for other folks all the time." He kissed his wife on her lips.

* * *

"They just like turkeys, Lord," Emma said. "They like tame turkeys out in the rain. They don't know they gon' drown lessen somebody take care of 'em and bring 'em in. If they need to run, the man can't run—not far and not fast. The woman ain't strong. We sho' can't keep on keepin' 'em here, and they want to go on up north to freedom. But where we sendin' 'em to? Man runnin' 'cause the mar'sar gon' sell 'im down to Miss'ssippi far 'way from his wife and churren. But how long 'fore they captured and sent right back where they come from? Maybe they catch 'em and beat all of 'em half to death in front of the other slaves—make a 'xample of 'em—'fore they sell every one of 'em to different places. Man ain't worth much to slave traders half cripple like he is now. Maybe his mar'sar kill 'im just 'cause he cripple and ain't worth much no mo'. They pitiful, Lord, and my heart right heavy for 'em. The chile that first come to me, the l'il boy, put me right much in mind of my Sammy. I wish you would perteck 'em, Lord, save 'em from harm."

"All creatures mine," the Lord answered. "You was a turkey, one of mine. How far could you run with that baby ridin' on your chest? You was in the rain many a time. You was even in the river and near 'bout drownded. Would've drownded 'cept your heavenly father took care of you and brought you out."

"I feel your love all 'round me, Lord," Emma replied. "You with me all the time and if I die right now, I know my struggles not in vain. Nary one of 'em, Lord. Every one of my sorrows through this whole life done shape me into your vessel. Long as I can he'p some of your churren every day, Lord, I'm blessed.

"But that family just left here got a long way to go to get to the north. Sposin' they get kilt or put back in slav'ry? What use is their sufferin', Lord? How their sufferin' he'p anything? If they gets caught or kilt, ain't what we tried to do to he'p 'em in vain—not for us, 'cause we tryin' to do your work—but for them?"

"All creatures b'longs to me," he reiterated. "The way I love you, that's the same way I love all peoples. Them folkses that just left here is just as loved as you, just as pertected. Whyn't they perish in the mud and swamp water 'fore y'all had a chance to h'ep 'em out? All y'all done to h'ep 'em is recorded in the mind of God and gon' be in his reck'nin' on the great jedgment day. Nothin' y'all done is in vain, not for y'all and not for them.

"Whether they live or die, whether they slave or free, their corner of life while they was here was brighten by all y'all done. God in the present, Emma. He *now*. The way you h'ep somebody today, the good in the way they live, b'lieve, love, hope *today* ain't never in vain. Tomorrow not promise to nobody.

"Whether them folkses 'live tomorrow or dead tomorrow, why their struggle, their sufferin' got to be in vain? When they was here—sick, runaway slaves—didn't you see no joy, love, courage, 'umbleness in them? As much as these signs of God was in their hearts, they was on the way to salvation and to life everlastin'. That's why I lived on this earth as a human bean and died on this earth as a human bean—to show that real freedom not in the hand of the world's well off. Real freedom in the hand of God who can heis' his folkses 'bove the worst hand that life gon' deal 'em. Real freedom in the hand of his folkses who done riz 'bove the worst that evil can do. Them who knows how to hol' on to hope and love done learnt the key to resurrection, resurrection of the spirit. God promise to resurrect the souls of the faithful, but every day folkses theirself decide whether their spirit, battered on the stormy, ragin' sea of life, gon' be lost or resurrected. No matter what sit'ation they in, they can decide to keep their spirit 'live and to he'p to keep others' spirits 'live. If 'cordin' to God's promise, nobody can kill the soul of them folks just left here, and y'all done he'ped 'em ressurect their spirit, what you worryin' 'bout 'em for? Who can harm 'em? What they, or you, got to fear?"

4

Abraham Laughed

Bringing the gifts that my ancestors gave,
I am the dream and hope of the slave.

from "Still I Rise," Maya Angelou, 1978

EMMA'S HAT WAS MADE of persimmon-colored felt. Its base fit snugly on her head, and its crown flared out like a flat-topped turban with two pheasant feathers stitched jauntily to its left side. She had dyed her hair using a mixture of aged white potato peelings and walnut hulls and wore it in ten tight underbraids that began at the hairline at her forehead and temples and continued to the nape of her neck. There, she had secured each braid with thin black ribbons of wool, leaving the ends of her hair to puff out and down to her shoulders. Her dress, a lightweight wool in a persimmon color to match her hat, was long-sleeved and collarless with a fitted bodice that buttoned up at the front and a skirt that draped softly over her rounded behind. Silas removed his wife's hat and placed it atop the wardrobe. Then he unbuttoned and removed her dress and hung it inside the wardrobe while Emma stood smiling at him. He placed his thumbs beneath the shoulder straps of her underskirt and tugged outward, causing the garment to fall from her body in a flimsy heap at her feet.

"I seen you every day for twenty-three years, and I ain't never seen you enough," he said. He bent to her breasts, filling his mouth, sucking her nipples, feeling them hard and round as crab apples, burying his face in her smell. He kissed her mouth, and reaching behind her, slipped his hand underneath the waistband of her bloomers, caressing her ample buttocks, cupping them, moving his hand to her breasts, to her stomach, along the sides of her thighs.

She had learned the ways to undress him and to spoon her body to his, to feel his life outside her and to urge its coming in. But today before he made love to her, with his eyes he swallowed her whole, and the heat and space between them were too large and too small for measure.

When they were done and lay tired upon the bed, Emma took Silas's face between her palms and stared into his eyes.

"You done give me a chile," she said. She was smiling, and to Silas she was a wonder of burnished cane and the water of life.

"I love you," he said. "We ain't had no churren in twenty-three years, and I ain't got no regrets. I been happy my whole life with you. God ain't seen fit to give us no churren, but he seen fit to give me you."

"Silas, God gon' give us a chile. I just feel it."

"It would be a mighty blessin'," said Silas, "but we old, Emma. I'm forty-five come Fev'ary. That make you forty-seven. Lord knows you look young and fresh as the mornin' dew. You always gon' be my beautiful Rose of Sharon, but don't you think we past ownin' churren?"

"I feel like God gon' give us a l'il baby, Silas, in our old age. Like he done for Sarah and Abraham. And this baby gon' be a fine boy, just like his papa."

In spite of himself, Silas was caught in the fire of Emma's joyous optimism. "If God give us a chile, could be a baby girl,

Emma. How'd you like to name her Arminta after Granny? You say it's gon' be a son? If God give us a son," he said, kissing her, "we gon' name 'im Minton. Boy or girl, I'm gon' call 'im Mint. Put me in mind of the smell that I smell right now on their mama, that make me want to touch her and taste her kisses, make me want to take her in my arms and squeeze her soft and gentle as a mama gorilla, make me want to hold her forever and be with her forever, and outlas' the stars and the sun and the moon."

* * *

Emma had made her new outfit, the persimmon hat and dress, and Silas's white cotton shirt and collar and his suit of navy gabardine, to be worn on what would be one of the three most important events of their lives. The first they counted as Emma's bold acquisition of her freedom in 1839. The second was her purchase of Silas's freedom from Reynolds Sutton for the rock bottom price of six hundred dollars in 1851, primarily with money that she had earned working for him for more than a decade and from sewing, domestic work, farmwork, and healing that she had hired out to do for white women and farmers throughout the county. And the third most important event of their lives was their purchase from Reynolds Sutton of forty acres of land located off Sutton Road in Chesterton in North Carolina's Chatham County on the Albermarle Sound on Saturday, January 6, 1863.

Transported by Reynolds Sutton in his horse-drawn buggy to Guilford, the county seat, Emma and Silas had duly placed their X's on the deed of ownership to the land. They had worked out the terms of payment with Reynolds Sutton far prior to the Christmas season, and Emma had picked Old Christmas as the auspicious day on which the land would be transferred. "It's the day of gifts," she had said to Silas, "the day the three kings come with precious gifts for the baby Jesus. Followed the bright star 'til they found 'im and give 'im his gifts from the east. This land our gift we givin' ourself."

When they had returned from town and had loved each other, and had lain entwined in each other's arms, and had dreamed dreams of raising a free child on their own land, they had not been aware that President Abraham Lincoln had signed and delivered the Emancipation Proclamation just five days before. Even though the War Between the States was raging and Emma and Silas had fed, sheltered, and cared for slaves and ex-slaves on their perilous way to Union lines where many of them would face illness and death from disease, starvation, and exposure, neither Emma nor Silas could know that with a stroke of his pen Lincoln had, in theory, freed three-fourths of the nation's enslaved people. They could not have surmised that in 1865, when the son that Emma would bear in nine months was two years old, no state in the Union would remain a slave state. Had they been aware of these things, perhaps the impact of anticipating emancipation for all blacks everywhere in the nation would have been enough to oil and spring the gates to Emma's womb, closed for a quarter of a century, allowing the seed of Silas's loins secure implantation. As it was, after twenty-five years of sex without conception, they made love in their bed and rejoiced in the blessings that touched their individual lives. Emma, convinced by instinct that she was pregnant, credited the mysteries of God and love and the conditions of humane treatment in her life for her certain fertility.

Playfully, she asked her husband, "You gon' still love me when my stomach pokin' out further'n my titties and my body stretched and ugly, and my ankles and feets swole and achin', and my face saggin' and tired and old lookin' as a ole hag?"

"I'll love you," said Silas, touching her again, aroused, nuzzling her, kissing her neck and ears. "Ain't got to worry 'bout that none. Anyhow, Granny use to say, 'Black don't crack.' Ever hearn tell of that?"

PART TWO

JUSTICE (1874-1914)

[Why] do people suffer? Maybe it's better to do something to give it a reason, any reason.

from "Sonny's Blues," James Baldwin, 1957

5

Idyll

[T]hey'll probably talk about my hard childhood and never understand that all the while I was quite happy.

from "Nikki-Rosa," Nikki Giovanni, 1968

ON THE WAY TO GUILFORD, county seat of Chatham County, where the road forks and leads to the little town of Chesterton, during springtime even today you can see orange ribbons of tiger lilies and the fuchsia of crepe myrtle, two spots of incongruous blossoms amidst poplars, oaks, dogwoods, a scattering of pines, and shorter growths of sumac, honeysuckle, and fox grape vines that line the road. Near the errant blossoms, under soil newly formed over the last thirty or forty years lie a few bricks, some shards of pottery, here and there a fragment of iron unsalvaged from ashes that had been a house. Under the spell of July, the thick heat rising from the recently blacktopped highway, the hum of frogs, the trill of cicadas and unknown birds flitting between dappled leaves, the current tarmac dissolves easily in one's imagination into the graded dirt road, narrower and given to curves, of the previous century. A pathway leads from the dirt road to the yard, an area kept clear of grass and recurrently swept clean of twigs and other debris that might hide poisonous snakes. The yard is further defined by a crepe myrtle bush to the far left and a cluster of tiger lilies to the right, progenitors of those wayward florals still flourishing among woods and weeds today. Toward the rear of the yard, there is an uncovered well with a wooden bucket on a rope attached to a well-side paling. The house itself is a small clapboard structure with a tin roof, a front porch stretching across the front of the house, one room for sleeping on each side of the hallway, a kitchen at the back. The steps at both the front and back of the house are single sections of barkless tree trunk. A dog lolls in the shade on the porch while chickens pluff their feathers in the powdery dirt underneath.

Some distance behind the house there is a smokehouse and, beyond that, a toilet whose detached door rests upon the ground, partially covering the entryway to its double seat. On the far side of the yard, what was once a garden lies unplowed, unplanted, and overtaken by underbrush. The only edible vegetation is a few stalks of "broadcast" salad, topped with yellow flowers promising seed. A few yards further stands a stable with attached barn and hay loft. The hog and cow pasture extends beyond a coppice of poplars to a branch where the livestock can find water. A black and white cat, its elongated teats trailing the groundcover of wild grass, buttercups, and clover, exits the pasture and heads with purpose toward the barn.

A child lives here—Justice, twelve years old—with her father, Elijah Holley. To Justice, from a distance the pasture is a yellow sea, its white clover blossoms capping waves of buttercups. Justice has seen the Albemarle Sound many times, though not the open Atlantic, and is familiar with the choppy grayness of its water in rough weather beneath the lacy meringue of its breakers. She much prefers the imaginary water of the pasture. She remembers falling into the sound when she was three or four years old, an event that her parents, obviously proud of her precociousness, had often suggested that she had been too young to remember. "You must of hearn me and your papa talkin' 'bout that time, Justice," her mother would say smiling. "You won't no more'n a baby."

"Ain't just hearn it, Mama," Justice would counter. "I seen it, and I sho 'members when I fell in the water—like to drownded. I 'members it plain as day."

* * *

Justice's memory, though flawed by suppression and the passage of time, harkened to a sunny July day in years past when she and her parents had gone to the sound for recreation on a Saturday afternoon. They had traversed a path through the woods to a small expanse of fawn-colored beach where two upside-down rowboats, in dire need of caulking, sunned their bottoms. Justice had run up and down the beach that day, wetting her feet and legs in the languid ripples lapping the shore. The water was dark amber, or else it was so clear that it appeared to take on the color of its tawny basin. Stretching as far as the eye could see, the width and seeming boundlessness of the sound set Justice ill at ease. When her parents entreated her to venture out into the water, she demurred, possibly feigning a great fascination with scooping up heaps of sand in the hollow of a turtle shell that Elijah had given her.

Leaving her on the beach, Elijah and Hannah cavorted in the blood-warm sound, their white cotton underclothes billowy and misshapen beneath the water's surface. They splashed each other and held each other, their two heads bobbing like twin ovoids on a shimmering, liquid table. Neither could swim, but the water so near the shore was not deep, and they called out to Justice on the little beach.

"Want Papa come get you?"

"Want Mama come get you?"

They took turns going to shore and admiring Justice's handiwork with the turtle shell. They marveled at the mollusk husks and pebbles that she gathered and her occasional discoveries of colored glass, which she called "di'munts," their broken edges worn smooth by sea and sand. When Elijah scooped Justice up in his arms and ran laughing with her into the water, he quickly brought her, clinging silently to his neck, back to the beach.

"I could feel her poor l'il heart racin'," he said to Hannah, out of Justice's hearing, when she had happily resumed her play in the sand. "She's powerful 'fraid of the water."

Imagine their surprise, then, as they luxuriated in the shallows, when Justice, backing up in their direction, did not stop when she reached the water's edge but continued her backwards trek, stumbled and fell, and was immediately under water. In the few seconds that it took Elijah to reach her, Justice had breathed sound water into her nose and, having opened her mouth as wide as she could, was gagging on its fishy, brackish taste. Elijah spread Justice face down over his knees while Hannah slapped her back to clear her lungs. Then, cradling and soothing their crying child, together they tried to ascertain what the evil force had been that had moved Justice to choose backing into the sound as a lesser peril.

She had seen a snake, a hooded dragon that slid in sinuous splendor upon the sand. Justice had been sitting almost motionless, her eyes fixed upon a scab on her outer left ankle, the thumbnail of her left hand gingerly raising its edges. She intended to pick it off, which she had been forbidden to do, since picking and scratching at mosquito bites had resulted in this and many similar scabs, the evidence of which dotted her legs and arms. "You gon' look like the small pox done got you," Hannah had warned her. "Them legs of yourn gon' stay that way, you keep scratchin' and pickin' them bites, and I'm gon' beat you." Even though the prevalent child-rearing philosophy of the day was "Spare the rod and spoil the child," neither Hannah nor Elijah had ever spanked Justice, who had little reason to attend to their threats of corporal punishment.

The snake—long, thick, and shiny black—lay upon the sand and contemplated Justice as she contemplated her scab. Under the irresistible pull of the snake's intention, Justice raised her eyes from her ankle and was consciously pinioned by the bloodless, reptilian stare.

It could be reasonably argued that the snake was merely curious about Justice or was interested only in protecting its patch of earth. But before the imaginative child's eyes, the snake appeared to raise its head higher and higher upon a body and back that seemed to be all neck. Its obelisk head, which widened perceptibly at its sides, darted toward Justice and back, its tongue flicking in and out to taste the air. And like a beast that has risen on its hind parts to war against the world, the snake stood tall upon its pointy tail and quivered and sensed and challenged from its height. Then its spring-hinged mouth flew open in the fashion of a woman's pocketbook and revealed the milk-white lining that matched its underside, a train of distinctly delineated scales of mother-of-pearl.

Justice could not speak or cry aloud before the towering menace. It seemed as easily capable of consuming the entire world by spewing fire and ashes as it surely was of whipping disobedient children with its endless tail. Justice stared into the unblinking charcoal eyes, their vertical pupils slits of black stone. Unable to call out to her parents or to avert her gaze, she began her backwards retreat into the water.

For weeks afterwards, Justice had frightening dreams about the sound and the "walkin' snake," and her parents would awaken and would take her into their bed where she would nestle in utter security between them. Oftentimes her father would lie facing her with one long arm stretching across her to rest upon her mother.

"Papa here and Mama here protectin' their baby," he would tell Justice, kissing her high forehead and playfully scratching her cheeks with the days old stubble of his beard. "Anything try to bother my baby, I'm gon' sho 'nough scratch 'em good, ain't I, Hannah?"

"Nothin' gon' mess with this baby," her mother would answer. "Ain't nothin' crazy 'nough to try to bother my sugar dumplin' again."

An adored child, Justice remembered the "walkin' snake" that almost "drownded" her as her only traumatic experience until she was nine years old when her mother died suddenly after the premature birth of her fifth child, the fourth miscarried over a secession of eight years. To the side of the garden, beneath a profusion of cosmos, larkspur, and hollyhocks, Hannah had buried the fourth baby in a tiny grave beside the graves of its siblings, gone back to her bed, and hemorrhaged to death in two hours. Her own body rests in the Chesterton Baptist Church yard in eternal separation from those of her children for whom she literally died.

At first people said that Elijah lost the will to live when he buried his wife. He began to shun company, quit going to Sunday school and church, and worked the fields even longer than the other sharecroppers did, plowing from the first light of dawn until pitch dark. He fed the mule by lantern light and ate the tasteless meals prepared by his nine-year-old daughter in virtual silence. "You doin' awright?" he would sometimes ask her in the dim lamplight of the kitchen. "Yassuh!" she would reply, her face toward her plate, in guarded hopefulness.

6

Promise Keeping

We stand there with this big smile of respect between us. It's about as real a smile as girls can do for each other, considering we don't practice real smiling every day....

from "Raymond's Run," Toni Cade Bambara, 1971

WHEN THE PERIOD of a year which the people had deemed acceptable for Elijah's grief had run out, they began to lose sympathy for him and for his little girl. Women who had fried chicken for them, made a sweet bread, persimmon pudding, or fruit cobbler, or boiled a pot of greens or beans with turnips or white potatoes forgot the heavenly rewards that such charity affords and began, instead—perhaps unconsciously—to hold Elijah indebted for their voluntary largesse. Women who had rubbed their knuckles raw aiding the hapless Justice in scrubbing his dingy sheets and boiling the acrid sweat from his shirts and overalls in hopes of attracting his manly attention grew disappointed, in time, and since their generosity did not exact from the devilishly handsome Elijah the price secretly set in their hearts, they gradually withdrew their efforts.

Some members of Chesterton's colored community argued, in hindsight, that Elijah could have regained his faith in God's merciful power and Justice her sense of childhood and joy if the community had continued to care, as Jesus admonished, without judgment of the bereaved. But what the community knew of the Bible most often had been learned from the selective sermonizing of slaveholding Christians. Sufficient to sustain the faithful through many tribulations, the Bible was a slippery tool that could be disregarded or used to prove an opposing point when expedience required. And since Elijah seemed unable or unwilling to get over his grief, most members of the community, busy with their own considerable concerns, appeared to get over him and Justice, too. Then one day the unthinkable happened.

The day, a Saturday, was a beauty. In the afternoon, most of the adult populace had taken off from fieldwork and had gone to Chesterton to buy food stuffs and dry goods that they needed and could pay for or could charge at the general store if they had an account. The men wore clean work shirts and overalls, outfits that would be put aside during church and visiting hours on Sunday but would see the wearers through five and a half days of the next work week. Women wore freshly laundered and ironed dresses or skirts and blouses, and many of the elderly among them covered the fronts of their outfits with heavily starched and impeccably pressed aprons. Tomorrow would be Sunday, and the women's Saturday apparel, like the men's, would undergo a few hours free of use. Indeed, the people's clothes, hard worn but carefully mended, were at rest far more than their owners were. Clothes were not overly abundant, especially among the poor of Chatham County, and most owners, including children, tried their best to preserve them. This awareness must have slipped the minds of June Rose and Ruth Ann on the lovely Saturday afternoon in question.

June Rose, a spritely fifteen-year-old, was deemed beautiful by blacks as well as whites throughout Chesterton. She was a slip of a young woman, with fawn-colored skin, aquiline features, large sloe-shaped eyes, and rivulets of luminous black hair that cascaded far past her shoulders to just above her waistline. Thin but shapely, June Rose was admired for her beauty and modesty by a great number of youthful black males who hoped to win her affection and possibly her hand in marriage.

Equally comely, some would have contended, was Ruth Ann, just six months June Rose's senior. The two had been great friends since childhood, but recently a coldness had risen between them. No longer did they sit together in church or Sunday school. They ceased taking pains to visit each other and to eat Sunday dinner, by turns, with the other's family. No longer did they comb each other's hair, conjure up elaborate plans for dresses that they wanted their mothers to make for them, or giggle about how silly the boys were that they had known most of their lives.

"I seen the way Tobey been lookin' at you," June Rose had said to Ruth Ann, whose thick, kinky hair June Rose was parting and weaving into a fancy under braid. "His eyes gon' sho nuff pop out further'n they already is when he see this braid I'm curlin' 'round your head."

"You know good and well I ain't studyin' 'bout no Tobey, that ole crazy thing! But can I get up a minute and see what all you doin'?" Ruth Ann queried. "You really think I'm gon' look real nice?"

"Yeah, you gon' look pretty as a early spring daffodill, and, no, you can't see what I'm doin' 'til I'm finished," answered June Rose. "You know I can't let go of this braid or it'll unravel on me. I gotta keep goin' 'til I reach the end. Then you can look in the lookin' glass, and I'm tellin' you, you gon' be mighty happy. This style suit your face to a T."

Ruth Ann's face was broad of cheeks, nose, and mouth. Her dark lips were plump, and her deep-set, kindly eyes were adorned by lashes longer than a Holstein cow's. Her forehead, with its pronounced widow's peak, and her chin, as pointed as the narrow end of a small funnel, gave her face the shape of a valentine. Her skin was smooth and dark, almost as black as molasses mitigated by dollops and dollops of finely ground ripe persimmons, evenly mixed in.

"Your skin pretty as blackberries covered in honey," her father, whose complexion was a little darker than her own, would tell her when she was younger and would complain about lighter-skinned children calling her black. "Light skin black folks call me black, too. Always did. But what you think white folks call them?" he would respond. "Think they call 'em white? If so many of our womens hadn't been taken 'vantage of by white mens, we'd all be black as the Af'icans brought all the way over here from Af'ica and sold into slav'ry."

"June Rose light skinned, and she ain't never called me black lessen it was behind my back," Ruth Ann had mused aloud, seeming somewhat unsure.

"All light skin black folks ain't crazy and rebby as po' white trash," her father had answered. "Common sense ain't clean dead in every light skin person's head. Don't rightly think it ever will be. That June Rose a nice gal. She smart, too."

On the Saturday when all hell broke loose, June Rose arrived in Chesterton with her parents. She rode seated on the buckboard with them, but she faced the back of the cart. This arrangement seemed to give her mother's wide hips ample room and to make for a more comfortable trip for parents and daughter. Clearly, June Rose had inherited her slender posterior from her father's side of the family.

"Ain't you comin'?" her mother turned around and asked when June Rose remained standing in the cart after her parents had dismounted and were about to head up the street.

"I be there in a minute. Y'all goin' to the general store first, ain't you? I be right there soon's I re-tie my shoe. These laces always comin' loose if they ain't tied tight enough."

Her parents departed, but June Rose stood staring up the street at the back of a man who was definitely Elijah. She could feel blood rushing to her head and the steady thudding of her heart. Her common sense fled, and she jumped down from the back of the cart fully intending to run after Elijah and tell him how "good" she loved him and always would. She reasoned that this might be her only opportunity to speak with Elijah practically alone since he hardly ever went to church or to visit anybody anymore. She knew that she was quite a few years younger than Elijah, but she had become determined to marry him and to be the mother of his little girl. She couldn't help herself, she told herself, because Elijah was such a pretty colored man, prettier than any white man that June Rose had ever seen, she reckoned. She believed that by marrying Elijah, she would ensure that her children would be at least as light skinned as she was, maybe even as light as Elijah. And they would have good hair like hers and Elijah's—none of that short, nappy wire grass that didn't fight hard enough at sprouting up through the rock hard surfaces of most black folkses' scalps. Some weeks ago she had had a dream where the family's mule had come into her room and nuzzled her awake with its wet, elastic lips. Its penis hung extended from its bloated belly as if it was about to spew gallons and gallons of foul yellow pee over her head, face, and the entire room. June Rose had been terrified and had tried in vain to run and to scream for God, Jesus Christ, the Holy Ghost, her earthly father, and her mother to come and save her from the monstrous mule. No one came. Then the mule became Elijah, gentle and beatific as the risen Lord.

"I wouldn't hurt a hair on your head," the mule, in the form of Elijah, had told her soothingly. "Not one hair."

She had awakened with her heart thudding as hard as it was now, her skin wet with sweat, her nightgown clinging to her cold body like an icy mist.

June Rose did not shift her eyes from Elijah's back. With the agility of youth, she jumped down from the back of the cart only to land on her former best friend Ruth Ann. Though Ruth Ann was heavier than June Rose, both girls lost their footing and tumbled to the ground. Their clean clothes were immediately spoiled by the profuse dry dust from the much traveled dirt street running through the center of Chesterton. Ruth Ann's right hand, extended to break her fall, landed in a damp pile of fresh horse droppings. June Rose picked herself up first and began beating the dirt from her wide skirt with both hands.

"Why don't you watch where you jumpin'?" Ruth Ann yelled, rising herself, and holding her soiled hand away from her body.

"Watch where you walkin'!" June Rose yelled back.

"I was watchin' where I was goin'! If I had known you was gon' throw your ugly bag-o-bones self on me, maybe I'd of moved further out in the street."

"Who you callin' ugly, and you standin' there lookin' like a ole dirty black sheep with shit all over one of your front sheep foots!"

"Take it back!" Ruth Ann demanded. "Take it back this minute or I swear 'fore God I'm gon' shove this here sheep foot down your yellow th'oat! I know you jumped on me, you blind bat, 'cause you was so busy lookin' at Elijah! I seen you! Think he gon' want you after I done rubbed horse hockey in your no-lipped mouth and all 'round your face?"

"Think he gon' want you smellin' like a shit house for mules?" June Rose's face was red as she advanced on Ruth Ann. "Can't nobody hardly see that mule mess on you 'cause it's 'bout as black as the palm of your ole black hands. Hands look like the sole side of bear paws! Why you think Elijah would want your ugly self, and he light skin enough to pass for white on a cloudy day? You the dumbest, stinkin'est, stealin'est, nastiest, blackest Af'ican fool I ever seen!"

Without warning, and so quickly that some fast-gathering

eyewitnesses later claimed they had been confused by the purpose of her instantaneous movement, Ruth Ann slapped June Rose's face sideways so hard that they expected her head to "keep spinnin' round and round and round faster'n a weathervane in a tarnader." June Rose's cheek and part of her mouth were smeared with the moist horse dung from Ruth Ann's hand. "How it taste to you?" Ruth Ann asked sarcastically. "Hope it's right good! Got to taste better'n your ole mama's cookin'!"

Once hit, June Rose had staggered, but after shaking her head like a wet dog, she regained her balance and succeeded in scratching Ruth Ann's offending arm, digging her finger nails under the skin and drawing blood.

"Umph!" they both grunted as they slugged each other and shouted accusations that the other one had been paying no attention to where she was "jumpin'" or "walkin'" because she had been "too busy lookin' at Elijah."

All the while, Elijah had remained oblivious to the two girls fighting over him and had continued on his way to take care of whatever business had brought him to Chesterton that day. When the small crowd that had gathered broke up the fight, Ruth Ann's skirt had been ripped down one side, and June Rose was forced to hold the front of her bodice and underskirt together to keep her small breasts from spilling out. Talk of the fight went on for as long as nothing more scandalous happened to divert the people's attention and give them something new to harp about.

"Why them churren fightin' in the street over Elijah like that?" grown women who had given up on chasing Elijah would ask incredulously, over and over again, after the fight. "What they think they got that none of us sho 'nough womens got to give a man like Elijah?"

"They better be glad nobody didn't call the sheriff on 'em and have their mess locked up in jail," some grown men opined, proving that those who claim males do not gossip are ill informed.

"Lord, ha' mercy!" other blacks complained. "Them two church-raised gals out there fightin' in the street like two strumpets, right in front of white folkses! No wonder they think we's a bunch of jungle monkeys and apes. Them gals just givin' 'em mo' dirt to pile on our heads, like they ain't got 'nough already. Why they brung bushels mo' shame on the whole black race, 'stead of liftin' us up? We glad they ain't none of our churren! Wouldn't be able to hold our head up in church or in town or nowhere else ever again. Got to feel right sorry for their mamas and papas."

Elijah had nothing whatsoever to say about the fight except to admit, when asked point blank, that he had been to town that day but hadn't seen or heard anything out of the ordinary. For him and Justice, life just kept on dragging one foot after the other, leading nowhere that any sane person, black or white, would willingly go.

7

Brokenness

I was broken in body, soul, and spirit. My natural elasticity was crushed, my intellect languished, the disposition to read departed, the cheerful spark that lingered about my eye died; the dark night of slavery closed in upon me, and behold a man transformed into a brute!

from *Narrative of the Life of Frederick Douglass,*
an American Slave, Written by Himself,
Frederick Douglass, 1845

NOT SURPRISINGLY, Justice's complete absence from school after her mother's death went unremarked. The county school for the colored was open maybe two months a year, but most children, needed in the fields to replenish the land owners' coffers, did not attend once they had reached the age for fieldwork. Instead of spending her days reading, writing, spelling, and ciphering, Justice labored in isolation in the home and in the fields, and her father, drowning himself in work to counter drowning in deep depression, did not miss her society. She grew ravenous for her mother's caresses, her father's doting attention, the frequent sound of human voices, and good food. She began to long for the society of ripening red and gold tomatoes, of roasting ears, their silk like angels' hair.

She missed the spiky blooms of onions above their rigid spears, the sculpted leaves of ruffled kale, the red-veined greens of beet tops, the fragrance from mint clusters and strawberry beds. She wanted to bring bunches of Hannah's flowers inside the house to restore its gladness and color. "Can we bring flowers from Mama's garden in the house again, Papa?" she asked Elijah. "No," he said quietly. "We don't go in that garden no more. We got a vegetable garden in the field, and we can get everything we need from there."

Tragedy may have been averted if Justice had received the loving support of relatives—grandparents, aunts, uncles, cousins—but she had no extended family. Indeed, an immigrant to Chesterton himself, Elijah had called Hannah his "found treasure," someone whom God had "put out on the road I was travelin' to open the path to my heart." Heading south from Virginia, he had rounded a sharp bend and there she'd stood, in the middle of the road, embraced by a sunset to rival Joseph's cloak. "Seem like I ain't never had time for just lookin' at the world 'fore now," she offered by way of explaining her transfixion when Elijah had almost reached the place where she stood and had gained her attention only after calling out, "Mighty pretty sunset, ain't it?"

Hannah had been evicted from the house where she had served since she was eight years old, almost half her life, accused of stealing two silver spoons that would later be discovered wrapped in coarse cloth and wedged kitty-cornered in a fine pair of the missus's shoes. One could give the missus, as culprit, the benefit of the doubt by surmising that she had honestly forgotten where she, herself, had put the silver spoons. On the other hand, she knew that Hannah had never been accused of theft before. Moreover, the missus was self-serving and hollow of compassion, and the spoons were part of a plot to render usable shoes that had been ill-gotten through the missus's customary deception. Acquired for a steep price and without her husband's knowledge, the beautiful, ill-fitting shoes had been paid for with money filched over a period of months from the family's wine and liquor account. It had been possible for the missus to stretch the supply of wine with home brew provided by Caesar, the loyal and reticent cook whose thick lips were sealed though perpetually parted by broadly protruding, gapped front teeth. Who could expect him to risk speaking what he suspected on behalf of that uppity nigger gal, Hannah, too proud to accept his advances and proffers of delicacies from the master's own table? Why couldn't she understand that he was no common field slave? He was somebody, and she was too stupid and spiteful to acknowledge it. "Thank the Lord for that!" he had said to himself when he heard the uproar from the missus and stepped out of the kitchen to witness Hannah's humiliation and tearful denial as she was being banished to live in an abandoned outhouse and to do fieldwork for the remainder of her days. That night someone picked the lock that Caesar had used to incarcerate Hannah and was gone or hiding before she could discover the identity of her benefactor. Then she, herself, was gone, swallowed by the night, as she began her trek away from that horrible place.

    Near nightfall on the day he found Hannah, Elijah threw a rock at a rabbit, nailed it, and led Hannah a good ways into the woods where, under cover of darkness, he made a fire and Hannah prepared their supper of spit-roasted rabbit and potatoes baked in the ashes. "Thank you, Lord, for this day," Hannah prayed before their meal, "and for this here food and this comp'ny. Guide our feet, Lord, and keep us in your hand."

    "You sure know how to cook a rabbit," Elijah said. "You cook like my mama, even without a pinch of salt for seasonin'."

    "You and God the provider," replied Hannah. "Without you there wouldn't be no king's supper like this. And these here new potatoes so good! Crispy hulls almost the best part. No grit on 'em at all."

"I'm partial to new potatoes myself," said Elijah, flushing with pride at Hannah's recognition of his ability to provide. "These here ain't so new no more, but brush the ashes off 'em, and they very good. As for grit, washed 'em clean myself gettin' ready for this journey. I try not to eat grit and raw at the same time, if I can help it. And I knew mostly everything I got to eat on this journey would be raw."

With hearts opened to each other, Elijah and Hannah abandoned their separate paths to undertake the business of loving, and Hannah turned her feet from north to south. They put a distance of ten days travel between themselves and the place—"too near that old haint that just as soon sic the paddyrollers on me as spit," said Hannah—where they met. Their southern trek took an easterly direction, and when Elijah found day work helping to build a house for a landowner's just-married son, the head carpenter, a black man named Silas, directed Elijah to a family of sharecroppers who took him and Hannah in. Though unaccustomed to field labor, Hannah gladly worked the crops with their hosts in exchange for a roof over their heads and three meals a day. Then Silas took notice of Elijah's strong work ethic and quick learning and offered him and Hannah a place to stay in his own home, two-and-a-half days' journey by horse from the building site, until they could find work to sustain themselves.

"Much obliged, Silas, for all you already done," Elijah said, "but I'm bound to find my brother."

"You say he was sold to a slave trader from Georgia a year 'fore you left home?"

"Yes, sir, that's right," said Elijah.

"He a slave trader from Georgia, but I bet he wouldn't 'of been sellin' no slaves down there. Who was he gon' find had the money to buy 'em, or crazy 'nough to buy 'em with the war ragin', slaves runnin' away right and left, and the mar'sars' women folks left home to manage by theirself? They was scared to death any strange nigger they see was gon' cut their th'oat. Your brother maybe ain't in Georgia. And even if he is, where at? Can he read and write?"

"Yes, sir. Mama could read and write and cipher good as anybody. She learned us both."

"Tell you what: You and your wife come on to my home 'long with me soon's this job's done. Then you write up a notice sayin' you lookin' for Philip. Say all what Philip look like and send it to papers in Georgia, like in Savannah and Augusta and Atlanta, maybe even Charleston, South Carolina. I can let you have the money—won't be that much no how—and you can pay me back when you can."

"Papers gon' do that for a black?"

"No need to let on that you black or that Philip's your brother. Folks runnin' the papers maybe gon' think Philip b'longed to you. They ain't gon' see you no way, and your money the right color."

"Never had no papa," said Elijah, "but you like a real good one."

Silas smiled. "Everybody got a papa, son. You take 'em where you find 'em. Ain' got to be no kin to you."

Then Elijah told Hannah what Silas had proposed. "What you think we ought to do, Elijah?" she asked.

"Silas got mighty good ideas," he answered. "Letters travel easier than folks, and it's true I don't know where Philip is. Now slavery's over, he could be lookin' for me hard as I'm lookin' for him and we just missin' each other. Think I'll send the notices out like Silas said. Send one to Massaponax, too, in case Philip find his way back home."

Elijah did not know the secret of Cadmus who slew a dragon and sowed its teeth upon the earth, teeth that sprouted into living souls and peopled Thebes; and since Elijah could convene neither the disappeared nor the dead, he and Hannah began anew in an unknown place devoid of kin.

* * *

Elijah had crossed into North Carolina from Virginia in 1865 carrying two dozen washed white potatoes in a tow sack. He had started out with sweet potatoes, also—now down to one—an array of cucumbers and muskmelons, and a few heads of cabbage. He had set out on a journey of indefinite duration, and while he planned to replenish his store of food along the way by working, bartering, even stealing when necessary, he did not want to arrive at his destination hungry, or with nothing to offer Philip in case he was hungry, too.

Elijah did not know his destination except that it was south. After the Civil War, throngs of newly freed slaves left the plantations where they had lived in bondage and struck out in search of a better life. Most would not have chosen to go south in pursuit of liberty and happiness. A few headed south inadvertently for lack of directional and navigational skills. But most going south shared Elijah's purpose of finding loved ones who had been sold away by their former owners. In some cases, those traveling south had themselves been sold and relocated north of their previous homes. Ignorant of his impending emancipation, Elijah set out from Massaponax, Virginia, on April 9, 1865, the day that Lee, sartorially splendid in defeat, surrendered to Grant at Appomatox.

Elijah had decided to run away in 1864, the day his brother Philip was sold to a slave trader from Georgia. Three years older than Philip, Elijah had taken to heart their mother's final charge: "Lijah, look out for Philip much as you can." Both boys had knelt beside her pallet, their heads bent low to hear her words. She held both their right hands in her own, and her eyes, sunken and yellow with fever, moved from Elijah to Philip and back. "Look out for one 'nother, and love one 'nother." They did not feel her breath, too shallow to reach their faces, but a detectable scent of metal emanated from her mouth, her empty stomach's final expulsions into the quiet air. Her name was Esther, and her sons did not know the moment that she died though they were right beside her. Her eyes closed, and so as not to wake her, neither of them moved from their knees beside her bed until her fingers ceased to clasp their hands. Only then did they get up to take away the pot liquor that they had not been able to get her to drink, and to put together such supper as they could provide for themselves.

Philip was sold three days later to atone for the sins of his mother. Esther had been a valuable slave, one whose handiwork as a seamstress was known into the northern reaches of Virginia and as far south as Richmond, farther in each direction than she had ever been or would ever go. The table and bed linens, the exquisite lace, the elaborate window treatments, even the ladies' parasols and fine undergarments that Esther created increased the master's wealth since he, John Holley, sold to shop owners in the more affluent neighboring towns all of Esther's fine handicrafts that his wife was able to part with. Considering what the prodigiously talented Esther surely saved John Holley in costs of his family's fancy clothing and household goods, one might think that he would protect his savings by protecting Esther, who had been born on the plantation from the union of his father and a slave mistress; whose softness and vigor visited his day and nighttime dreams; who had given him two strong sons; and whose cost per year was merely a slave woman's rations.

When John Holley dealt Esther what would turn out to be her death blow, he went too far, much farther, as a man who prided himself on his head for business, than he had intended to go. But she had forced his hand by going too far, he vainly sought to console himself, by running away with the incontrovertible intent of stealing his rightful property: herself, her sons, and all that they were. When she was trapped—the memory caught in his mind like the sob that hung tangled in the paralyzed muscles of his throat when he saw her caught. The cloth that she had tied around her head had fallen from her profusion of hair, which spread in silky tendrils across her face. Finding her way through the woods the night before, she had been startled by a poacher who had not seen her but had heard her rustling in nearby underbrush. His dog had treed a raccoon, and its beady eyes beheld them from a leafy branch high in an elm tree. The poacher had shot and bagged the raccoon, thinking of how glad his wife and children would be, thinking of the smells of coon roasting, sweet potatoes roasting, and kale and dumplings boiling in the pot. He did not see the woman, Esther, who saw him, dropped to her hands and knees, and crawled over a carpet of pine needles away from the hunt. When she had gone a short distance, she got up and ran, her dark-clad form moving like a frightened animal in vague and unfamiliar surroundings. Then she realized that in dropping to the ground to flee by crawling, she had abandoned her flour sack of provisions. She could not go back and risk capture, not even for food and samples of her artistry that could be sold or used to advertise her craft. She did not know that the hunter's dog, released from urgency by the already dead raccoon, had followed its nose to her deserted sack and the hastily wrapped breads, fish, and meats that it held. The hunter retrieved the sack, remembering the noise that he had heard before shooting the raccoon, and surmised that what he held had been the possession of a runaway slave. The fish was fresh herring, fried in a coating of cornmeal, its sides notched to better disburse the salt and black pepper seasoning through its flesh. The hunter ate two of the fish and a cake of corn bread as he made his way out of the woods in the direction of his home. "Niggers sho can cook!" he said to himself. It had crossed his mind that he should chase the runaway, bringing him or her in for perhaps a steep reward that his family could certainly use.

"Sposin' it's a bunch of 'em," he argued with himself, "and only one of 'em lost their bag. Sposin' it's a gang of crazy nigger bucks and they manage to get my gun from me and kill me with it and then go have their way with my wife and kill my churren."

The hunter knew that in less than an hour, it would be daybreak, so he shifted direction and began the thirty-minute trek to the sheriff's house. "No need to let that reward money out the county," he said to himself. "The sooner I let the sheriff know 'bout them runaway niggers, the sooner he can catch 'em, and the sooner that reward money is mine. Won't hurt 'im to get his fat ass out the bed early for once." The hunter thought about eating another herring but deemed it imprudent to eat up more of the evidence before he had claimed the prize. Besides, if the sheriff had no objections, he'd take the rest of the slave's food home with him.

Esther was apprehended less than three miles from the Holley plantation. As soon as he saw the contents of her sack, the sheriff knew who he was after, and he sent a slave to fetch her master, who could verify that Esther was missing as well as help to bring her in. "Anytime you can have the owner present at a slave capture, you're at a great advantage," the sheriff had long taught his deputy. "With the owner present, there'll likely be no questions of how you treated the property, and they can have the pleasure of doling out all the punishments theirself."

When John Holley saw Esther, she had flattened herself against the far side of a large oak tree that clearly had been chosen to hide her from the clangorous pursuit of hounds and men. Her hair unbound, her bronze-colored face damp with sweat, she had spread her arms backwards around the tree, the inner side of her arms and her palms touching its bark. She had become a human cross, its transverse beam pliant and plastered against an ancient oak. She wore an ivory tunic and a blue jacket, sewn by her own gifted hands, cinched around the waist by a knotted cord. Her flared skirt of cedar green stopped just short of her shoe tops. Both her jacket and tunic were open at the throat, and John Holley could see the violent rise and fall of the hollow at the base of her neck, marking the agitated evenness of her breathing. To Holley, even at thirty-five years of age, two years younger than himself, Esther was more beautiful than she or anyone else had ever been before, and when he tried to call her name, he could not speak.

The sheriff grabbed one of her arms. "See to the dogs," he said to his deputy. "Don't try to run or do anything foolish while we put these irons on you," he said to Esther.

"You don't see me tryin' to run nowhere," said Esther. "Runnin's over for now. And y'all can do what you will." Her ordinary words dripped hatred, not despair, hatred that flashed in her eyes when she looked at John Holley, who managed at last to speak her name.

"Esther, you can believe me on this: You'll be mighty sorry for what you've done before this is all over," he said to her.

"Already sorry," she said. "Sorry you alive. Sorry I was ever born. Sorry I done brought two churren into this life of misery. Sorry I didn't cut your evil throat a thousand chances I done had." Esther bent her head slightly, never breaking eye contact with him, and spat upon the ground.

Holley stepped directly in front of Esther and slapped her hard, but she did not fall. His palm left an imprint upon her face that was as red as his own visage, twisted with shame and rage at her words. "Tie her behind that mule!" he shouted to the sheriff's deputy. Then to Esther: "You gon' walk back, and you gon' keep up with that mule!"

"Prepared to walk farther'n that," came her heated reply. "Prepared to walk all the way to freedom in a Yankee state! Prepared to make fancy things and sell 'em and save up the money to buy my sons! Prepared to get a white man, a abolitionist, to buy 'em for me. You'd sell 'em, greedy as you is, 'cause I would of offered so much money for my churren. You wouldn't of known it was me no how, and I wouldn't never have to look in your evil face again. Ain't no man look out your eyes. Satan look out. Satan done et up your soul. He eats it some more every time you force me. I hate you for all you ever done, and you can kiss my ministratin' ass!"

This time he hit her with his fist, and she floated, a billow of blue and cedar green, unconscious, to the ground. In the end, she could not stand, or refused to stand, and John Holley lifted her onto his horse and carried her, slumped backward onto his chest, home to the plantation.

"That sharecropper of yourn's gon' be lookin' for a reward for helpin' us find Esther, you know," the sheriff said to Holley as they rode along. "Mentioned it to me this morning 'fore I left. You offerin' anything?"

"You can tell 'im I'm offering him the coon he poached out of season without permission on my land. I never could stand no lazy, thieving, stinking, dirty, no 'count, poor white trash, and that's all he is. Always trying to beat something out of somebody. Tell 'im he so much as mention a reward regarding Esther and I'll have the law on him faster'n that broke down wife of his can spit out another of them ugly, cross-eyed, hungry, inbred young 'uns they always havin'. Talkin' rabbits is what he and that wife of his are."

John Holley intended to deter Esther from ever again considering that running away to freedom was a viable option for her or her children. At the same time, he intended for Esther's flogging to convince his other slaves that running away had been a foolhardy move and that death would be better than the thirty lashes he planned to inflict upon her. Every slave that John Holley owned was summoned and accounted for to witness Esther's punishment. He used an old leather strap with iron buckles on each end whose original function had been to gird a horse or mule's underbelly from one side of the saddle to the other. It was a few inches wide, thick but pliant. Under its force, Esther lost consciousness before the tenth stripe. Her son Philip, fourteen years old, broke from his brother's arms to intervene on his mother's behalf. Elijah regained hold of Philip, and two other male slaves helped to restrain him. John Holley was certainly aware of the disturbance but too tired, perhaps, to flog Philip for his audacity, or maybe his thirst for blood and for power over Esther's spirit had been sated. Quite possibly his heart recoiled momentarily from pummeling his own offspring, for Philip's face, though younger and darker tinged, was nearly John Holley's own.

Esther lay inert, and abruptly her master left off beating her, signaled the overseer to disperse the slaves and to move Esther to her cabin, and headed for the pump at the back of the great house. He would remove as much as he could of Esther's blood before entering the sanctity of his home where (and he did not yet think this thought; that would come later) she had spent every day and where every room bore the stamp of exquisite beauty that her boundless mind had envisioned, her hands created, and his wife— still hidden deep in a dressing room to escape the reach of Esther's cries—enjoyed.

John Holley sold Philip without one word about the matter having leaked to the slaves. Esther did not witness in any earthly form Philip's being shackled and loaded onto a cart for transport toward Baltimore. The iron teeth in her master's horse belt had entered and re-entered her side and back with the ease of greased bullets, and she had suffered multiple punctures to her right kidney and lung. Yet, her spirit clung stubbornly to her body for three days.

8

Innocence

[O]ne of the plantation slaves was brought to town . . . and Dr. Flint ordered him to be taken to the work house, and tied up to the joist, so that his feet would just escape the ground. . . . Never before, in my life, had I heard hundreds of blows fall on a human being. His piteous groans, and his "O, pray don't, massa," rang in my ear for months afterwards.

from *Incidents in the Life of a Slave Girl,* Harriet Jacobs, 1861

IN THE FALL after her twelfth birthday, as Justice struggled to prop the sagging clothesline against the weight of dripping wash, Jack Askew, the nineteen-year-old son from a neighboring household, appeared as if by magic at her side. His smile was white in his sun-tanned face, his gray eyes hooded from squinting in the morning light. "Let me he'p you with that," he said, taking the pole from her skinny hands and lifting the clothes to safety on the tautened line. "Thank you, suh," she said and stood back, looking at the ground.

"Now, don't be scared of me," he said. "No need to be scared of me. I ain't gon' hurt you. I know your papa. Knowed your mama, too. Where's your papa at now?"

"In the pea field down to Jones Place.

"Looks like that old cat of yourn got business in the barn."

"She got kittens, suh."

"Well, show me your cat's kittens," he said. "How many she got?"

"Got five," said Justice. "You can go on and look at 'em, suh."

"I ruther for you to go with me," he said. "Sometime mother cats get mean when anybody they don't know come 'round their kittens. Might try to scratch and bite, thinkin' they gon' harm 'em, but I ain't gon hurt 'em any. I just want to see' em. I like kittens. Had me a cat once."

Justice looked at the young man's slitted eyes, at his hay-colored hair and bright smile, and the message of fear sent from her stomach to her brain was written on her face.

"Do you like ginger snaps?" he asked, and produced a crisp paper bag from the deep pocket of his cotton pants. "I've brung you some," he said, opening the bag and handing it to Justice. There could have been as many as eight or ten of the pungent little cookies in the bag. Justice had never tasted ginger snaps, but she smelled their molasses and spices and she remembered the rich molasses breads that her mother had baked, the dark sweetness that had filled her mouth and lingered in her nose even after its passage to her stomach. She was ravenous for the past, for the society of humans, and for good food; and not comprehending the cost of the white man's offering, she swallowed her trepidation and followed him into the barn.

Pushed against the mountain of dried corn, she tried to run. She could not gain her footing, and the man was on her, crushing her thin body against protruding corn cobs, his mouth locked to hers, his white teeth parted, his tongue down her throat blocking her scream. Then, his left hand pressing hard against her forehead, he spoke in whispers of her beautiful skin and her mouth like honey, and warned against sound or ever speaking of that day or her father would surely die just as her mother had. He could not know the horror of her mother's death, of the nine-year-old Justice digging the shallow grave while her mother wrapped the bluish bundle in a sun-bleached feed bag and stumbled with it from the bedroom to the flower bed. He could not see the child half supporting her mother, whose double trail of blood marked her way from the house to the garden and to the house again. Justice had placed a folded quilt on the bed, under her mother's buttocks, and wedged an ample edge between her thighs, but the bleeding would not stop. It soaked the crazy crosspatch, rendering blues and greens and yellows a stiff and fecund red. With cool water from the well, Justice had bathed her mother's forehead and waited for her to awaken, as she had before, from troubled sleep.

When he had finished and the child lay bleeding upon the cornhusks, the man took a single ginger snap from the bag that Justice had dropped in her struggle. "You better eat the rest of these way 'fore your papa get home," he said. He crumbled the hard cookie between his thumb and fingers and kneeled to spread its pieces near the bed of the week-old kittens. The black and white cat, sprawled on her side to accommodate her suckling offspring, appraised the man with fleeting interest. And sensing that her kittens were not the ones endangered by his presence, she had forgotten him before he quickly stood and left the barn.

Finding blood between her own thighs, Justice may have expected to die her mother's death, but courage born of sorrow compelled her resolution to save her father's life. First, she disobeyed him by entering the garden to bury the bag of ginger snaps, including the crumbs scooped from before the cat's lair, near the graves of the four aborted fetuses. Then, with a slab of lye soap, she bathed herself in the murky water from the day's wash. She used the discolored cloths that Hannah had worn during her monthly periods to fashion for herself an awkward pad. The first that she had ever needed, she drew upon remembrance of her mother to knot the pad to a belt of slender rag.

She remembered, too, that Hannah had taught her love of God and of all people, including one's enemies. Now, surely forsaken by God, she loved only memories and her father. And first among those she hated was herself.

When Justice was six months pregnant, Elijah saw that her stomach protruded under her mother's dress and that her breasts were full on her boyish frame. She said she could not name the father of the child. She tearfully protested remembering that any man had ever touched her and insisted that her body had suddenly swollen with fat. Perhaps it was her lying—Elijah's perception that the child who had never been deceitful before was now treating him as a fool. More feasible, it was fear for his daughter's life prompted by a mental flashback to his wife lying dead from childbirth on a mattress soaked with blood, her waxy face swathed by Justice, unaware that she was gone. It could also have been suspicion that the child, recently become a woman, had let the evil of lust into their home, rending the threadbare fabric of their lives. Or it may have been that he simply snapped under the ancient strain of God's pride and anger when disobedient woman consorted with the snake. Whatever the specific cause, Elijah began to beat Justice with his fists and, dragging her to the smokehouse by her arm and the waistband of her dress, he bound her wrists with rope that he snared on a meat hook impaled for butchering hogs beside the door.

At first, hanging against the rough hewn boards of the smokehouse, her chin drooped upon her chest, Justice was silent. But when her father had fetched the leather reins from the stable and had begun to flail her length with cutting blows, she pleaded again and again, "Ha' mercy, Lord! Ha' mercy, Lord! Don't, Papa! Please stop, Papa! Save me, Lord!" The force of each swing propelled Elijah to his toes, and the crack of the leather on his daughter's body was a slashing counterpoint to his rocking dance. The dress that Justice wore in tatters, her body torn and bloody, her head and face unspared since she could not shield them with her arms, her bare feet drawn beneath her dress in useless search for harbor, she cried out, "Mama, he'p me! Please he'p me, Mama!" And from the graded dirt road, two giant steeds in billows of dust swung neighing into the yard. Their manes were like windswept snow, their white hides glistened with sweat, and the heat and force from their thundering hooves threw sparks into the languid air.

Dropping the horse reins, Elijah froze, and Justice lifted her gaze to the horses who stopped in front of her. She would recall their eyes as golden suns, their fleshy nostrils long and pink lined, their lips pulled back in awesome scowls from block-like, ivory teeth. They reared over Justice and her father, and she saw the cavernous hollows between their flanks and massive chests. She saw the perfect juncture where their hair met down their middles, and she felt the sure protection of their powerful, pawing hooves. Then they stood still before her, their icy breath stanching her bleeding and easing the clinging tatters of her dress from her open wounds. When Elijah had lifted her from the meat hook and held her in his arms, as swiftly as they had come, the horses departed forever, melting in snowy whiteness into the woods.

It was then that Elijah reached out to his neighbors by seeking the aid of Emma Sutton, the midwife and healer who had ushered the infant Justice into the world. Carrying her bulk, her paraphernalia, and the majesty of the aged, Emma cringed at the sight of Justice, a mass upon the bed. As if she had time on her side, she swept the steps and the doorways, drew a sign upon the lintel, and with arms stretched toward the darkening sky, she called on the name of Jesus. She howled out to God the Father, "You got to be here, Lord! You said you would, almighty God and true redeemer!" She cried out to the Holy Spirit to throw off the yoke of suffering on that house, to stomp the forces of Satan, and to breathe the breath of healing on the child. "Start right now, Lord! Move through this here house, Holy Spirit!" she prayed. "I done swept the way clean for your holy feet, but I can't do this by myself, Jesus! We need you to come in here right now, Lord, and he'p me, Lord, 'cause I'm jus' your poor servant! You know it was you who done fed us, Lord, when we was hongry! You know you done strengthened us when we was half dead to hold our l'il chirren to our breas', Lord! You know how many times you done kept the mar'sar's whip from off our backs, Lord! You know you done lifted us up from slav'ry, Lord! You done lifted that yoke! You done washed us clean in yo' blessed river, Lord, and we needs you, Lord! We needs you right now, Lord, to he'p this chile. In the name of Jesus."

And then, sending Elijah into the night, she fetched a basin of water, cut the child's clothing from her body, laid out her herbs and unguents, and, strengthened by the power of proof that God is merciful, she began the daunting task that lay ahead.

She dressed the child's wounds, stitching the worst tears, and murmured quiet reassurances during Justice's fevered outbursts about hunger, a white man who had hurt her and would kill her father, about little molasses cakes, and kittens in the barn. During the long night, Emma's hands received the pale-skinned mummy from Justice's ruptured womb, and she realized the terrible truth of the child's misfortune.

* * *

In the morning Emma Sutton, called by God to midwifery and healing, summoned the red-eyed Elijah in from his sleepless night, related the harrowing details of Justice's delirium, and held the blond-haired remains before his eyes. Then understanding smote Elijah's broken heart, and he rushed blindly from the house.

In the three weeks that it took to find Elijah—his overalls caught upon a jutting tree root, his flesh bloated and gnawed by crabs, his rotting scalp listing against the clayey bank of the Albemarle—his body had been washed four miles downstream where a fisherman, hoisting his flounder catch, had seen the sodden blue of his denim shirt. Women from the community had taken turns helping Emma to care for Justice, but when Elijah's death was known, Emma fashioned in her cart a mattress of corn shucks covered in tow sacks, directed her son Mint to carry Justice out of her father's house to the makeshift bed, and with Mint walking alongside the mule holding its bridle to keep it gentle, she moved the broken Justice, under a mound of covers, to her home.

9

Found

Ere sleep comes down to soothe the weary eyes,
  How all the griefs and heartaches we have known
Come up like pois'nous vapors that arise
    From some base witch's caldron, when the crone,
To work some potent spell, her magic plies.

from "Ere Sleep Comes Down to Soothe the Weary Eyes,"
Paul Laurence Dunbar, 1895

JUSTICE SLEPT ON A BED of horizontal slats, narrow boards spread far apart on a sturdy frame. Of Mint's invention, the bed, without covers, allowed for optimal airflow to Justice's wounds. Airflow aided healing, enhanced the strength of the tinctures that Emma painted twice daily over Justice's body, and hastened the entry into her lacerations of gelatin made from aloe, rose hips, and strawberry leaves. Under Emma's careful ministrations, the arnica extract that Justice swallowed turned traitor to the deadly poisonous role it often played in less accomplished hands, and Justice began to recover. When teas brewed from the snakeroot plant, or from wild ginger root, or from pennyroyal leaves had finally cured her fever, Justice became aware of her nakedness.

Her bed stood before the fireplace in the kitchen, a large room added by Mint to the original structure of the house. It was a pleasant environment—or would have been if Justice had been alert enough to notice it. On the wall opposite the fireplace, dried gourds of various colors, sizes, and textures hung from pegs. Underneath them, shelves of pickled beets, cucumbers, peaches, and watermelon rinds, along with canned meat, beans, peas, fruit, corn, tomatoes, and preserves, lined the wall. Clusters of garlic and of onions hung alongside bunches of herbs, wild flowers, and medicinal plants strung around the tops and sides of the room's two paneless windows, wall openings with heavy plank shutters. The smells of beans cooking in the iron pot over the fireplace, or of chicken and dumplings on the kitchen stove, or of apples or pumpkins baking sometimes permeated Justice's stupor and began to awaken her appetite.

One morning as the gray light of dawn slipped beneath the kitchen door, Mint, up before his mother, moved between the slat bed and the fireplace to stoke to life the dormant flames. In the firelight, her lids practically closed, feigning sleep, Justice observed Mint as he studied her. From his kneeling position before the fireplace, Mint had shifted his body to face Justice and was gazing at her left foot where she had sustained a wide gash. He saw that it was healing well, and his eyes moved to her left side, her belly, and her left breast where the reins had dug deeply. Only when his gaze had traveled up her neck and to her face did Mint notice that her whole body was trembling, and from their cavernous sockets, her petrified eyes stared wildly up at him.

"Mornin'!" he said softly. "How you feelin'? I b'lieve you finally 'wake."

Justice did not answer. She had covered her breasts and pubic hair with her hands and arms.

"Mama!" Mint said loudly as he rose to his feet and backed

away from the bedside. "She's woken, and I b'lieve she's wantin' cover!"

10

Lost

You are loved, awake or dreaming,
You are loved.

from "Response," Bob Kaufman, 1965

THIS NEW LEVEL of consciousness was a milestone for Justice. In the nether world that she had inhabited for weeks, she had seen a recurrent montage of troubling visions. One followed the other in rigid sequence, a pantomime of life unerringly relived to the last detail of its predictable doom. In this world of dreams, there was no mystery of events—only a mystery of meaning—and Justice had struggled mightily to awaken from it to peaceable times.

In the dream, Justice saw Elijah lying asleep in a bed. He lay in a strange house by an open window, and a dove, white as birch bark in a dark forest, came to the window and hovered there. Far larger than the house in which Elijah slept, the dove's head was all that was visible in the window frame. Its eyes were like cold gray pebbles from the bottom of a crystal stream and in its beak it carried a gray-eyed baby who turned into a writhing serpent before the dove, opening its beak to speak, let it fall to the ground.

"Go east, Elijah, and hide by the great water and drink of its bounty," the bird's voice thundered, "and I have commanded all manner of fowl to bring you meat and bread to eat in the morning and in the evening, and you shall never know hunger or want!" At the sound of the bird's voice, Elijah awakened and was very afraid. Then Justice saw her mother come into the room where Elijah lay. In her hands she carried a cake of meal and a flagon of water. "Don't be afraid, Elijah," she said. "I have food of which you may eat and drink," and she handed him what she had brought.

When Elijah had eaten, Justice saw her mother fall on her knees before him. Weeping loudly, she said, "Please, husband, Man of God, heal our child!" And Justice saw her own body lying dead in her mother's arms, and her father, realizing that it was he who had killed her, ran from that house to the great water where ravens drank his blood and ate his flesh.

And again Justice saw her father lying asleep in a strange place when the landlord, carrying leather reins, came and woke him. The landlord's eyes were stormy water, his voice a rusty bellows, and his lips a skull's grin. "Take these reins," he said to Elijah. "Go and harness the mules and horses and drive them to water that they might drink. For these acts you will be forever blessed and pleasing in my sight."

But when Elijah had opened the stables, the mules and horses broke free and scattered. As they galloped, their hides took on a gray-white hue, and their bodies grew larger and larger until they covered the sky. Then they turned around from fleeing and came back toward Elijah at a ferocious speed. Now they wore the faces of gray-eyed monsters with blood red muzzles and patchy, yellowed manes. Their tongues were darting flames, their hides scabrous and scaly, their nostrils fiery tunnels spewing ashes instead of breath. Elijah was greatly frightened. He looked for a place to hide, but, finding none, with his bare hands he dug a shallow grave beside a clump of burdock and lay within it. Then he called on Christ Jesus to come and cover him up.

Then Justice saw her father walking alone in a desert where he had sojourned for some time, and a gray-eyed man came to him in a cloud of swirling dust. "Go call your friends and neighbors and tell them to come and aid you, for your wife has died and left you, and your child will surely die. Tell them that I will provide a banquet in your honor—a savory feast of suckling pig and venison and beef and fowl and fish and breads and wine and all manner of vegetables from the fields and sugar and ginger sweets. And tell them that I will do these things to prove that I am I."

But Elijah was doubtful that such a feast could be provided, for the rains had not rained and the fields had long been dry. The larders were almost empty in the homes of his friends and neighbors, and the landlord who had a plenty was not about to share.

"Where will you find provisions," he asked with incredulity, "when all the people are hungry and their children cry for bread? If I deliver your message and the banquet is not laid, the people will all be angry and will slay me as punishment."

Then the man stirred up the dust and hid his cold, gray eyes, and he spoke from the billowing cloud: "Remember that I provide! And if any turn against you, I will raise you in a wind to safety beyond the narrow reach of mortal man."

Elijah turned from the desert and entered his homeland and brought his friends and neighbors together to share in the promised meal. But food was not forthcoming. Instead, the banquet cloths were strewn with newly dead infants, their glassy, gray eyes open in their bluish, wrinkled faces. And Elijah's friends and neighbors quickly grew exceedingly angry. They turned into vicious dogs that fell upon the infants and tore them limb from limb.

Then Justice saw her father riding on a horse of fire that raced around the sun at lightning speed. Time and again she saw

Elijah upon his fiery steed as he circumnavigated the brilliant eye that never closed its lid or went to sleep. But that was later in his journey. Some time before, aboard a hoary boat, he had skiied over frozen oceans, ascended snowy mountains unknown to vegetation or other worldly life. Descent had been endless dropping, the wind a constant moaning, the air a sharp and steely ice-edged surgeon's tool. And when an egret lifted Elijah up in its knotted claws and flew him through vast spaces of stars and hails of comets, his spirit and body rested, not least of all his feet. In heat too thick for cutting, on molten, running sand, a water globule opened and closed around his form. Then black winds came and blew him from that sere and burning desert and set him down for good. And Elijah, in moisture perfect as that inside the womb, resumed his journey walking and landed in a room of joy and peace enduring, and he lay down and slept.

11

Guidance

I have wrapped my dreams in a silken cloth;
I hide no hate; I am not even wroth
Who found earth's breath so keen and cold. . . .

from "For a Poet," Countee Cullen, 1925

IN A WAY, the morning that Justice became conscious of her nakedness was a milestone for Mint, too. He had seen Justice without clothes every day. He had helped his mother to nurse her, lifting her naked body, turning her from her back to her stomach, from her stomach to her side. To keep scar tissue from forming on her face, he had used his calloused thumbs to abrade the thickening ridges of her knitting flesh. He had lifted her left leg onto his lap to massage his mother's salves into her foot wound with no apparent interest in the clearly visible cleft between her thighs. He had neither bathed Justice nor tended the gash along her stomach or the one crossing her breast, but he had not turned his back as his mother had cared for the child, and he had studied with great interest her speedy improvement. Now her terrified eyes and skinny hands that sought to hide her nipples and the sparse hair between her legs from his view marked the need for care in how he presented himself in her presence. He sensed her terror of him as a man, and his heart grew heavy with pity.

He surprised her with a little box that he had made, the top of which was formed from different colors of wood in various sizes and shapes that fit together like a puzzle. He told her it was to put her keepsakes in, and when she declared that she had none, he brought her such treasures as he could find: a blue bird's feather, a piece of purple quartz, a four-leaf clover, a mirror. Mint had a set of checkers, and in time that he had to spare from work and tomcatting, he taught Justice to play. From Emma she would learn the craft of excellent cooking and would delight her own reluctant palate with her culinary skill. She would learn to fashion men's, women's, and children's clothing without patterns, to create dyes from "shumake" leaves and berries, indigo, and walnut hulls, to form baskets and chair bottoms from rushes, and to make soap and candles as smooth and soft as sound water in summer.

Mint never asked anything of Justice, and Emma never had to because Justice was eager to learn and to please. But she showed no interest in or aptitude for healing, and when Tim Brantford, married one year, came in great agitation to seek Emma's help for his pregnant wife whose water had broken, Justice became so upset that she lost control of her bladder and stood in the pool of urine that formed around her feet. Mint walked to the waiting mule and cart with Tim and Emma and did not return to the house until he had given Justice ample time to clean herself and the floor.

"Let's talk about what's the scariest things to us," he said to Justice.

"Oh, you not scared of nothin'," Justice said, raising her eyebrows in mock exasperation.

"You wrong, girl," Mint replied. "I'm 'fraid of too many things to count."

"Like what?"

"For everything I tell you 'bout, you have to tell me 'bout somethin'."

"Well, what you gon' tell 'bout?"

"I ever tell you 'bout my papa?"

"Naw."

"Well, you never knew him 'cause he died when you would of been real little, when I was 'bout your age now. My papa worked in the log woods sometimes durin' the winter to help make ends meet—you know, times he didn't have to be in the field every day. And you know how two people get on either end of a saw to saw a tree down? Well, my papa was on one end and Henry Burke was on the other. Henry was a young guy, 'bout fourteen at the time, and he hadn't done a lot of loggin', and he wasn't too strong, either. Well, it had got cold and had snowed some. There was a thick layer of snow on the ground over the leaves, and the snow and the leaves and stuff had got wet and slippery. And my papa pulled the saw to his side, and then Henry pulled it to his'n, but then Henry lost his footin' and when he fell, he let his end of the saw go, and it whipped roun' some way and caught my papa—'cause he was bent down in the position to pull the saw back to his side—and it caught 'im just in the vein on the side of his neck. That's what Henry said he thought happened, but it happened so fast and he was fallin' and couldn' see what happened. But the people said that saw couldn' of whipped 'roun' like that. They said Papa and Henry had just started sawin' the tree and the saw must of buckled out of the tree and Papa must of slipped and his neck got hit. They was far back in the woods, and Henry yelled for the others and they carried my papa out, but by the time Mama got to 'im to he'p 'im, it was too late. . . .

"They say that snow was jus' red. And Henry was sick over it for the longest time. Prob'ly still is. But you got to let it go."

Justice sat very still. "I didn't know 'bout your papa. I'm sad to hear it, Mint. . . . What you 'fraid of, Mint?" she asked quietly. "You ain't said what you 'fraid of."

"You know I'm a carpenter," he said. "I 'prenticed with my grandpapa and Ole Man Joe Taylor. I was with Ole Man Taylor when my papa died. Certain times a year, I use saws almos' every day the Lord send. And I can handle saws, but so could my papa. Maybe somebody else's mistake'll kill me. You don't know how you gonna go. But every day you got to get up and go on out and do what you got to do. You got to make a livin', you can't hide from the world, you got to forgive people, you got to get over bein' scared. I'm scared somebody might make a mistake and kill me with a saw like what happened with my papa, or I might be the one to make the mistake and kill myself or, worser, I might kill somebody else. But there's a hundred million other things that I could die from, or could cause somebody else to die from. But I don't go 'round every day bein' scared of 'em, and that's just 'cause my papa didn't die from 'em. What I'm tryin' to say is saws ain't no more dangerous than plows or mules or anything else I use to make my livin', and 'cause my papa died from a saw don't mean I'm goin' to."

"So you ain't mad with Henry Burke no more for killin' your papa?" Justice asked.

"I ain't mad with him a bit. Never was, and I loved my papa. It was a accident. Whatever happened, Henry didn't 'tend for it to happen."

"Now, s'posin' he had done it on purpose. I bet you would be mad with him then. Prob'ly would of tried to kill 'im yourself. You'd still be hatin' 'im!"

"Maybe. I can't rightly say. But I don't think so 'cause I just can't see no good come from hatin'."

"Even if they 'tended to hurt you?"

"Every thing people do 'cause they 'tend to, they got a reason for to do it. May not be a good reason to me or you, but it's their reason. Sometimes folkses' reasons are so bad, you have to feel sorry for 'em. Take men who 'buse their wives and churren and don't hardly feed 'em or get 'em clothes to wear. Use what little money they can get to run women and buy corn liquor 'stead of feedin' their family. The reason they do like that is 'cause something's made their soul sick. Maybe they so unhappy with their life and feel like they can't do nothin' 'bout it, so they get mad and lash out at the only people they ain't scared gon' hurt 'em back. They want to feel like they big, like they got some power over somebody, but here they grown men and can't even feed their family, put clothes on their churren's backs. They worked hard all their lives, and they saw their own papas slave, and none of em ever was able to take care of their family like a man, or to keep white folks from beatin' 'em and sellin' 'em off. They so mad with white folks for cheatin' 'em and keepin' 'em down. It ain't slav'ry they angry 'bout in particular; slav'ry been over twenty-three years, since I was two years old. They angry 'cause even though we been freed, we ain't been freed enough. We still livin' under the white man. Some of us too weak for it, so we turn on our own family. And we turn on our own self 'cause we can't get at the folks we mad with."

"What about white folks, Mint? They got everything. They ain't got no reason to be mad. They got the land and the stores and all the money. They own near 'bout everything, so why they hurt us, Mint? Why they 'tend to hurt us?"

Mint cupped Justice's chin in the fingers of his left hand, and with his thumb he brushed away tears that were brimming from her eyes, and he kissed the flat scar on her left cheek. "White folks' souls sickern' black folkses', Justice. They so lazy and greedy. They want to own everything, but they don't want to work for it. Want us to do all the work for 'em and let them have the profit. That's bad 'nough, but then they try to fool theirself and black folks, too. Claim we lazy, but they the ones don't do no work worth a cuss. Claim we nasty, but who clean their house and raise their churren? Claim we steal, but they the ones steal most of what money the blacks s'posed to get for their crops. Claim we want their women, when they the ones want somebody else women. Claim we ugly, look like gorillas. If our women ugly, why they been after 'em since they got off the slave ships from Africa? Why ain't their women 'nough for 'em? You see, Justice, they treat us bad 'cause their soul is rotten, and it's rotten 'cause they live a lie, pretendin' they don't treat us no worsern we need to be treated 'cause we ain't real people. Near 'bout everything they do is a lie. People who lie to theirself so they can feel better 'bout all the bad things they do got sick souls that get sicker all the time. The Bible say, 'If the devil is your father, you will follow the lusts of the devil, and you won't dwell in the truth 'cause the truth ain't in you. And when you tell a lie, you and your father the devil both liars.' White folks done made the devil their father, 'stead of the Lord, 'cause the Lord dwell in the truth. The Bible say we gon' be like God and know good from evil, but white folks be like the devil; they confuse good and evil. When the Bible say, 'Some learn but never come to the knowledge of truth,' that's white folks. And when it say, 'Evil shall slay the wicked,' that's white folks, too, cause through their evil, they slayin' their own soul."

"The Bible say, 'Hate that which is evil,' and white folks evil! You just as much as said so yourself, Mint, and I hate 'em!" Justice exclaimed, though she had likely not fully understood the scriptures that Mint had quoted, if, indeed, he had quoted them reasonably correctly or had understood them fully himself.

"Hatin' don't do no good, Justice," Mint said. Again he took her chin in his hand and held it. "I wish nobody never hurt you." There was a sad little smile around his eyes and on his lips, and Justice gave him the ghost of a smile back. His gaze held her, and the love and understanding in his eyes were a slow river whose great length she began swimming in the direction of salvation.

Though she shed bitter tears in the darkness of her bed, that night Justice was not visited by disturbing dreams.

12

Baptism

Drove to . . . the same little Baptist Church that the school is held in. The people came in slowly. About eleven they had all assembled. The church was full. . . . I enjoyed nothing so much as the singing—the wonderful, beautiful singing.

from *Journals*, Charlotte Forten Grimke, 1862

IN JUSTICE'S SOCIETY, a twelve-year-old child was thought to have gained the level of understanding and responsibility required to become a member of the church, but Justice did not join the Chesterton Baptist Church until she was fourteen, a little late— in her case, especially— for just the right blend of understanding and acceptance of God's mysterious ways. She was clear, however, on the secular benefits of church attendance and looked forward to the monthly church services and the weekly Sunday school and prayer gatherings. She saw church pragmatically, as an extension of the joys of life, and music was one of life's greatest joys. On any given Sunday, from any point in the church yard or from the road leading toward it, you could hear the clomp, clomp, clomp of the congregation's shoe heels striking the wide planks of the church floor, instrumentation for the hymns and spirituals pouring from full hearts. Beating out the rhythm of the singing, the heel stomping was most audible at the end of a line of song:

> *I wanna go back with 'im,* clomp,
> *I wanna go back with 'im,* clomp,
> *I wanna go back with 'im when he co-o-o-me,* clomp, clomp,
> *He'll be comin' on a clou-oud,*
> *Every eye shall see him,*
> *I wanna go back with 'im when he come,* clomp, clomp, clomp!
> *You can't make me doubt 'im,* clomp,
> *You can't make me doubt 'im,* clomp . . . .

On any endless day of fieldwork, maybe you would be picking cotton under the scorching sun, your legs, back, and arms near to breaking. You would be powerfully thirsty, and two young children would appear, struggling to carry a bucket of water and a dipper between them, and you would drink. Then, some rows away from you, maybe further down the field, a voice would ring out in song:

> *Some glad morning when this life is over, I-I-I will fly awa-ay!*
> *When-n I die, hallelujah, by and by-y-y,*
> *I-I-I will fly away!*

And you and everyone else in the field would join in the singing, and your hearts would take flight with your voices and escape the world, soaring up to the skies where God and angels would surely witness you on earth. Joy would fill you and the hours of work would fly. And your pain would not be so painful, and the future would not be so dim, and wondering what to cook for supper would lose its edge. In the evenings or on Saturday nights you might hear the men playing the guitar and blowing the "juice" harp or a comb or a jug and singing stories of love, disappointment, and bad luck. And the sorrow in their singing would join with your sorrow, lifting it up and making it seem easier for you to carry.

Justice loved music, and she could not imagine not going to church, but joining the church presented her with problems. First, church membership required going to the mourners' bench where you sat every night during the week of revival meeting until the Holy Ghost descended upon you and you shouted in the ecstacy of receiving God as your personal savior. The spirit came to those on the mourners' bench at the prompting of the church's holy members who would gather around the bowed heads of the unanointed, singing, praying, moaning, and beseeching God and his son Jesus to touch the children and cleanse their hearts. Justice knew that she would never rise from that bench simply because the "shiver of the spirit" moved her to rise. She was not expectant of the Holy Ghost. For her, the required shouting would be an embarrassing performance of compliance staged so that she could gain membership in the church. She disliked calling attention to herself, and the prospect of being observed on the mourners' bench with children two or three years younger than herself—jumping and waving her arms, hollering "Thank you, Jesus!" and "Yes, Lord!" when what she felt was dread—was most distasteful. But how could she continue to live among Christians, and in the home of the godly Emma and Mint, if the community believed she was damned to hell through the deliberate omission of church membership?

Then there was the problem of baptism. Justice had never felt the desire to learn to fish or to swim. In fact, she was afraid of deep or wide expanses of water, and after her father's death, she had come to see the sound as a dark and irresistible force that beckoned her to an abyss of cold nothingness. She knew that on the eve of revival's final day, those who had graduated from the mourners' bench would be taken to the sound with most of the congregation in tow. The preacher would wade out into the water, perhaps up to his waistline. Then the penitents, lined up and waiting their turns, would be ushered out to him, one by one, by an unsympathetic deacon who would turn them loose, their legs unsteady against the water's pulse. The preacher, familiar only from the distance of the pulpit, would grab the child by the upper arm and pull her close while intoning with calculated passion, "I baptize thee, my sister, in the name of the Father, the Son, and the . . ." and you would no longer be in a world that you knew. Trying not to breathe, trying to keep your eyes and mouth shut, feeling the murky water flood into your ears, your lungs bursting, the smell of fish and lichens present in your brain, you would resist the urge to bite, scratch, and kick the preacher's disembodied arms during this interminable captivity under water. Once he had sung out, "Hoooo-ly Ghooooost!" to the last reverberation of its extended syllables, the preacher would stand you on your feet and you would be delivered, like a half-drowned rat, to your triumphant folks waiting on the shore. To Justice, fear of baptism was even greater than fear of the mourners' bench.

But her greatest fear surrounding joining the church stemmed from her loss of belief in God, a secret that she kept hidden from the world. She simply saw no connection between an all-loving God and the everyday realities of her life. As things were, she went to church and Sunday school services for their social and spiritual—as opposed to their religious—benefits. Not wanting to dismay Emma and Mint, she participated in praying at home to draw attention away from her non-belief. Bible study required no pretense since she genuinely loved the scripture's richly textured stories. Had she been committing her soul to sickness by living a lie all along? Would pretending to receive the Holy Spirit, a deliberate communication of fraudulent convictions, complete her certain conversion to evil? She knew that the culmination of revival would consist of formally enfolding the new converts into the bosom of the church. For the first time, they would eat and drink of the body and blood of Christ, an act so awesome that baptized Christians were admonished before each communion to search their hearts and to judge honestly whether they were worthy to partake of the holy meal. What level of pretense, Justice wondered, would render her soul indistinguishable from that of a white person? In spite of her anxiety, when Emma had stated quite reasonably that it was time for Justice to join the church, that it shouldn't wait any longer, Justice had not been able to voice a single salient argument against it.

* * *

After Justice had sat through two nights on the mourner's bench, not expecting deliverance from God, she sought Emma's wisdom in solving her predicament. They had risen before day on Thursday morning to prepare breakfast and enough dinner to feed them supper, too. They would spend the day in the packhouse grading tobacco, but that night, after a cold supper of boiled cabbage, side meat, white potatoes, and cornmeal dumplings, Emma would resume her hopeful vigil over Justice's abject form on the mourners' bench.

"Miz Emma?"

"Yeah, baby?"

"You know how white folkses' souls is sick 'cause they hypocrites?"

"Hypocrites 'mong all folks, white and black, baby."

"But you know how white folks treat us bad and their souls sick 'cause they lie and claim they don't treat us no worser'n they should 'cause we ain't real folks?"

"Yeah, I know, 'cept that ain't all white folks. Them ab'litionists that he'ped free the slaves didn't treat us bad, and they white folks. And President Lincoln that freed us, and all them union folks from up north come down here and fight for to end slav'ry, most of them's white folks. And you know Miz Avery? I been workin' for Miz Avery a long, long time. Well, reason Mint can read the Bible and write and cipher like white folks is 'cause she learned 'im when he was little. Said it ain't right how the l'il black churren not 'lowed to learn like the whites. She give him near 'bout all them books he got in there he all the time readin'. And you should of seen what she done when we lost Mint's papa." Emma stopped bustling about the kitchen, and her face took on a dreamy quality.

"It was a hard winter, very cold, lot of snow, and a lot of times Miz Avery was the one made sure me and Mint had 'nough food. True, I always he'ped her whole fam'ly out much as I could. But Miz Avery ain't no hypocrite. Why you say all white folks hypocrites, chile?"

"Well, Mint 'splained to me how wh. . . how some folks live a lie so long their soul get sick, and I don't want to be that-a-way."

"What you worried 'bout, chile? You the blessedest daughter anybody could want! You a good chile! No need to worry 'bout your soul gettin' sick!"

"But I don't think I can shout in church like I'm s'pose to, and I'm scared of the water. My papa died in that water! Miz Emma, I just don't think I can go in there!"

Emma crossed the kitchen to take the sobbing Justice in her arms.

"Don't cry, baby," she said. "I tell you what. . . . God a merciful God, and he can forgive anything, but if you can go through with the mourners' bench just so we can hold our head up in this here community—cause you like my own daughter, you know—I'm gon' go every step of the way with you in the water. Miz Emma gon' walk you to the preacher and stay by your side. You got to be baptized, baby, and the Lord knows we's all afeared sometime.

Sometime we lose our faith 'cause we weak. But as long as we continue to call on the Lord Jesus, he will reveal hisself to us and show us that he ain't never left us even when we think we lost our way. And he ain't never gon' leave us! Ain't the Lord good, baby? Ain't the Lord good?"

Just then Mint came into the kitchen, back from feeding the livestock by lantern light, and his mother's voice lost its soothing tone.

"Mint, don't you scare this chile not one more time with all your stories 'bout white folks and sick souls! Got her near 'bout too riled up to go to the mourners' bench and be baptized! And you know she got to be baptized!" Mint's mouth had dropped open. "Well, shet your mouf 'fore a fly flies in," Emma chided him, "and sit down and eat this here food, scarin' this poor chile and you a grown man, twenty-five years old! Ought to be shamed of yourself!"

Mint looked from his mother to Justice, whose tear-streaked face expressed both apprehension and embarrassment. He washed his hands in silence, sat down at the table between the two women, and with his arms stretched out to either side of him, he clasped his mother's right hand and Justice's left in his own, thanked God for his bounty, and asked his blessings upon their meal. Then, raising their hands to his lips—first his mother's and then Justice's—he kissed them before devouring his breakfast, as he usually did, with great appetite.

13

Doubt

I have a cookbook copyrighted around 1901. When this old black woman cook was asked for her recipes, she said, "I'll give you the recipes, but cooking is just like religion. Rules don't no more make a cook than sermons make a saint."

from *I Dream a World,* by Brian Lanker,
words of Leah Chase, 1989

THAT EVENING, Justice was the first to fly from the mourners' bench in a deliberate frenzy of short-lived shouting. Afterwards, as long as she did not allow herself to dwell on the impending Saturday baptism, she was free to immerse herself in the music and pageantry of the service. Amid shouts of "Amen!" "Ho, Lord!" "Thank you, Jesus!" and "Bless you, chile!" Justice had been led to a pew with the other newly converted who held their heads low, preserving unction. In time, Justice began to look furtively at the congregation. She was not surprised to see that Mint and most other young men and women had absented themselves from the service, probably immediately after the sermon, to fraternize in the near darkness of the church yard.

This was one of the cherished by-products of a revival meeting, an event which offered something for almost everyone. It provided a venue as well as a worthy excuse for celebration every day of the week over a one-week period once every year. For the devout, it prompted repeated catharsis, opportunity for paroxysm after paroxysm of repentance and retribution. It gave the hardworking adults rare respite from seemingly endless labor and the children a chance to cavort with those who were not their own siblings. Before and after services, men smoked and talked, some even drank whiskey, congregating near—or making suspiciously steady trips to—a cart by the edge of the woods. Teenagers and young adults cast their nets for amorous trysts, and during the daytime services on Saturday and Sunday when each family brought their dinner to church, women spread homemade covers upon the grass and served heaping plates of fried chicken, boiled ham, sweet potatoes, collards, cabbage, kale, snap beans, corn field peas, stewed tomatoes, corn bread, yeasty rolls, fruit cobblers and pies, cakes, and herbal teas—hearty repast from the county's best cooks.

After the service, Justice had hurried from the church intent upon finding Mint to express, out of Emma's earshot, remorse that her words that morning had earned him an undeserved tongue-lashing from his mother. She found him standing near the back of the church house, his lips joined hungrily to those of a woman whose legs were wrapped around his thighs and crossed behind him, framing them both against the billowing skirt of a rose-colored dress that Justice had recently made. One of Mint's arms, hidden beneath his companion's buttocks, supported her weight. The other, cradling her back, shoulders, and head, made an upright bed upon which they seemed to lean. Lost in each other, maybe they did not hear Justice gasp, and then she was gone—back to the front of the church where she mingled with the congregation exiting its doors. When Emma had given and received commentary on the many wondrous aspects of the service and she and Justice had made their way to their mule and cart, Mint stood there alone, waiting for them. As he always did, he lowered the two-rung step ladder that he had made to ease his mother's climb into the cart, but when he turned to lift Justice, she brushed aside his proffered hands and clambered, unaided, into the cart and onto the buckboard.

"Lord, the service sho' was good tonight," said Emma, "and come Sunday, we gon' have ourselves a new member of the church. We mighty proud of you, baby!"

"Mighty proud," said Mint. "Now, let's see how long you gon' keep all that religion you got, Justice."

"I just love that story 'bout them dry bones in the valley, Miz Emma," Justice said, referring to the night's sermon. Throughout their ride home, she kept up a cheerful chatter, and though Mint joined in the conversation, not once did Justice address him. Week after week she continued to shun him as much as she dared.

But how thoroughly could she avoid him since they lived in the same house, worked in the fields and on other farming chores together, and ate their meals together where, as likely as not, Mint held her hand during the blessing and surely felt the trembling that coursed throughout her limbs? Sometimes she was surprised that the current from her own body did not jolt through Mint's and on to Emma's, whose hand he also held. She worried that Emma, as wise as the biblical sages, would read with unlettered eyes the words in her heart. She worried, too, that Mint would challenge her new behaviors in the presence of his mother, however covert and subtle she tried to make them seem. She saw no ready resolution to her increasing distress. She had started, in fact, to become quite dizzy whenever Mint prepared to leave the house to call on his female friends.

There was nothing new in Mint's courting except Justice's reaction to it. Though he had never married, he was old enough to have had a wife for some years and handsome enough to have had many. Emma said he took after his father: tall, over six feet, a chiseled face and broad but pointed nose, deep-set dark, dark eyes, strong teeth as white as skimmed milk, and dark black skin. His wide mouth was quick to smile, its corners turning upward, his high cheekbones pushing laugh wrinkles around his eyes. The hard physical exertion of farming and carpentry, the genetic heritage of African royalty, the forced breeding of slaves for physical power—all were stamped upon his frame. His muscles and sinews rippled like horse flesh against his clothing, and women, understandably, found him compelling. "Ain't no myst'ry why Mint ain't never married none of these gals yet," Mrs. Sadie Hebron had announced to Mary Evans, her neice, as if Justice, picking the next two rows of cotton, was not able to overhear every word she said. "Born in his mama's old age like Isaac to Sarah, and she done spoilt 'im to death. He sho' ain't wantin' for no woman to take care of him. And as for wantin' more'n cookin' and cleanin', if a man gettin' all the milk he want for free, why he gon' go buy a cow? He ain't gon' do it! Any gal wantin' to ketch Mint better keep her legs crossed 'til she sho' nuff got 'im!"

* * *

During late fall, winter, and early springtime, Mint built house furnishings, rowboats, cabins, barns, coffins—anything commissioned by blacks or whites within miles of Chesterton. His industry was a relief to Justice, whose coldness had melted to a shy sullenness, enabling her to carry on a poor substitution of their former easy relations. One day in mid December as Justice was picking up pecans under two giant trees marking the boundary of the yard, Mint accosted her on his way to the house for supper.

"Justice, somethin's been botherin' you a long time. What is it?"

"Nothin'."

"It is too somethin'. You been actin' curious since you got baptized."

"Nothin' botherin' me."

"Why you treat me like this? Like you mad 'cause I done somethin' to you. What I done? If I done anything to hurt you, I beg your pardon. Just tell me what it is."

"It ain't nothin' you done to me," Justice said, her head cast downward.

"You ain't still scared your soul sick?" Mint asked and smiled in spite of himself. "Look at me," he said, and Justice raised her eyes to his. She seemed so vulnerable to Mint, and an idea of horrible proportion entered his head. "Ain't nobody hurt you again . . . or scared you? I'll kill 'im, so he'p me God!"

"I'm just scared you gon' leave!" Justice blurted out.

"Gon' leave? Where you get such a foolish notion from? And where I'm goin'?"

"S'posin' you get married?"

Mint smiled. "Who I'm gon' marry? Don't you think you still too young for me to marry you?"

"S'posin' you and Miz Louvenia get married?"

"Me marry Louvenia?!" Mint's face was lit with laughter. "Why you think I'm gon' marry Louvenia?"

"Don't y'all love each other?"

"Justice, Louvenia young, but she already married. Her husband ole man Sam Wofford. Didn't you know that?"

"That ole, ole man come to church sometime with a cane? Sets back there behind the deacons?"

"Yep! So where you get such a notion from?"

"She so pretty, and I seen her lookin' at you all the time. Even when she come over here for me to sew for her, she be lookin' 'round for you," Justice lied—and Mint knew that she was lying, though he knew also that what she said was true.

"She pretty, but I sho' ain't marryin' no Louvenia, and I ain't leavin', so don't you worry your pretty head!"

"I ain't pretty!" Justice said softly, her head bowed. Her fingers stole up to touch the scar on her cheek.

"Look at me, Justice," Mint said. "You mighty pretty! Don't you know that? You one of the prettiest girls 'round here." He gave her an encouraging smile. Then he bent and kissed her full on her mouth. "Now, let's go eat Mama's vittles!" He grabbed her basket of pecans and, draping his massive arm around her shoulders, he teased her good naturedly about trying to give his mama's baby to Louvenia Wofford as they went in to supper.

14

Belief

White men would walk the trails where we had to go wash at the spring and if they caught a girl alone there, they'd just rape her. Parents was afraid to say too much about it. You might be visited by the KKK that night.

from *I Dream a World* by Brian Lanker,
words by Winson and Dovie Hudson, 1989

ONE EVENING in late spring as Justice hurried to bring in the morning's wash before the dew fell, a white man rode up to the house on horseback, leading a mule. He was wearing a wide-brimmed hat that he lifted from his straw-colored hair when he spoke.

"Evenin', miss. My wife's 'bout to have a chile and some of my neighbors told me to see if Aunt Emma Sutton would he'p us. Is she home?"

He dismounted, and Justice could see the flinty gray of his eyes. Wordless, she turned and ran into the kitchen.

"Miz Emma, a white man want to see you!"

"Well, awright, baby. Watch my corn bread for me. Supper 'bout ready. Know who he is or what he want?" Emma wiped her hands on her apron.

"He said his wife havin' a baby. Didn't say his name."

"You doin' awright, Justice? You lookin' mighty peaked, chile." Emma stopped on her way to the door, her eyes riveted on Justice's face.

"L'il hot, I guess," said Justice. "I'm gon' get me a drink of water. I'll be awright."

"I be right back," said Emma.

As Emma talked with the visitor in the yard, she heard the tin dipper strike the wooden bench where the bucket stood. She heard it clatter against the flat irons that sat on the floor beside the water bench. In her mind's eye, she saw Justice swoon, and she listened intently for the actual thud of Justice falling.

"'Scuse me, suh. I got to see 'bout my daughter. I'll he'p you, but I got to see 'bout my daughter 'fore I do." She hurried into the kitchen where Justice was rising slowly from the floor.

"Wait a minute, baby! Don't get up yet. Let me pull up a chair for you to set on.

"Mister!" she called to the man outside. "Can you come in here, please, suh?"

"Can I he'p y'all any?" The man stood in the kitchen doorway, and Justice, seeing him there, fainted again.

"Lift her in there to the bedroom for me," Emma said, moving the corn bread from the fire. "She mighty light, but I ain't young and strong as I used to be."

The man laid Justice on Emma's bed, and Justice awakened, coughing from the pinch of snuff that Emma held under her nose.

"How you feelin', baby?" Emma asked.

"Aw right," Justice murmured.

"You need a drink of water, and Miz Emma gon' get you some.

"Come on in the kitchen, suh," she said to the white man. "We sho' do 'preciate you, and I'm gon' go see if I can he'p your wife soon's my boy get here. You unnerstan I can't leave my daughter by herself right now."

"When you think he gon' be here?"

"Any minute. . . . Where you live at?"

"Not far. Two farm places up the road. Next to Kimbry's."

"You can go 'head on if you want, and I'll come 'long behind you soon's I can," said Emma, but just then they heard the clop, clop, clop of the mule as Mint rode into the yard.

* * *

After he had fed the livestock and eaten supper, Mint washed the sweat and grime of fieldwork from his body while Justice cleaned the kitchen. When he had dressed himself in clean work clothes, he went into his mother's room and sat on the side of the bed where Justice rested.

"You goin' off?" she asked him, her eyes frightened, her face pinched and bloodless.

"Nope. I'm gon' stay right here with you 'til you get ready to go to sleep. How you feelin' now?"

"Can I tell you somethin'?" she asked, and he could see that she was beginning to cry.

"Anything." He touched her hand.

"I'm so scared, Mint. I got so scared when that man come up here for Miz Emma. He put me in mind of that one that hurt me. I know he ain't the same man. He bigger'n the other one. And he don't sound like 'im. But he got the same eyes, the same hair, and I just got so scared. I get so scared when I see somebody that look like that, I don't know what to do."

"I'm so sorry, baby," Mint said. He picked Justice up and held her on his lap, cradling her. "You say the man who hurt you looked kinda like this man?"

"Smaller," said Justice. "Not as old. Bad. Very bad. I'm

scared of 'im, Mint! I wish he was dead!"

"You ever seen him since then?" Mint asked calmly. He was rocking Justice slightly to and fro, and in between his questions and her answers, he was feathering her with little kisses to the top of her head, her forehead, her eyelids, her cheeks salty with tears.

"I ain't never seen him but that one time. I'm scared, Mint, he gon' come back for me! I been scared all this time!"

"He ain't comin' back, Justice," Mint said. "I know who hurt you. Name's Tip Askew. Figured it out, kinda, two years ago. Now I'm sure who done it, and he's gone. They moved. Trashy folks. Farmin' for Mr. Haskins and just left in the middle of the night. Left the crops in the field. Stole two of Mr. Haskins' best horses. If they ever come back here, Mr. Haskins gon' have 'em put in jail, prob'ly hung. If that boy ever come back, they won't hafta hang 'im 'cause I'm gon' kill 'im. Don't you worry none. Don't you be 'fraid of him no more."

"Mint, he done took so much from me! Sometime I wish he'd of kilt me 'stead of what he done. He ruint me inside, and then my papa ruint me outside, but that man made 'im do it! Mint, sometime I wish I'd of died like my mama's other churren! Why you think I lived for, Mint? Why I lived?"

"For me," he answered. "For my mama. We love you. You part of our family. Mama wanted you to be her daughter, Justice, and I want you, too. I can't even dream of what it would be like without you. I can't recollect what it was like 'fore you come here." He brushed her lips with his.

'Miz Emma like my mama," said Justice. "The only thing make me happy, Mint, is bein' here with you and Miz Emma. Sometime when I think 'bout my papa, I just want to go out in the water and never come back! He died 'cause of me, Mint, and I'm so sorry!"

Mint lay Justice on the bed and leaned over her, his face nearly touching hers. "Believe me, Justice," he said, "you not to blame. Only person whose fault it is, is the one who hurt you. He the only one to blame. Not you. . . . You no more to blame than a little slave chile sold away from their mama and papa 'cause the mar'sar want some money. You no more to blame than Joseph when his brothers sold him and tore his coat and told their papa he was dead. You no more to blame than Jesus Christ when they hung 'im on the cross and he hadn't never harmed no one. You not to blame, Justice. . . . You hear me?"

"Sometime I feel like I'm bad, Mint, and that's why my face ugly and my body ugly and my insides is ruint. And that's why I ain't got no folks left."

"Your face beautiful, Justice. You got one scar on your neck and cheek, but it's flat. Folks can't hardly notice it. But I love it. Do you b'lieve me? I love your scars, all of them. They mine. They brought you to Mama and me." He kissed the length of the scar, from her cheek to midway down her neck. "Your eyes deep as the spaces between the stars, Justice. In the night, I dream of them. In the daytime when I'm plowin' or whatever I'm doin', I dream of your eyes. Your skin like ripe brown pears. Your lips plump as sweet plums." He kissed her lips softly and repeatedly, and he licked them, tasting her.

"Your body beautiful, Justice. You got a woman's body now." He placed his palms over her breasts and felt her nipples rigid against her clothing. He cupped her breasts in his hands, and his index fingers played back and forth across the dark circumference of her nipples. His fingers trailed down her rib cage, and he bent to kiss her navel. Then he traced both hands across her belly and onto her thighs, his fingertips touching each other at the mound between her legs and descending it, reaching inward. Then he raised the hem of her dress and kissed her thighs. He touched the backs of her legs and kissed her shins and ankles and the broad scar on her left foot, dusty from the chores of the day.

"Your body beautiful, Justice," he repeated. "It don't feel

ruint to me. And if you can't never bear churren, many churren in this world already, always will be, who need a mama and a papa to raise 'em and love 'em.

"And don't be 'fraid of love. The coward who hurt you didn't do nothin' to you in love. What he done got nothin' to do with love or with lovin'. It's got nothin' to do with what's between me and you and has been between us and always will be between us. Even though he may have thought he kissed you, he did not kiss you. He did not make love to you. This is a kiss, Justice." And he raised her up and kissed her, and her mouth opened to him. But when she placed her hand instinctively between his legs and caressed him, he reluctantly turned away.

"I love you, Mint," she stated, reaching for him, kissing him.

"I know," he said, shaken. "But my need for you is great, and before I let you touch me, I must teach you what to expect... How old are you now, Justice? Fourteen, still? I think we have to wait."

PART THREE

BESS (1890-1967)

I bore you one morning just before spring—
My head rang like a fiery piston
My legs were towers between which
A new world was passing.

from "Now That I Am Forever with Child," Audre Lorde, 1976

15

Birth

[O]ne of my friends told me in the middle of recess that his baby brother had died the night before of an evil spirit brought in by the wind. . . .

from *Dreams from My Father*, Barack Obama, 1995

SHE LAY AMONG SWEET GRASS at the edge of the great water, her feet lapped by ripples, her body facing east. In the night, the Albemarle Sound had gained the shore and had washed her legs, arms, breasts, and stomach, over and over, in phantasmagoric repetition of the ritual duly bestowed upon her own mother, by her grandmother, at her birth. In a foreign place, in the absence of relatives, when it was time for the baby to be born, she lay near the water, the sun loosened the reins of gravity, and the sound reached beyond its basin to caress her through the night.

She lay in the company of her ancestors' spirits, scores of them, who stood upon the water shielding her from the eye of evil. Between sky and sound, she saw the Hatteras tribe joined by the English from Roanoke's Lost Colony, and heard the tellers from both sides tell their history of cultural collaboration so spectacularly successful that it had never been accepted by experts of civilization. She heard their prophecy that in the twenty-first century, forensic science would trace the blood of the Lumbee tribe to their own ancient Indian and English blood. The English told of the struggle after their arrival on Roanoke Island in the summer of 1587, too late in the year to plant the crops that could sustain them over the months of winter. They related how, bedazzled by the artistry of words and of pictures and by cunning, wanderlust, and greed, they had been lured without adequate provisions from their homes across the Atlantic to Roanoke Island, which had purged its shores of English settlers less than two years before. They related how, cold and starving, they desperately dispatched John White to England for relief, and how they were rescued by the Hatteras people and how they placed the C-R-O-A-T-A-N mark upon the tree. The Hatteras told of how they and the English had melded their cultures and traditions over time through pragmatic selection: the language of the English; the livelihood of the Hatteras; the housing design and materials of the English; the foods and medicines of the Hatteras; qualities and practices from each side as needed; respect for practicality in great abundance from both. They told of their retreat inland, for purposes of safety and seclusion, to the area now called Sampson County, and then on to the Lumbee River in 1650 where they lived, protected by moats of swampland, in peaceful uniqueness. Then they told the pain of their later treatment by the government and by the settlers and sang of their own courage, strength, and endurance against bigotry and hate. And as soon as they foretold a time in 1953, over six decades into the future, when their rightful name, the Lumbee, would be recognized among the nation's people, Bess was born.

    Bess was born in the early morning in 1890, in the half light before sunrise, with a blistery rash like the meat of scarlet pomegranates covering her ears, knuckles, and neck, the places on her body where her true complexion would first be evident. How could she be buried in the water when signs of her paternity could not be read? Who could drown her when the spirits had taken due heed and had come to witness her arrival, to provide her with protection and subliminal knowledge of her maternal line, and to welcome her to the village of humanity—as they would do for any Indian child? Bess's mother could not hold her under the water, and neither could her mother's husband, so Bess was allowed to live. And when the fire had faded from her skin some six months hence and evidence of the rapist was clearly stamped upon her, neither possessed the flintness of heart to banish her fledgling spirit from the world.

16

Weight

if you would stand fire
rather than difference
do not hesitate
move
away

from "move," Lucille Clifton, 1993

FOR FOUR HOURS the child and her mother stood in August's midday sun waiting for the man to come. Two hours after their arrival, when the child had begun to fidget, her mother had motioned her toward the outhouse that stood a ways behind the general store, a half moon cut into its door. The mother did not relieve herself, or sit, and barely moved during the hours that she and the child waited for the right man.

The man came when the store's shadow said two o'clock. A god of a man, he spoke to his mule and patted it above its muzzle after he had tethered it, and he nodded a greeting to the mother and the child as he walked in their direction to enter the store. When he came out some twenty minutes later and crossed the sandy yard with his tow sack of groceries in one hand and a can of kerosene in the other, the mother and her child stood waiting for him at his cart.

The woman was tall and pretty, her lustrous hair in a single braid, her high forehead and cheekbones intercepted by deep, luminous gray eyes. The child was clearly part black, her hair long but frizzy, her skin brown, her lips thick. But her eyes were the deep and luminous gray eyes of the woman.

"Good evenin'," said the woman. "This here is Bess. She is four years old, a good, healthy child who loves playing, dancing, and music. She's a big help to me, but I can't keep her. I have to leave her, and I want to give her to you."

He could not bear to look at the child, holding what probably were her worldly possessions in a pillowcase, as she listened to her mother speak pleadingly about her inevitable abandonment.

"Ma'am," he said when she had enumerated the child's virtues, "I don't b'lieve I ever seen you before. I don't b'lieve you know me. Why you want to give me this chile? Who she b'long to?"

"She's my child, but I'm gon' leave her. I got to. We Indian, and this here child a half-breed. I was forced by a black man. We goin' back to our home, and she can't go.

"You the one to take her. I seen you in a dream, and my dreams speak truth, so I come here with the child to wait for you to come. I seen you in my dream, and you don't have no chil'ren 'round your hearth. Me and my husband will have other chil'ren, and, besides, I know your heart's a good heart. I see it, and the child sees it, and she needs to live with her own people."

The woman spoke in tones to make him see that if he did not take the child, she would simply walk away and leave her where they stood. He forced himself to look at the little girl, whose heart's blood seemed to have emptied out, whose salty tears seemed to have formed a lining underneath her skin. She was bewildered, afraid, an earthbound creature whose safety lay in flying. She was a doomed soul without expectation of mercy. "This is almost like the slave chile," his mind told him, "uprooted from family, feelings cut clear through, nobody to love 'em or soothe their cry." He gave the child his dazzling smile, his mouth lifting upwards at the corners, a smile that encompassed his eyes. His face was open and friendly, and when he spoke to the child he stooped down to be at her level. "My name's Mint," he said. "I'm mighty pleased to meet you, Bess. I'm mighty glad you comin' home with me to be my little girl."

Throughout her life, Bess would remember this moment as one of her greatest treasures. In her times of deep sorrow, or insecurity, or humiliation, or fear, or regret at feeling unloved, she would summon this view of her beautiful father, and whatever load she carried, or imagined that she carried, would be made lighter.

But now it was her mother's leaving that was Bess's burden. Taking the child's hand, the woman led her daughter to the back of the cart and lifted her over its tailgate. Then, wordless, she turned and walked away. Mint and the child watched as the mother walked past the store and down the road to the west, retracing their steps from the morning. Her back was straight, her shoulders squared, and her long thick braid bumped gently against her buttocks as she walked. Perhaps she felt in peril of turning into a pillar of salt, for as she journeyed away from her firstborn child, not once did she look back.

***

Bess did not bring harmony into her new home.

"Somethin' terrible wrong with me, Mint," Justice said. "I'm shamed of it and of myself. And you know somethin' wrong, so I might as well tell you."

"It's the chile," Mint answered. "It's Bess. You and Bess ain't takin' to one 'nother."

"Bess love you, Mint. You the one saved her, and she

prob'ly a l'il bit jealous of me. And I don't blame nobody for wantin' you all by theirself."

Mint laughed and kissed her. They were lying on their bed without covers, since the night had brought little relief from the summer heat wave that had stretched into October.

"Now, don't tell me you jealous of no baby," he said. He kissed her again, and she sat up.

"Don't do that, Mint," she said. "You know I can't think when you do that."

"I can wait," he said, and smiled.

"I could be jealous of her," Justice admitted. "But what I'm shame of is somethin' else. I'm shame 'cause I'm scared of her eyes, Mint. They so gray, just like that man's eyes that hurt me that time. Maybe she his chile, and I know I couldn't stand to have his chile 'round here. I just couldn't. She stands back and she looks at me like she don't like me or she scared of me. And I feel all dizzy lookin' at her gray eyes. I feel like she evil or somethin', and I feel scared. I don't think I like her, Mint."

"The scoundrel that hurt you not her papa,' said Mint. "Her real papa a black man. Her mama the one look like she white, say she a Indian. She say she was raped, remember? Give the chile a chance, Justice. No such thing as a evil chile. She only been here—what—two months? I can't give her back to her mama; she gone. She didn't want her, remember? And how would you feel if your mama had give you away or let you know she was gon' walk off and leave you 'cause she don't want you? No matter what her reason was for not wantin' you, you would feel terrible. And if your mama was raped and you was born as a result of it, would that be your fault? And if you had a child from a rape, would you want to keep that chile, Justice?" Mint knew that he was hurting Justice in a way that he had never hurt her before, but he did not stop. "Bess done had a hard, hard time, Justice. Just lookin' at her that day put me in mind of what could've happened to me if I'd been born a slave and snatched from my mama and sold Lord knows where to Lord knows who."

Justice lay back down beside Mint. Her voice trembled when she spoke. "Everything you say is right, Mint," she said. "I'm gon' put my heart and mind to doin' better."

"Thank you, Justice," he said, but he did not reach for her. She waited until the rhythm of his breathing indicated that he was fast asleep before she started to cry.

* * *

The next day Justice made Bess a sky blue jumper and a white blouse, but the child did not warm to her. "Make her a rag doll," Mint suggested, and when Justice presented Bess with the beautifully crafted gift, the child clearly loved it, but her reticence toward Justice was not affected.

"Miz Emma," Justice said one day when Mint and Bess were building a feeder in the backyard for the winter birds, "you the only mama I had for most of my life, and I need a mama's he'p."

Emma was in the kitchen preparing herbs to treat a neighbor's gout. "Sit down, baby," she said. "I don't want to get in young folkses' business, but I been wonderin' if you and Mint is awright."

"We not awright," Justice answered, "not since Bess come to live here." She unburdened her heart to Emma, telling of her fear of the child's eyes and her belief that Bess was driving a wedge between her and Mint. "I love Mint more'n I love my life," said Justice, "and I think he's turnin' 'way from me. Miz Emma, please he'p me to 'cept the chile in my heart. Mint know my heart; he can see it, and if I can't feel love for Bess, he gon' take his love from me. I know he love me, but I think he gon' stop."

"Sometime life seem hard, baby," Emma said. "But God

don't put on us no mo' than we can bear. And all that he put on us he'p us to be mo' like him. I'm sayin', baby, that God give us trouble sometime so we can rise up above it. Trouble give us the chance to be godly. And there's flat out blessin's in trouble, too."

"I know you right, Miz Emma," Justice replied, "but I can't hardly see no blessin' in this. We got this chile that I can't seem to be comfortable with, and she can't seem to be comfortable with me, and it's tearin' me and Mint apart. I'm hurtin' Mint, and maybe I'm hurtin' the chile, and my heart feel like a fist of ice just squeezin' it every time I think Mint losin' his love for me."

"You know what I think, baby?" Emma responded. "I think, s'pose you can gain the victory over bein' feared of folks with gray eyes. That'll be a blessin' straight from the Lord. Long as you still scared, the devil still got control, and he can keep punishin' you by scarin' you. Now, he like that, but you ought not to let him. He done punish you enough. And see what he doin,' he punishin' you, and Mint, and Bess, and even me. That's how the devil work. It ain't just one soul and spirit he after, but many as he can get. If he can bring sorrow to one of God's churren, he hope he can use that one to bring sorrow to everybody they love and everybody that love them. The devil smart and powerful, but he ain't no match for God's love. I tell you what you do, baby—and I know this gon' take time—but you try it; just work on it. Even though you scared to do it, you just look at l'il Bess' eyes every chance you get. By and by, you gon' see there ain't nothin' in gray eyes to be feared of. Might take a while, 'cause Lord knows I ain't never got over bein' feared of rats. Rat come in here, Miz Emma gone! But I b'lieve God gon' he'p you lose your fear of that chile eyes. It ain't folks with gray eyes that do bad things. It's folks with any color eyes. It's even folks ain't got no eyes. I don't know much, Justice, but I know folks with gray eyes no worser'n nobody else, and God gon' bring you to knowin' it, too."

"I'm gon' try to stop bein' scared, Miz Emma," said Justice, "but I can't wait no long time. I can't take the chance of losin' Mint. I know the women folks after 'im; I been knowin' that. I thought I was gon' have to fight that ole Mary Evans, and I would, too—I don't care how much bigger'n me she is—if she didn't leave my husband 'lone. But them womens ain't gone nowhere, Miz Emma. They just backed off, waitin' to see their chance."

"Here's what you got to do, baby," Emma said. "I b'lieve God want you to be just as lovin' and kind as you can be to Bess even though you feared of her eyes. The devil choose fear, but you choose lovin' kindness. That's the way of Christ. Whatever it take for you to show love to that chile, you give what it take, and God will give you the glory. And your heart that's full of fear, God will empty the fear out and fill your heart with love."

"But, Miz Emma," Justice protested, "I don't think the chile like me. How I'm gon' make her to like me?"

"That chile done been through a lot, baby," said Emma. "I think maybe you ought not to care too much whether she like you or not. Long as you nice and lovin' to her, that's all God 'spect you to worry 'bout. Love her with the love and patience of Job. Bess ain't got to give you your reward. God gon' take care of that on the great jedgment day. You think you can do these things, baby?" Emma asked.

"Yes'm, I do," Justice assured her, "but I ain't so sure 'bout how to keep Mint from turnin' 'way from me. I feel him bein' angry with me, and I can't stand it if he stray from me."

"My boy love you to death, baby," Emma said. "But I got to tell you somethin' 'bout Mint's papa. Baby, Silas was a beautiful man, just like Mint, lovin' and kind, just like his son. And when I come here, it look like the womens already got their clutches in 'im. And Silas and me got married, but I knowed this ole gal had 'ranged for Silas to go meet her one night. So when he gettin' ready to go, I say, 'Silas, ain't you gon' stay home with your wife tonight?' And he say, 'I be on back soon's I go check on the curin' tobacco.' And I say, 'I b'lieve I'm gon' go with you 'cause I don't want to be by myself in the bed tonight.' And he say, 'Naw, Emma, you stay on here to the house and I be back soon's I can.' And I say, 'Silas, even God jealous.' And he say, 'If God know who love 'im, seem like he know who he ain't got to be jealous of. Seem like if you know somebody love you, ain't no need to be jealous.' And Silas laughed. And you know what I done, baby? I say to myself, 'I know Silas love me, and I can't watch 'im all the time, and he picked me to marry over all the rest, and I know nobody don't rightly belong to nobody else, only to God, and you can't force a man to be faithful, and I'm gon' have to just trust and pray that he gon' be faithful, but I'm gon' give 'im a l'il bit of he'p tonight 'cause God he'p them that he'p theirself. Silas,' I say, 'you the greatest blessin' of my life. I be here when you get back, keepin' your bed warm.' 'Thank'ee, Emma,' say Silas, a li'l surprised I'm givin' up so easy, lookin' hard at me. And I say, 'I'm feelin' kinda tired. I think I'm gon' turn in right now,' and I done like this: Emma began to yawn and stretch like an unhurried cat, extending her arms sinuously over her head, thrusting her ample breasts outward, and opening her legs far wider than necessary to rise from her chair. Then, standing, arms akimbo, she twisted her torso as if to limber up her back. From left to right she swivelled, her pelvis arched and ready, leading her fleshy rump in a fluid grind. Then she bent forward from her waist, her behind facing the imaginary Silas, and pantomimed the untying of her shoes.

"And what he say, Miz Emma?" Justice asked, laughing and clapping her praise of the seventy-nine-year-old Emma's flawlessly executed acrobatics.

"Why, he 'lowed that the curin' tobacco'd be awright 'til the mornin'," Emma said and winked lasciviously. "That ole gal out there in them bushes somewhere waitin' for 'im could still be out there for all I knows or cares. I b'lieves in usin' what I got, and if the Lord had blessed me to still have Silas, I'd still be usin' it, too."

Justice believed her and began immediately to plan the ongoing seduction, beginning that very night, of her own husband.

* * *

By nightfall, Justice had lost much of her resolve. After supper, she examined her body by lamplight and, again, saw in it no reason that Mint should prefer her over every other woman he knew. When she raised her arm to examine, again, the scar that ran across her left breast and down her side, he walked into the room.

"You admirin' my beautiful wife?" He shut the door behind him and sat at the foot of their bed, looking at her.

"I didn't 'tend for you to catch me," she blurted out truthfully. "I'm tryin' to see what you see in me. I'd do anything to be prettier, to be a better person, to deserve your love more'n I do." She knelt in front of him, her arms resting on his thighs, and trained her eyes upon his eyes. Then, remembering that she was naked to her waist, she began to struggle back into her clothes.

"Don't," said Mint, touching her arms to still them, touching her shoulders, her face. He kissed her temples, her eyelids, and her neck, his tongue traced the outline of her ears, and his lips caressed her earlobes. "I been missin' you so much," he said. "Life ain't long enough, Justice. We ain't got time for us to be distant from one 'nother."

"I promise you," she said, "that you gon' be pleased, for the rest of my life, with the way I'm gon' be by our daughter. Both you and God gon' be pleased, Mint. I have that power to love."

"I know you do, Justice," he answered. "I'm already pleased. I see how you do for the chile. I see how she take more to me than she do to you or to Mama, and I see how she take more to Mama than she take to you. I know that must hurt your feelings, but I see you goin' on and not paying it no mind. I'm proud of you, baby, and I didn't think I could love you no more'n I already did, but I do. I love you more."

"You truly love me?" asked Justice. "You satisfied with me, Mint? Why you satisfied with me, handsome as you are, good as you are?" She took his face in her hands and she smiled bravely at him, but he could see the moisture building in her eyes.

"You the only woman, 'cept my mama and grandma, I ever loved. I didn't marry nobody, Justice, 'til I found the one I wanted to marry, and that's you. You ask me if I'm satisfied. I wouldn't even say 'satisfied.' I say I'm just as happy as I 'magine any man could possibly be with his wife. And it's more to it than the fire that burns between us. I seen your struggle, Justice. I seen your courage. I seen you get well when most folks would of died 'cause it would of been easier. I seen you go on when you had lost everybody and everything you knew and loved. I been watchin' you fight your own fear so you can love Bess with a mother's love. I know Bess takin' out on you the hard feelin's she hold for her own mama. But she a little chile, and she gon' grow out of that. I seen you swallow your hurt when other women primpin' and preenin' like male peacocks in front of me, and I got to treat 'em polite. All this make me love you even more.

"Why you cryin,' Justice? Don't cry, baby." He brushed away her tears and kissed her cheeks and her lips.

"'Cause I'm happy, Mint. 'Cause I want so much for you to love me. I'm just cryin' cause I can't he'p it. I guess I'm just weak."

"You not weak, Justice. You and Mama the strongest folks I know."

"You sure you don't just think you love me 'cause you feel sorry for me, Mint?" Justice smiled to hide her fear as she asked the question, and Mint read her heart.

"I know you think that sometime, but it ain't true. I don't

feel sorry for you, Justice. I admire you. There's a difference. The same things that happened to you could've happened to all kinds of people by the thousands. I would feel sorry for anybody that had something bad happen to 'em. But I admire how you faced everything hard in your life. You special not because of what happened to you but because of the spirit and courage that you pulled out of your heart and mind to have a fightin' chance in this world. And you so honest! Justice, you ain't no good at lyin', and I love that." Mint was smiling broadly.

"That's 'cause I don't want my soul to get sick," Justice joked, and they both laughed, and then Mint was serious again.

"The reason I adore you, Justice, is that everything about you speak to my heart. There's a cord between us, tyin' us together. I think God ordained that we love each other. I think my love for you is a gift that God gave me. It's a gift to me, Justice, 'cause it put so much more meaning in my life. I never needed nobody else 'til you came, and I ain't never wanted nobody else since you been my wife. But I don't think I can explain lovin' you," he said. "Maybe it's like grace from God that I didn't have to earn or deserve. Maybe he just opened up my heart out of his own love for me. . . . What you think, Justice? Why you love me?"

"I love you, Mint," Justice said without hesitation, "'cause you the closest thing to God on earth that I'm gon' ever see, or know, or touch." She reached up and kissed him, her tongue exploring his, one hand fondling him, the other beginning to disrobe him.

"And when I'm inside you, I am in heaven with God, and I have all the pleasure of the angels," Mint replied smiling, as he undressed her. And he lifted her up on top of him and they entered, by his own definition, heaven's gate.

17

Courage

Throw the children into the river; civilization has given us too many. It is better to die than it is to grow up and find out that you are colored.

from "Tired," Fenton Johnson, 1922

TWO WEEKS AFTER the Salem boy was lynched by a mob in Washington County for trying to register to vote, his penis and testicles hacked off and stuffed in his mouth, the skin below the rope around his neck purple and bulged as a link of boiled sausage, Justice went to the home of Mrs. Patricia Williford, a white woman for whom she worked, to deliver the sewing and ironing that she had done. Bess accompanied her, carrying a basket that held Justice's handiwork of delicately stitched cotton handkerchiefs and linen table scarves with borders of tatted lace. A throwback to the customs of her African ancestors, Justice carried a large basket on her head, and she could smell the starch in the shirts, blouses, and dresses and the freshness of the cedar fronds that kept her flat irons clean and smooth. As they walked, Justice told the seven-year-old Bess the story of the rabbit, the fox, the bear, the tar baby, and the briar patch where the rabbit had been bred and born.

When they arrived and John Williford had let Justice into the sanctum of the wood-paneled hallway to his study, rather than placing the three dollars that he owed her in her hand, he took her outstretched palm and brought it to his lips.

"I 'clare, Justice," he said, looking at her from rheumy, pink-lidded eyes, "I been wantin' to do that a long time. And I been wantin' so much more." He tried to draw her to him.

Justice's eyes were wild with terror. She snatched back her hand, grabbed the silver candlestick from the hallway's gate-leg table, and brandished it in front of her as she backed toward the door. Dislodged from its base, the heavy, unlit candle fell to the polished floor and rolled into Justice's path, leaving a wake of waxy flakes. When her feet encountered the candle, she did not look down but kicked it, lifting it with uncanny force and precision from the floor and in the direction of Mr. Williford's chest. He ducked, and his rabbit eyes widened with respect and heightened excitement.

"Please," he said. "You're so pretty, and who needs to know? And there's money and pretty things for you. . . . And who gon' do anything to us if they find out? . . . We free to love and enjoy. The white man and the colored woman the freeist folks there is."

"I'm gon' kill you," said Justice. "You so much as touch me, and I'm gon' break your temple open with this here candlestick. I don't care if they kill me for killin' you. I don't care if they hang me from a tree, rope 'round my neck. I don't care 'cause you gon' be dead awready."

"No need to kill nobody," Mr. Williford said, his ardor checked by her vehemence. "I ain't gon' force you. . . . Here, take your money," but Justice did not glance in the direction of the money he offered. She seemed not to notice that he had stopped pursuing her. At the back door, she reached behind her to let herself out and bolted down the steps.

"Come on, Bess," she said to the child playing with the

husk of a June bug in the shade of an ancient rose bush. Justice grabbed Bess's arm to hurry her along, and the child resisted, escaped Justice's grasp, and fell sideways into the rose bush where the thorns, unlike those in the briar patch of Uncle Remus's tale, were not welcoming. Throwing the candlestick on the sand and crabgrass near the rose bush, Justice helped the child to her feet, "Come on, Bess!" she said, near tears. "We got to hurry!"

Two days later, when Mr. Williford saw Mint at the general store, he gave him five dollars to give to Justice. "Would you give this here to Justice from Mrs. Williford?" he asked, smiling amiably. "She forgot and left it on the table when she brought back the laundry the other day. And tell her Mrs. Williford say she sure do a fine job."

"Thank you, suh," said Mint. "I'll be sure to pass it 'long to her."

18

Discord

Nothing can console me. You may bring silk
to make skin sigh, dispense yellow roses...
still, ...
nothing is sweet to the tooth crushing in.

from "Demeter Mourning," Rita Dove, 1995

IT TOOK TWO FULL WEEKS for the thorn embedded in Bess's leg to begin to poison her. When it had been impacted for a week and Justice had noticed that the child seemed to favor her right side, she asked Bess if her foot hurt, if she'd bumped it, if anything had bitten her. "No'm" was Bess's reply to each of her mother's questions.

"Ain't you limpin'?" Justice asked.

"No'm. I'm awright," Bess answered. But when her father came home that evening, she met him in the yard and showed him her swollen leg, a head of white pus already formed around the black hole where the thorn had entered. He picked Bess up and carried her inside, and he and Justice examined the child's leg in the lamplight.

"How long your leg been like this?" he asked.

"Since Mama push me in the rose bush over to Mrs. Williford's," Bess promptly responded. Her gray eyes hooded, she did not look at Justice.

"Your mama wouldn't push you in no rose bush, Bess," Mint said. He looked at Justice, who stood holding the lamp so that he could better inspect the child's injury. He could see that her eyes were suddenly weary, and when she spoke, there was pain in her voice.

"Bess was near the rose bush playing when I told her we had to leave, and when I took her arm, she pulled 'way from me and lost her balance and fell. I got her out of the rose bush and didn't know she got hurt like this. I saw she got a couple of scratches, but I didn't see nothin' look like she got a thorn in her."

"Why didn't you tell your mama you was hurt?" Mint asked Bess.

"It won't hurtin' me 'til you got home."

"I noticed her limpin' earlier, and I asked her 'bout whether she hurt herself and she said she won't hurt," Justice offered.

"Well, this a job for your grandmama, and she ain't here," said Mint. "Won't be here 'til Sat'day. That's a couple days off. Let's see what we can do for you." He stood up from the bed.

"I can heal it," Bess said brightly. "Grandmama done showed me when I hurt my arm that time. All I'm gon' need after I wash it is some salt and some jimson weed and a li'l honey."

A week later, when fever and thorn had been banished from Bess's body, Emma, back from midwifing, praised her as a healer. "That baby got a gift," she said as the family ate their supper. "I been thinkin' maybe she gon' take over for her ole granny one day," and Bess beamed.

* * *

That night, as Justice lay in her husband's arms, he surprised her with an astute suspicion. "I bet you anything Bess wanted her leg to swell up," he said. "Didn't want nobody to know 'bout it 'til it was good and swole to try to make you feel bad for makin' her leave her playin'."

"She must think I really 'tended to push her in that rose bush," Justice said. "Poor thing." And she kissed him to stop his words, for she did not want him to ask any questions about that day. She never wanted him to learn what had happened in the Willifords' hallway. She would gladly assume the blame for ten thousand large or petty sins that she had not committed as long as Mint did not suspect what Mr. Williford had done. She realized that she actually could endure much worse than Mr. Williford; for the first time, she understood that she could endure a second or a third or any number of rapes if doing so could protect her husband from the lynchman's noose. In her mind's eye, Justice had seen the Salem boy's body when the mob had defiled and mutilated his flesh. And it was clear and easy logic for her to conclude that the black man's right to protect his wife from a white lecher was a far more threatening consideration in their society than the black man's right to vote.

19

Learning

And then I saw him read. I was never so surprised in my life, as when I saw the book talk to my master, for I thought it did as I observed him to look upon it, and move his lips. I wished it would do so with me.

from *A Narrative of the Most Remarkable Particulars in the Life of James Albert Ukawsaw Gronniosaw, an African Prince, As related by Himself,* James Albert Ukawsaw Gronniosaw, 1772

IN SPITE OF LOVE, Bess was a headstrong and grudge-bearing child who developed, over time, into a headstrong and grudge-bearing adult and, ultimately, into a headstrong and grudge-bearing septuagenarian. As a child, she was a clam that closed its shell in self-protection against the possibility of hurt. While her biological mother had succeeded in rejecting her, her adoptive mother would never be able to do so since Bess, seizing the upper hand, had rejected her first. Unlike Christ, the light of the world, Justice proved ill prepared to redeem the imperfections that Bess had perceived in her biological mother and harbored in her memory. That Justice had no responsibility for those imperfections was an unfactored detail, perhaps, in Bess's estimation, so she lived most of her life without forgiving Justice for what her birth mother had done.

Quite possibly her loving relationship with Mint was the closest that Bess ever came to rising above the circumstances surrounding her first four years in the world. Maybe she could love Mint because she did not hold her Indian father, her birth mother's husband, responsible for her eventual abandonment. Maybe she did not believe that he was indebted to her since the seed from which she had inopportunely sprung—like a feckless, accidental tadpole trapped in a ditch of mud—was not his. Perhaps her rapist father, an amorphous shadow too unknown for consideration, lacked the substance to accrue significant enough debts for someone else to pay. For whatever reasons, no figure loomed between Bess and her father, and she never disclaimed his love for her. Yet, he managed to mightily displease her many times, especially on the subject of education.

In 1900, when Bess was ten years old, there were over 28,560 black teachers in the nation and 1,500,000 black students, but Bess was not one of them. She had barely gone to school at all that year, shunning the company of most children, pretending that she was attending school but foraging the woods and pastures all day collecting medicinal herbs. When she was finally discovered by her mother, her satchel full of brittle vegetation, she had obstinately refused to return, claiming that the children terrorized her, called her "ole red Indian girl," threw rocks at her, refused to play with her, and beat her with sticks.

"Do you try to play with the other churren?" her father asked her.

"Nawsuh," she replied. "They don't like Indians.... I told Mama I don't like school."

When Mint voiced his intention to go to the school and speak with the teacher about Bess's allegations, she howled with anger and said she would rather "run away like a ole slave" than go to that school, and he had sent her to bed, even though it was barely six o'clock, where she could enjoy the solitude that she professed to cherish and contemplate without interruption the falsehood that she had perpetrated by pretending to go to school.

"We raisin' a chile who ain't gon' be able to hardly read and write," Mint said to Emma and Justice. "It's gon' be harder in ten years for black folks to make a livin' without a education than it is now. I just can't understand why Bess so 'gainst book learnin'. She don't even want to get the lessons out we give her here."

"You sho' won't like that," said Emma. "Justice, you ain't never seen no chile apter'n Mint. Miz Avery use to say he smarter'n ary chile she got, and he ain't even had the chance to go to school. She use to say he catch on quicker'n a flea can hitch a ride on a dog."

Justice smiled. "I know he smart, Miz Emma. I wish I could understand all them books and 'splain 'em like Mint can. I done learned more from you, Mint, than I ever did the li'l I went to school."

"And I ain't never been to school a day in my life," said Emma, "but bein' round y'all, hearin' y'all talk 'bout all them books and papers Mint done ordered, I feel like I come to know the world more. And when I see Silas again in glory, and he find out Mint done learn me to write my name, he gon' be mighty proud, mighty proud."

"He already know you can write your name," said Mint. "He already proud of you, Mama. He know you smarter'n I ever been. Now, tell me what you think we ought to do 'bout that chile in there won't go to school. Seem like a cryin' shame. All these black churren can't get no schoolin', and she flat out refuse to go."

"She half Indian, Mint," said Justice. "She like to be outside. She been raised like that almost half of her life, travelin' round from place to place. She prob'ly don't like to be cooped up in no school with a lot of churren. There's a lot of black folks who got some Indian blood, but they been raised all their life like they black, so they don't act out like Bess do."

"That's true, Justice," said Emma. "Just like all them black folks got black mamas and white papas. Don't matter if they got white blood, they raised like they black. And if you took 'em and put 'em with a white mama and papa, they prob'ly start actin' up like Bess done tonight. Seem like how you raised count more'n your blood."

"Well, 'less Bess go off and live with the Indians, she gon' be black the rest of her life," Mint replied. "Even if she do go live with the Indians, she gon' be black. Occurs to me, that's what she doin' here in the first place. Her mama say she need to be with her people, meanin' black folks. And if Bess tellin' anything near the truth, li'l black churren tellin' her she a Indian girl. I don't think she rightly know where she b'long, and I feel sorry 'bout that. But we got to think 'bout her future."

"Will it be so bad if she don't get a education?" asked Justice.

"Well, maybe she gon' be able to heal folks and birth babies like Mama and do housework and fieldwork like both of y'all. And maybe she can learn to sew like y'all, too. Maybe if she learn to do like her mama and grandmama, she'll be okay. But I don't know. Things changin'."

"Gon' be hard to make much of anything from healin'," said Emma. "White folks usin' doctors more, and the po' blacks ain't hardly got 'nough money to keep body and spirit together. You have to he'p 'em for nothin' or what li'l they can give. 'Cept for folks who can't pay you, I think healin' work gon' dry up."

"We get 'long better'n most 'cause we own the land and the house," said Mint. "I'd like to buy some more land, but who I'm gon' buy it from? Nobody own land much 'cept white folks, and they ain't sellin' it, and when they do, they not sellin' it to no black person."

"Most black folks can't scrape together the money to buy land no how," said Justice, "and them few that got the money ain't 'lowed to spend it on what they want. Black folks need to figure out how to get money. They work hard 'nough to have some. And then they need to figure out how to make white folks sell stuff to 'em just like they sell to their own."

"You right, Justice," said Mint.

"Y'all get 'long good 'cause y'all save," said Emma, "just like me and Silas. And both of y'all do other work to he'p out what you get from farmin', like me and Silas done."

"You and papa set a great example," Mint said to his mother, and he reached across the kitchen table where they sat and patted her hand. "And even though I could be a farmer and a carpenter if y'all hadn't kept sendin' me and encouragin' me to learn readin' and writin' and 'rithmetic from Miz Avery, bein' able to do them things make my life so much more enjoyable. Mama, I thank you and Papa for that every day."

"Lord, baby," said Emma, "who get any more pleasure out your readin' than your mama? Now, I love that Mr. Dunbar and that 'Jump Back Honey, Jump Back,' and that 'Malindy Sangin',' and that 'Moses' poem. And seem like I couldn't hardly wait for suppertime to be over every day when you was readin' us that book 'bout Frederick Douglass and how he riz up out of slav'ry and learned readin' and writin' and 'bout how he had it so hard. And I just love that book 'bout Harriet Tubman and how she had a pistol and brung all them peoples to freedom and she faintin' sometime and can't read and write no more'n I can. And, churren, them books make me think 'bout my own journey from slav'ry and how the Lord done bless me to have my wonderful son in my old age and bless me to raise him all the way up to a grown man, and he ain't never give me or his papa not one minute of trouble. And the Lord done bless me to have both of you wonderful churren by my side every day. And

I never forget the day he done carried me all the way 'cross that muddy river to freedom, and to my husband, Silas, and to do the Lord's service, and I sealed sorrow up in a li'l patch somewhere in my heart, and I ain't never gon' turn back."

Mint smiled at his mother through his tears and kissed both her hands, and Justice threw her arms around Emma and buried her face in Emma's neck.

"Miz Emma," she said, "you come from the past, but I feel like you the future. You got the love and strength black folks gon' need to make somethin' out of theirself in the future."

"Y'all churren talk so sweet and pretty to me," Emma said.

"Justice tellin' you the truth, Mama," Mint said. "You see the future as clear—moreso— than a lot of the educated folks, black and white, that's writin' books. I just read that every black person ought to learn how to do somethin' needed in the world, that they ought to learn to be business folks and make their own goods to sell. The book say that if a black person make the best product and sell it for less, white folks gon' buy it; that they ain't gon' care that they doin' business with black folks 'stead of white folks."

Justice laughed.

"Now, who in the world said that?" Emma asked. "That'd make sense if the world was fair, but it sho' don't make no sense in the South."

"He's from Alabama, Mama, from the Tuskegee Institute. Name's Mr. Booker T. Washington. He's a real smart man and a good man, but I knew you were gon' have somethin' to say 'bout that idea of his."

"Why he think white folks gon' buy what black folks make just 'cause they make it real good and it don't cost much? And white folks makin' it, too?" Emma asked incredulously. "What them ole rebby white folks gon' do is they gon' tell them black folks to close up shop or they gon' burn it to the ground. Get them Ku Klux Klan folks in them sheets to do it. Same kind that's been burnin' crosses and lynchin' all them black mens that ain't done nothin' but try to live decent, and they killin' 'em. Tell whoever wrote that book that ole rebby white folks hate black folks more'n they hate spendin' money."

"I don't like them no more'n they like all us black folks, 'cause I sho' wouldn't buy nothin' from no Ku Klux Klaner even if they was givin' it away for free," said Justice somewhat illogically, and they all laughed.

"And why they got to have crosses and long white robes like they Jesus or somethin'?" Justice added.

"'Cause they hypocrites and their souls sick," Mint said, and the laughter continued.

"When God gon' get tired allowin' all this lynchin' of innocent peoples who ain't hurt nobody, Miz Emma?" Justice asked, suddenly serious.

"Folks the ones doin' it, baby, and folks the ones 'lowin' it," Emma answered. "That ain't none of God. He just givin' folks free will, just like he said he would."

20

Emancipation

If there were seven blind men
one of them unable to hear
would be father . . .
promising to deliver
what never arrives.

from "Conditions," Essex Hemphill, 1986

IN 1905, the year before Emma died at the age of ninety-one, Bess ran off with a red-bone Negro whose nappy hair was harder than ball bearings and whose finest attribute may have been his self-proclaimed role as a "sport." She ran off on a Wednesday when everyone except Emma was supposed to be out of the house working and Bess, herself, wanting to earn some extra money, had hired out to chop cotton for Preston Cobb. Of course, she did not come home for supper that night, having run off, and Justice, Emma, and Mint would have worried themselves senseless had Mint not gone up to the general store in Chesterton and learned that Bess had been seen heading west out of Chesterton that morning with Tommy Maben, her erstwhile boyfriend who, her family had believed, was out of her life. Emma and Justice discovered that her clothes were missing from the bedroom that she had shared with her grandmother for eleven years. She had left no note, said no goodbye. The following day, instead of returning to their own fields with Mint, Justice was in Preston Cobb's back yard at 6:30 in the morning to apologize for Bess's absence and to make up for it by helping his "hands" chop cotton in Bess's stead for the rest of the week.

"I know y'all got your own crops to take care of," Mr. Cobb told Justice. "Seem like everybody's fields just ate up with grass, all this rain we been gettin'. I 'preciate you comin' and lettin' me know not to count on your daughter, and I sure thank you for bein' willin' to he'p out here, but ain't no need. I think I can get one of Clara Mae's girls. They prob'ly ain't doin' nothin' much. I 'clare, churren these days are 'nough to keep you wake at night no matter how tired you are when your head finally hit that pillow. And it don't matter 'bout color. White bad as black. My own churren given me and the missus a thing or two to worry 'bout, b'lieve you me."

* * *

Bess came back on a Saturday twenty-nine months later with a nine-month-old baby on her hip, another child in her belly, and Tommy Maben in tow. After a fine dinner prepared by Justice—fried chicken smothered in gravy, boiled cabbage and white potatoes, stewed corn, onion-flavored corn bread fritters, apple turnovers, and mint tea—Tommy moved their belongings, contained in two feed sacks and a cardboard suitcase tied together with twine, into Emma's room. Mint and Justice learned later that the cardboard suitcase contained Tommy's clothes and that the baby, a beautiful little girl with a mane of unruly hair, owned just two shirts and four diapers to her name.

"Y'all stay here long as you want," Mint told Bess, who had seemed paralyzed with grief when she learned of Emma's death. "I know Mama so pleased you and your family back in you all's old room."

"Thank you, Papa," Bess said, "but Grandmama stood on her own foots. She ain't never been beholden to nobody, and I'm gon' be the same. Tommy goin' out first thing Monday mornin' and find some work and a place for us. We ain't gon' be layin' up here on you and Mama. You gon' find a place to farm, ain't you, Tommy?"

"Yeah," said Tommy. "You ain't hearn of nobody lookin' for a tenant, is you?" he asked Mint.

"Let me think on it," Mint answered. He knew of one track of land without a sharecropper, but he was not prepared to mention it.

"I been thinkin' 'bout goin' up north," said Tommy. "Seem like the colored can't make no decent livin' down south."

"We ain't goin' up north," Bess retorted. "We done hearn 'bout it, Tommy, and we seen folks lost their jobs, churren hongry, and they back down south lookin' for work. We ain't goin' nowhere where we can't hunt and fish and grow a garden. Helen got to eat, and this here other baby gon' have to eat."

In the darkness of their room that night, Mint and Justice talked in hushed tones about Tommy's prospects for finding work.

"Bess can get work cookin' and cleanin' for somebody, but she prob'ly can't do too much fieldwork right now," Justice said. "But where Tommy gon' find something, Mint? I been tryin' and tryin', but I can't come up with no house or land that's vacant right now, and if Tommy can't get a crop somewhere, I don't know what they gon' do."

"The house you was born in just come vacant," Mint answered, "and Mr. Haskins gon' need somebody to take over that crop allotment. But you ain't been in that house since me and Mama carried you out of there. If Bess livin' there, how you gon' feel 'bout goin' back?"

"Tell 'em 'bout the place first thing in the mornin', Mint,"

Justice replied. "Tommy got a family to take care of. This ain't no time for foolishness from me 'bout somethin' that happened twenty years ago. And bad things done happened near 'bout every place folks done been, I 'magine. It ain't the places' fault."

The day before Bess and Tommy moved, Justice walked alone through the front door of her childhood home and into the room where her mother had died. And she beheld Emma, leaning over the bed to cut the rags from her body, and Mint, lifting her like a baby and carrying her out of the house. And her mother rose and walked with her to the spot where the children lay in what had been the garden. And Elijah took her memory and peeled back her pain like layers of an onion, and the tears that she shed were from the acrid fumes. And he led her to the barn and to the smokehouse where she beheld a vision of her most hurtful past. But what had been her pain was now Elijah's, absorbed of his own free will as restitution for all that she had suffered and for what he had given—his life—which had been all that he could give in his twisted state of sorrow. And then Mint was with her in the brilliant sunlight, and he held her body to his, and they did not speak. Then she walked with him to the front yard where the crepe myrtle trees and tiger lilies were in blazing color, and Mint broke a sprig of the purple blossoms and placed it in her hair.

That house would be Bess and Tommy's home for the rest of their life together, except for an unspeakable period of two years when they lived in their own house, on their own land, and Tommy was his own boss man. The house that they were now moving into was where six of their eight children would be born between 1907 and 1921. And when it burned to the ground in 1964 from a bolt of lightning that struck the pitch of its roof and split the house in two like a halved pecan, Bess was able to step out of her bedroom into the powdery earth beneath it and walk to safety at the far edge of the yard. She stood under the purple night sky and watched as orange flames lit the world around her and destroyed the awkward sections of her home. When the timbers were mostly ashes, the heavy, low-hanging rain clouds began to beat the earth with furious dollops of water. A barefoot old woman draped in an exquisitely crafted quilt handmade by her mother over fifty years before, Bess trudged off to the barn and, cocooned in Justice's handiwork, burrowed atop the corn and slept the sleep of the righteous. In the morning when the sun had barely touched the horizon, she awakened to the noise of her own stomach growling from hunger. Then she wrapped her feet in tow sacks, caped her body in her mother's quilt, and began her halting pilgrimage to her daughter Esther's home.

21

Signs

Nobody eber help me into carriages, or ober mud puddles, or gives me any best place. . . . I have plowed, and planted, and gathered into barns, and no man could head me. . . . I have borne thirteen chilern and seen 'em mos' all sold off into slavery, and when I cried out with a mother's grief, none but Jesus heard. . . .

from "Ar'n't I a Woman? Speech to the Women's Rights Convention in Akron, Ohio," Sojouner Truth, 1851

THE FIRST TIME Bess caught Tommy engaged in sexual intercourse with another woman was in the summer of 1912 when she was heavily pregnant with Esther, their fourth child. Afterwards, she would think ruefully that she had been forced to bear the humiliation of discovering Tommy violating their marriage vows in their own bed because she'd had to pee. However, the truth in her cause and effect ruminations was merely literal, for Tommy was prone to seek sex outside their marriage, and he had never bothered to hide his actions from his wife. A more accurate reading of why Bess caught Tommy in coitus is that she failed to read his signs.

"Read and respect my signs, woman," he had told her angrily many times. "And if you don't and you run into somethin' you can't handle, you ain't gon' have nobody to blame for it but yourself."

Over time, when Tommy was preparing to go out, Bess had learned not to ask whether he was going somewhere, where he was going, or when he was coming back. A "sign," for example, was his sprucing up on a Saturday or a Sunday or after a half or a full day of work. "Readin'" his sign was understanding without coaching or explanation that he was "fixin' up" because he was "fixin' to go off." "Respectin'" his sign meant accepting it without question or comment. Bess had "run into" the back of Tommy's hand on several occasions when she had failed to "read" or "respect" his signs. Once, in the dead of winter, she had appeared not to have read his sign that he wanted conjugal sex, and her face had "run into" his fist and she had had to search the frozen hedge rows and ditch banks of the land they farmed to find enough of the cocklebur plant to treat her dislocated lower jawbone.

Bess caught Tommy pumping hard to reach orgasm, his yellow behind clenched and thrusting with the detached rage of a motorized ram, his hands splayed against the mattress like duck feet, sweat pouring from his helmet of tightly coiled hair, his mouth slightly open, his eyes staring straight into the headboard, a man traveling nowhere, alone. The woman underneath him clutched his back like a life raft and moaned in wily encouragement to row him safely to port. She was a whore. Her two teenaged daughters were whores. What was most humiliating for Bess about the situation in which she found herself was that Tommy had brought a whore into her bed.

At the time, Bess was working as cook and housekeeper for Mabel Haskins, the wife of their landlord. On most mornings, Bess would cook breakfast and dinner for her family before reporting to her employers' place to prepare and serve their breakfast and clean their house. She would cook and serve their dinner at noon and clean up after the meal, leaving preparation of a light supper to Mrs. Haskins. Bess would then head to her own home to spend the rest of the afternoon doing fieldwork before cooking supper for her family. On the day in question, rather than taking her hoe from the yard, leaving her smock and shoes on the porch to save the time that it would take to put them inside the house, and going straight to the field as she usually did, because she had the irresistible urge to pee, she altered her pattern and began the straightest route—through the central hallway of her shotgun house—to the toilet. The children were being looked after at a neighbor's house by their ten-year-old daughter, and Tommy was supposed to be walking behind the mule, hilling up the tobacco. But the sounds coming from the room where she and Tommy slept clearly indicated that the house was not empty, and Bess pushed open the door.

She had not read the signs. Tommy's brogans, their soles thick with dirt from the freshly plowed tobacco field, stood empty on the front porch, just outside the front door. The door to the bedroom had been pulled to, and Tommy's straw hat hung on the doorknob outside the room.

"What you think it was you hearn in here?" he had shouted at Bess when his hired partner had climbed hastily into her clothes and left the room and Bess had protested that she had simply not seen his signs because she had to pee. Naked as the day he was born, his face suffused from anger or from exertion or both, the veins in his neck and forehead engorged but his sex withered, Tommy impressed Bess as representing a whole different species from that of her father.

"He a snake," she said to herself, and though she did not speak aloud, her wet gray eyes measured him and flashed the hatred that had long been growing in her heart.

"You got to pee so bad," Tommy said, pulling on his shirt and overalls and clearly hating her right back, "what you standin' up here for? Gone pee!" And he quickly left the house to follow the whore out to the road.

22

Murder

You may leave and go to Hali-ma-jack,
But my slow-drag will-a bring you back,
A-well-a you may go but this will bring
you back.

from "You May Go But This Will Bring You Back,"
sung by Zora Neale Hurston, 1935;
music and original lyrics by Ben Harney, 1897

SAMUEL LOWREY shifted his eyes from Solly's face and squinted at a gaggle of Canada geese skimming the air in V formation against the steel gray sky. Father and son sat on Samuel's back porch on rocking chairs that Samuel himself had made when Solly, named Solomon, his eldest by five minutes, was a boy. Solly was intent on relating the events surrounding a murder to his father, and he knew that Samuel was listening, though Samuel's eyes followed the armada of sailing geese that had the vast ocean of sky to itself.

"They're not spelling out vacation," said Samuel. "They know where they're going, and nobody ever needs to go find even one of them. Most folks are nowhere near as smart as geese."

"If they were, they wouldn't cause half the trouble they do," Solly responded. "Now a goose'll shit on you, but it's unintentional. Hitchy Askew planned to do what he did, and this time he's gonna pay."

"What're the new developments in the case," asked Samuel, "leaving out all the personal stuff? Seems like we got to treat this case like it don't have anything to do with us. To be fair, you know."

"We can't overlook the facts, Papa, and fact is that this case has got everything to do with us. It *is* personal. Mama's broken up over it, and you are, too. And Mabel and I, well, it's almost like one of us was lost. I'd want to do anything possible to bring justice to this case even if Annie Mae hadn't been connected to us the way she was. But she was a part of this family, and I'm prepared to go beyond what looks possible."

"You sounding like an old Hatteras medicine man," said Samuel, chuckling.

"That's who my father is," answered Solly. "Why should I be different?"

Samuel smiled. "That's more like your mother, only she's a woman. And I've talked with her, and I've seen as she told it what she's seen in her dreams. Talked with her this morning while she was sealing and fluting the top crust over an apple cobbler she's cooking for dinner. And we pieced together what came to her in dreams with what we already knew. Here's our story, your mother's and mine, if you care to hear it, for what it's worth:"

* * *

Hitchy Askew lay on his side under the front room of Annie Mae's house. He could see the lamplight slip between the floorboards where the rag rug did not reach and reflect weakly on his outstretched legs. He had lain there, cramped and wary of bumping his head and alerting Annie Mae and Acey Phillips of his presence. For well over an hour, he lay there as Annie Mae courted and carried on with Acey, that half Indian, half black, serving him her special cake that she called sweet bread and mint tea laced with sugar. When Acey finally left, Hitchy stretched out flat upon his back beneath the house, instead of crawling out as he had planned and taking off through the woods, the same stealthy way he had come. He lay still beneath the two rooms of Annie Mae's home, and his mind visited the bygone nights from three years before when he had held her, her chest upon his, and had fallen in love with her, a beautiful black pearl, before abandoning her because, one mind said to him, "The times, they what they are."

"I don't want to be like my papa," he'd told Annie Mae right before he left her. "He had a powerful hankering for blackberries—that's what he called juicy young black gals—but he used to steal what he wanted. He never took responsibility for the hurt he brought on other people. He grabbed children, even, and this started a long time before he married my mama and I was born. Knowing who you come from helps you look out for what you need to steer clear of in yourself."

"I ain't no chile," Annie Mae responded.

At the time, Annie Mae was already a woman, a laundress and housekeeper for other people, and head of her own home that had been secured with the help of her benefactors, Samuel and Mary Lowrey. They had taken her in when she was orphaned at six years of age after the deaths of her mother and father in a house fire of unknown origin. Perhaps a banked ember had leapt from the fireplace to the dry planks of the main room's floor, and had tasted crackly resins dormant in the wood for decades, and had nibbled in covert constraint until it gained the power to fully consume. Annie Mae had been saved because her father, awakened by the smell of fire, had opened his eyes to a dust storm of smoke roiling into the room.

"Get up, Arlice! House afire!"

He ran into the hallway, but the smoke coming up the ladder muffled his nose and mouth and drove him backwards into the room. Arlice had awakened Annie Mae, and she and Thomas had worked wordlessly but in tandem, as if of one mind, as they prepared their daughter's life-saving cocoon. They sandwiched her between two pillows, then rolled her in a quilt. Thomas broke out the window panes in their loft bedroom, gashing his hands and arms because he could not see in the heavy smoke, and he and Arlice shoved the bundle that was their daughter through the only safe exit. Then the air from the broken window rushed in and fanned the fire to heavenward heights. Safely on the ground, Annie Mae had wriggled out of her cocoon, coughing and crying, and had dragged it with her a safe distance from the inferno that engulfed the upper rafters, its tongues of fire reaching towards the clouds seeking wetness and death. In the morning, it was Samuel who found her curled atop her cocoon where she had fallen asleep with her thumb in her mouth. On the ground at the side of the house where the loft's window had been, Samuel discovered the white bones of her parents, clothed in a covering of black and gray ash.

When Samuel entered his kitchen carrying the sobbing, petrified child, he handed her to Mary, who was chopping vegetables for the day's dinner. "A terrible thing's happened," he said to his wife. "The new colored family's house burned down, Tom and Arlice's. I found their little girl at the edge of the yard. She'd been out there for hours—had to been—since the whole place is ashes, just ashes."

Mary had taken the little girl in her arms and had carried her to and fro in the kitchen and had begun singing an ancient song in the ancient language that they no longer knew. "Heart is hearth, heart is home, love is hearth and home," she sang in the words of the Hatteras, and the child had closed her eyes and gone to sleep.

The second night that Hitchy hid under Annie Mae's house, he could hear her and Acey kissing as if trying to suck the marrow from each other's bones. To Hitchy, the kissing seemed to start the minute Acey got in the front door. He heard their declarations of love for one another and Acey's marriage proposal.

"You ever been in love before?" asked Acey.

"Once," answered Annie Mae, "but not like this. Nothing's ever felt like this."

"I never been in love before," said Acey. "No way, no how. This is it, first time and forever!"

Then Hitchy had to listen to their endless smacking and murmuring until Annie Mae said, "No, Acey. Stop. Stop."

"Well, you gon' marry me?" Acey asked.

"Soon as you want me to." And Hitchy had to listen to them as they made their foolish plans: how Acey would move into Annie Mae's house and would add another room—two more if she wanted—before the start of winter. Hitchy knew that Acey was a builder mostly of fishing boats and rowboats, and sometimes of canoes. But it sounded to Hitchy as if Acey thought building onto a house was easy as snapping his fingers. Hitchy was not a builder at all, but his own shortcomings did not affect his mounting disdain for Acey and Annie Mae's grandiosity. Then he heard them making love, not waiting the way they had said they were going to do. Their happiness choked him, and his heart struggled to rise from his chest and burst through his clothing. He crawled out from under Annie Mae's house, crying soundlessly, and headed to his campsite, thinking that Acey would surely stay the night in Annie Mae's bed. He could not bear to hear any more of their rooting into each other like hogs in a pile of rotting squash.

But Acey did get up and go home. He did so to guard against anyone's seeing him leave Annie Mae's in the morning—maybe some gossiping witch bent on spreading nasty stories about them throughout the community. Annie Mae was going to be his wife, and he would protect her from the acid slander of gossipmongers. He headed home not the way he had come, but practically as the crow flies, through the woods in the same direction that Hitchy had taken.

At around 9:30 the next morning, when Annie Mae had not come to work at her never-once-late time of seven o'clock, her employer, Miss Carrie Smith, decided to ride over and see if Annie Mae had fallen ill. She knocked on the front door of Annie Mae's house and received no answer, so she opened it, calling, "Annie Mae! You in there?" She noticed blood-stained shoe prints on the yellow pine boards of the narrow hallway leading to the back door. Since the steps led away from the sleeping and sitting area, she looked there first. Annie Mae lay in her bed with her throat slit, her head almost severed. Her gown had been bunched up around her waist, and a deep gash opened her abdomen and the layer of flesh over her pelvic bone. The scene stunned and nauseated Carrie, who felt her knees giving way beneath her, and she reached out to grab the bed and steady herself. Her hand closed around Annie Mae's left foot, grown hard and cold as a metal shoe last. Carrie staggered from the house and hastened to notify Sheriff Crawford of the murder. Dr. Mansfield, who accompanied the sheriff to Annie Mae's home, discovered that her clitoris had been cut out and was no longer with the rest of the body.

"It's the worst, sickest crime I ever seen in this here county or any other place in near 'bout twenty-eight years in this job!" Sheriff Crawford declared.

* * *

"Since Acey's in jail for cold-blooded murder, a crime for which he'll surely hang if he's convicted," Samuel said to his son, "why wouldn't he make up a story about running across a campsite on his way home from Annie Mae's and hearing someone scurry away from the area when they heard his approach? He didn't actually see anybody, so he can't identify anybody. And, yes, the sheriff says it looks like somebody camped there a couple of days and left in a hurry. It could've been a drifter, and it could've been Acey himself, setting the scene."

"You're right, Papa," said Solly. "But, you, Mama, and I know that Hitchy Askew was sneaking around Annie Mae before he up and left here three years ago. I think he came back and killed her for taking up with somebody else, somebody that he would see as inferior to himself, since he's white and Acey's from an Indian father and a black mother."

"True," responded Samuel, "and his family history supports what you're saying. Everybody knows that Old Man Tip Askew was the scum of the earth and had reverence for just about nothing. He had a criminal mindset against black women, not against the women of his own race. He never once raped a white woman that I ever heard tell of, but he raped three different black girls who spoke out about it, all of them very young. Used to try to tempt 'em with gingersnap cookies; too cheap to buy any other kind, I reckon. And he set one of 'em's house on fire because her father spread word that he was going to kill him when he least expected it. That evil old man set that house on fire when the whole family was inside, already gone to bed, but some of them hadn't fallen off to sleep and they heard something and the dogs were barking up a storm, and the man went to check and saw the porch on fire. Everybody got out safely, and they were even able to put the fire out before the house burned down, with the help of neighbors and their buckets and with the river nearby. That's when the old man was run out of here. But Hitchy wasn't like his father, and that's why nobody bothered him when he stayed. He just left on his own three years ago. Nobody seems to know why—or why he would've come back to murder one of the finest young women in these parts, black, Indian, or white."

"Maybe that's it. Maybe he killed her because she was beautiful and was going to marry Acey."

"She ever tell you she was going to marry Acey?"

"No, sir."

"She never told your mother or me or Mabel either, far as I know. Now, like I told you already, your mother's dreams showed Annie Mae telling Acey she'd marry him. But every detail in a dream, even your mother's dreams, ain't got to prove true. And you know better than I do that dreams are not permissible as evidence in any legitimate court in this country."

"Acey says he had just asked her on the night she was killed."

"He admits he was with her the night she died. Nobody else admits to that. The murder weapon, just dropped on the floor, was her own butcher knife. He could have picked that knife up in the kitchen, taken it in the house, and killed her as easy as anybody else could."

"Why would he kill her if he's telling the truth when he says he loved her? His whole family says he was crazy in love with Annie Mae."

"Most killing's done in the name of either craziness or love, son. When somebody hurts those you love, you just might go crazy enough to kill them. They might deserve to die. But Annie Mae didn't hurt anyone, unless she rebuffed Acey's marriage proposal and hurt his feelings. He's a mighty fine young man so far as I've ever been able to see. But he needs some hard evidence in his defense or he's going to be just as dead as poor Annie Mae."

"I think there just might be one tiny piece of hard evidence in his favor, Papa."

"What's that?"

"When I went back by the house this morning and got the sheriff to let me look in at the shoe prints in the hallway—you know, they've got the place padlocked and everything—well, it's the same kind of shoe sole that's on almost every man's brogans, and the size looks kind of average, but it looked to me like the shoes were so run over that the outside of the heels didn't get much blood on them. Every print is missing an edge where the heel would have been worn down the most."

"Acey run his shoes over?" asked Samuel.

"I don't know yet," Solly replied. "I asked the sheriff to look into it, keeping in mind that lots of men run their shoes over."

"They probably don't have the fingerprint results yet, do they?"

"No, sir. Not yet. But since Acey and Annie Mae started courting, his fingerprints are likely to be all over the house."

"Well, unless he's been helping her with cutting up meat for cooking, they ought not to be on her butcher knife."

* * *

Some people claimed that Acey got out of jail because he had the good luck to be a black man who'd only killed a black woman. After all, he ran his shoes over—proof positive, they said, that he was the killer. He stayed out of jail because not one of the fingerprints detected on the murder weapon was his. There was some talk of lining men up and fingerprinting them to see if a match could be found to those, other than Annie Mae's, on the knife used to kill her. That turned out to be just talk, since Acey was the only real suspect at hand, and he had been exonerated without any sign of a trial. "He could'a wore gloves," more than one citizen argued.

"Folks think you can just fingerprint the whole community, cats and dogs, too, I reckon," complained Sheriff Carter. "You can't just haul men folks in for fingerprinting when you ain't got no probable cause against 'em. And just 'cause they got this newfangled way of helping to catch a criminal don't mean it's the only way, or that it's cheap. This ain't Raleigh. It ain't even Wilmington, and we ain't got nothing like the king's mint over here to draw from. Some drifter prob'ly stopped through here and killed a nigra. We've done got the word out: anybody notice anyone strange or suspicious round here's s'posed to notify me first thing. Don't y'all think I'm sleep on solvin' this here case. No, sirree!"

* * *

"Some things are better left alone, son," said Samuel. "You cannot know all the comings and goings of any man or of any man's heart. If a man commits an evil deed, does that make him evil and deserving of our harshest justice? God saw fit for David to prosper after David sent Uriah to his death at the front of battle because David wanted Bathsheba, Uriah's wife. And God saw fit to punish David for his sins. But it was God's punishment, not man's."

"I'm as tired of thinking about the white man's God as I am

of thinking about his justice," answered Solly. "I'm ashamed of his blood running through my veins. When have whites ever done fairly by other races? When have they punished murderers among their own people for killing blacks or Indians? Annie Mae's murderer will never be brought to justice if doing so is left to Sheriff Carter. I believe Hitchy Askew's hand is in her murder. Since Hitchy's white, the sheriff isn't going after him. Like his father, Hitchy thinks he can live a life of crime and never pay, but I'm going to make him pay. You heard Mabel talk about Old Man Askew raping that little black girl when he was a young man living with his folks over in Chesterton. Well, Hitchy's—"

"Think a minute, son," Samuel interrupted. "You're a lawyer, so think like one. That was so long ago, I'll bet nobody remembers the straight of it. And it was Hitchy's father, not Hitchy. . . . He wasn't even born, wasn't even thought about in those long-ago days. Mabel wasn't born or thought about—you either—and everything she says on the subject is hearsay warmed over a thousand times. Mabel says she knows the daughter of the black woman that Hitchy's father raped, but that doesn't make her an expert on the crime. I doubt she even knew the alleged victim. In fact, that woman could've been dead way before Mabel and Lawyer Haskins got married and he moved her to his home over in Chesterton. Before that, your mother and I were pretty near the only folks around here who'd ever heard of Chesterton, let alone been there—not counting the Askews, of course, and they came here later and didn't stay all that long, considering."

"You and Mama? When had the two of you ever been in Chesterton?" asked Solly, very surprised indeed by this unexpected revelation.

23

Grief

This little light of mine,
I'm gonna let it shine.

from "This Little Light of Mine," Negro Spiritual

MABEL HASKINS walked out to the spread of trees beyond her yard where Bess and her children were harvesting pecans that local merchants would later ship to markets throughout the mid- and northern Atlantic states. During their leafy season, the four acres of trees formed a broad canopy that kept most sunlight from reaching the ground and nurturing the stubborn weeds and grasses struggling to grow there. Undeterred by differences of race and class, Mabel Haskins's son and daughter, absent today because of school, spent joyous summer and autumn hours cavorting with Bess and Tommy's older children under the trees.

In the virtual absence of ground cover during summer, the children played fearlessly in this wonderland of little vegetation where sun-loving snakes dumb enough to look for shade could easily be spotted. On windy days in winter, the deserted trees stood like marooned prisoners waving their bony arms and hands in scratchy supplication to the sky. The pecan husks, blackened and dry before the harvesting season, released their hold upon the nuts by splitting in four equal parts and stretching each newly formed tentacle towards a different corner of the world. The husks hung on with great tenacity, some for most, if not all, of the winter, perched like topsy-turvy blackbirds throughout the expanse of trees. Sometimes they struck the eye as gnarly hairdos on pin-headed stick figures, but to Mabel Haskins they were black stars, jewels bedecking the slate blue robe of Sky Woman, an exquisite beauty who fell to earth through a hole in the filament of heaven. Mabel mesmerized her children with the tale of earth's creation from a small bit of dirt on the back of a brave and generous turtle. The turtle had taken the patch of dirt upon his back so that Sky Woman could make a soft landing and would have a place to live after her fall. When Sky Woman landed, the earth on the turtle's back expanded and expanded until it formed the entire landmass of the world. Before the coming of Sky Woman, there had been nothing but water, as far as the eye could see, inhabited by birds and animals. When Sky Woman fell, she brought in her hands seeds of trees, grasses, and all manner of plant life from Sky Land. She sowed the seeds upon the earth, and they began to grow. The pecan orchard, Mabel loved to tell her children, was an ancient gift from Sky Woman just for them.

Like Sky Woman, Mabel Haskins was a beauty. With large gray eyes, long, wavy blonde hair, and pale skin, she looked more aristocratic than did most members of the oldest, wealthiest families in all of Chatham County. She was married to one of the county's richest men. She went to church, her children were brilliant in school, and she was both sought after and responsive to high society, sometimes carrying out civic services such as hosting parties for forward-thinking aspirants to political office. But if one paid attention, one could see that in various small ways, Mabel Haskins distinguished herself, perhaps unfavorably, from other genteel persons in the area. Socially generous, she spoke with warmth and interest to equals and unequals alike, regardless of their social status or race, wherever she met them. She rode horses more than other women did, and she owned a thoroughbred named Millie that Mr. Haskins brought all the way from Kentucky for her twenty-fifth birthday. She took care of her children herself, rather than hiring black women to do so, and from the age of five or six, her twins could be seen cantering on their horses under their mother's instruction. She taught them to ride bareback as well as in the saddle, and both the boy and the girl had bows and arrows that they used expertly for hunting wild game. Perhaps Mrs. Haskins, who did not hunt, had not taught the children this skill. Certainly their father had not. As a large landowner and gentleman farmer never known to pursue any type of hands-on animal husbandry, and as the head of his own law firm in the bustling town of Guilford, Mr. Haskins's interests and acumen lay in directions quite removed from archery or horsemanship. It was rumored that the children's aptness with the bow and arrow had been handed down from generations of kinfolks in kilts or tunics and tights who practiced those arts long before modern times. The children's free spirits, however, were derived directly from their mother, and their long blonde manes, floating behind them as they raced on horseback, were smaller renditions of her own. "Look like they ought to cut that boy's hair, big as he is," some people complained. Perhaps the most telling difference between Mabel Haskins and her peers was her seeming unawareness that grown women did not run around playing with their children as if they were children themselves; and even if they did, they certainly did not do so with their hair flying behind them, wild and free as a horse's tail.

  On the day that Mabel Haskins walked down to the pecan grove to commune with Bess, she observed that her own daughter, considerably younger than Bess's older daughters but almost as tall, had clothes, books, and toys that the beautiful little black girls could use. Surely her son had much that would be of value to Bess's sons. Mrs. Haskins had recently returned from Annie Mae's funeral, and her heart was crushed by grief. She wanted to reach out to someone in need, and it seemed that the Holy Spirit had set Bess and her children in Mabel's way to need and receive her aid. She headed to the pecan grove carrying a basket containing three dozen freshly baked tea cakes and a quart-sized fruit jar of sweet mint tea.

"It won't hurt anybody for all of them to drink from the jar," she said to herself upon deciding not to haul glasses to the grove, and she smiled remembering the time, years ago, when she, Solly, and Annie Mae had drunk two quarts of scuppernong wine that Mabel had stolen from the cellar. They had sat on the ground with their backs propped against the rough boards of the smokehouse and had passed the jars back and forth until the wine was gone. Mabel and Solly had retched like dogs disgorging poisoned meat, frightening Annie Mae, who was not similarly affected by the brew, into running to Mary for help. Mary had marched Mabel and Solly to the pump, forced them to stand barefoot in the lichen-carpeted water trough, and had pumped cold water over the backs of their heads until their emptied stomachs had settled, the hammering on their temples had ceased, and Mabel had grown afraid of sticking permanently to the trough's slimy bottom. Later, through Mabel and Solly's telling, the event became known as "Cat Mama's Murderous Attempt to Drown Her Own Dear Kittens," a joke that neither Mary nor Samuel seemed to appreciate. But they were good sports.

"Should've left you there for that old half-blind Hobbs to lick you to death, thinking you were salt blocks, nasty and sweaty as you were," Mary would retort.

"If Bossy'd got her tongue around the two of you, she'd 've lodged you up those bushel-basket nostrils of hers, and we never would've seen you or heard of you again. You'd 've lived off eating nothing but her snot. Think about that! Y'all got off easy,"

Samuel would add.

At the time, Mary had removed her apron and used it to wash her twins' faces and to clean the purple vomit from their clothes.

"Fire and water don't mix," she'd warned them before turning to resume her duties inside the house. "Thank you, Annie Mae, for being the one with some sense around here. And you're by far the youngest, too."

"I don't have no sense, either, ma'am!" Annie Mae had exclaimed in deep consternation that Mary had judged her innocent.

* * *

"Here come Miz Haskins, Mama," said Helen when it was clear that the pecan grove was Mabel's destination.

"When she get here, you all be quiet and polite and keep workin' like good churren, you hear?"

"Yessum!" the children murmured.

"And don't eat one pecan while she here!"

Soon enough, Mabel Haskins was upon them, smiling her wide-mouthed, friendly smile. "Good afternoon, Bess, children," she said, setting down her basket. "I thought you all might like a little refreshment. I baked some tea cakes while the children are at school, and I've brought you some, and some mint tea."

The children stopped working and looked hopefully at Bess.

"Thank you, Miz Haskins," said Bess, deeply moved by this unexpected kindness. "We much obliged. Churren, speak up and thank Miz Haskins for this treat."

The aroma of buttery cookies wafted from the basket when Mabel whisked away the white damask napkin used to cover them. The children stepped forward, heads down, murmuring, "Thank you, Miz Haskins."

"Our hands dirty, Mama," said Helen, looking at her palms stained by blackened pecan husks, her nails with lines of grime beneath them.

"We all a little dirty," said Bess, "but if Miz Haskins kindly hand us a tea cake, the dirt on our hands ain't gon' hurt nobody one bit."

"You all go on and help yourselves. My mother always said a little dirt in your food won't hurt your body like an unclean heart will. She claimed that every healthy person's going to eat a peck of dirt in their lifetime. Said it makes 'em stronger!"

"No wonder I'm healthy as a ox," said Bess, laughing with genuine pleasure before the affirming kindness of this rich white woman. "And, I 'clare, I don't think I ever would have remembered it 'fore this minute, but my mama use to say the same thing."

"One thing I know," said Mabel, "is all good mothers are more alike than different. Come on, you all, have some tea cakes and tea. If you can't eat them all now, take what's left home with you for later."

The children remembered their manners, and Bess, given the jar of tea first by Mrs. Haskins, drank and then served the children.

"This mighty fine tea," said Bess. "Taste like sun tea. No touch of bitterness from boilin'; just soothin', coolin', calmin' freshness in your mouth and down your throat." She looked off to the horizon and fleeting pain swept over her face.

"Tea cakes mighty good," said Tommy Lee.

"Help yourself," said Mrs. Haskins. "I'm glad you like them. . . . And you're absolutely right about the tea, Bess. Mama's always said it slips down your throat, soothing your taste buds, healing what ails you when you don't even know you're sick."

"Your mama seem like a mighty fine person," said Bess.

"She is," answered Mabel. "How I wish you could meet her."

Bess looked at Mabel Haskins, certain, because of the sincerity in her voice, that she had gone crazy. "Maybe in gloryland," she responded. "But in this life, ain't no fine white woman other than you want to meet me just for pleasure sake. If you don't mind me sayin' so, you not like most folks, Miz Haskins!"

"You don't know my mother. She and my father raised a colored girl, almost like she was my sister. She passed away recently, and I just came back from the funeral yesterday. I was up there"—she nodded toward her home—"in that big house by myself, and I just felt so sad and wanted to reach out to you and the children in my time of sorrow."

"We mighty sorry 'bout your loss, and I'm ready to do anything I can to he'p you, Miz Haskins. Just let me know what it is."

"Do you think you could help me with some cooking and some housework a few hours a day? I'll pay you better than anyone else around here would. And I have lots of clothes and toys and shoes from my girl and my boy, too, that you are welcome to for your children."

"We thank you for whatever you give. Lord knows the churren can use just 'bout everything. They grow so fast! And toys!" Again Bess looked off to the horizon. "When can I start, ma'am?"

"Tomorrow, if that's not too soon for you. If it is, soon as you can."

"What time you want me, ma'am?"

"Mr. Haskins likes to eat around 8:30. But I know you have your own family. I can get his breakfast; he has a light one anyway."

"I'll be there tomorrow mornin' eight o'clock, if it's all the same to you, ma'am. I'm gon' get all your cleanin' done and whatever cookin' you want. This job comin' to me when my fam'ly really need it. May God rain his blessin's down upon you, ma'am. I'm gon' bring your basket and things back tomorrow mornin'."

It was then that Mabel Haskins shocked both Bess and the children. She walked over to Bess and embraced her. "Thank you,

Bess, and may God bless us all!" The two women stared into each other's stormy eyes, and the bonds of compassion and understanding were strong between them.

24

Loss

When my life becomes a burden,
And I'm nearing chilly Jordan
O thou Lily of the Valley,
Stand by me, stand by me . . .

from "Stand by Me," C.A. Tindley, late 19th Century

BESS LIVED LESS than two miles from her parents, who delighted in her children. Mint and Justice kept clothes on their grandchildren's backs, shoes on their feet, and food in their stomachs, especially during the winter when the garden was dead from frost or during hard times when Tommy had taken the money hoarded by Bess from her housekeeping wages, leaving her unable to purchase flour, sugar, dried beans, rice, or other staples. Justice and Mint took them jars upon jars of canned meat, fruit, and vegetables. Bess knew how to can, having been taught by her mother and grandmother, but between working for the Haskins and shouldering more responsibility than Tommy ever did for the farm work, and bearing and caring for all their children, Bess ran out of time each year to "put up" as much food as the family would need to tide them over. Justice began canning three or four times her usual amount to ensure that her daughter and grandchildren would have food to eat. To provide milk for the children, Mint gave Bess and Tommy a heifer, but shortly after she had freshened, she disappeared, her tracks mysteriously ending in the front yard. It was after the heifer vanished that Tommy was able to purchase a broken down Model T. Mint resorted to his old habit of bringing milk to the children, and Bess resumed lowering it in canning jars into the cool depths of the well.

Bess could have packed up her children, left her sorry husband, and moved in with her parents. Emma's room was still empty, and Mint would gladly have added another room to the house to accommodate the children. The children certainly would have been pleased to move into their grandparents' home, especially Helen and Tommy Lee, who were old enough to comprehend somewhat the negative effect that their father exerted on the quality of their lives.

"We want to stay here," they would plead when they had spent a day and night or two at their grandparents' and it was time for them to go home.

"Why can't we go live at Grandma's?" the eight-year-old Helen begged her mother in late August of 1914. Justice had just presented the little girl with three beautiful dresses for the start of the school year. The pink one had a white collar and a garland of red roses embroidered around its hem. Justice had also made school clothes for Tommy Lee, who was six years old, and one outfit each for Booker, Esther, and five-month-old Mary. While such gifts may have influenced Helen's request, undoubtedly pertinent was the fact that she had watched from the kitchen window that morning as her father, angry because her mother claimed not to have any money left from the wages Mrs. Haskins had paid her, hit her mother in her lower back before cranking his car and driving off. Helen had seen her mother stagger, and then she had straightened up a little and come into the house.

"I hate Papa, and I want to go live at Grandma's," Helen

said to her mother. She had a serious little face and gray eyes that seemed old beyond her years. She was feeding the baby a sugar teat and standing at the kitchen window.

"What you want to go stay with her for?" Bess snapped. "She mean, too. Pushed me in a rose bush one time when I won't even old as you."

Two months later on a Sunday morning after Mint and Justice had eaten their breakfast and were almost ready for church, and Mint had told his wife how beautiful she was to him, and had held her in his arms and kissed her deeply, and had let his right hand caress her breasts and her behind, and she had kissed him back and told him, laughing, that if they started that they would not make it to church, and he had smiled and said that the church was in her and between them, but he had sat on the bed and watched as she put on her hat, then he had lain back on the bed and died. He was fifty-one years old.

After Mint died from the massive stroke that came out of the blue, and Justice had arranged his funeral, and Lucky Holton's voice had lifted the words of "I'll Fly Away" to the very gables of the church house, and Christine Smith had filled the hearts of the people with the strength and promise of "Power in the Blood," and Reverend Jones had encouraged their spirits and stirred their sorrow with the story of Mint's grandparents, and of Emma and Silas, and of Mint's unceasing aid to the people as teacher and lawyer and bondsman and banker and scribe and friend, and as God's true emissary, and as the unwavering helpmeet, protector, and lover of his wife, and after Justice, dry-eyed and wooden, had seen the mound of dirt shoveled onto his coffin, and had gone home with the entire church following, and had accepted all their condolences and good wishes and prayers, and had convinced Bess and the children that she would be just fine alone—actually needed to be alone—she had straightened up the house and crawled under the covers on Mint's side of the bed and dreamed of lying in his arms and of feeling his heart beating against her skin and of his smile and his teeth and his laughter and of his eyes looking at her. In the morning, she simply did not wake up.

25

Deprivation

Cheer up, my brother, live in the sunshine,
We'll understand it all by and by.

from "Farther Along," Anonymous,
Arranged by Barney E. Warren, 1911

ON THE FIRST OF NOVEMBER, Bess and Tommy moved with their children into their own home on their own farm inherited by Bess as their next of kin from Mint and Justice, purchased by Emma and Silas from Reynolds Sutton in 1863. Bess and Tommy gathered the corn on the Haskins place, and Tommy settled with Mr. Haskins for what they were owed for the year. Many sharecroppers at the time, and their children after them, were little more than serfs tied to their crooked proprietors for their entire lives. Cheated shamelessly by their landlords, tenant farmers and their families often found at the end of a year of hard labor that not only were they not due any payment for their work but that they were actually in debt to the landlord. The sugar, salt, and flour, and the occasional coffee or piece of side meat that they had bought at the proprietor's commissary or at the general store in Chesterton where the landlord covered their account, the seed corn and peanuts, the tobacco seed and muslin needed to start the tobacco beds, the cotton seed and fertilizer required for planting—these and various other expenditures more than consumed the benefit of their labor over a year's time, or so they were told. In spite of the abject poverty in which they and their children had lived—their children's bellies distended from malnutrition, their legs and arms spindly from rickets, their teeth rotted from a lack of vitamin D and calcium, their eyes dull and listless, and their intellects undeveloped—in spite of these conditions and more, many families learned that they had lived so "high off the hog" that they could not leave the landlord to seek better opportunity elsewhere because they owed him and had to remain in his employ until their debt was paid.

Mr. Haskins, however, was far more honest than most. Nevertheless, when the time came in the early spring of 1915 for Tommy to make the purchases necessary to start his crops, he had certainly spent on liquor, women, clothes, and his old car all that he and Bess had earned over the previous year. They had no landlord to front the costs of planting, and when Bess dipped into Mint and Justice's savings to buy what was required, Tommy learned of this windfall and, asserting his right to their inheritance, he began, forthwith, to deplete it.

Had they been living, Mint and Justice would not have been surprised. After the milk had mysteriously disappeared from their grandchildren's mouths, they had debated the most practicable course that they could take to help their daughter and the children.

"No need of flat-out givin' 'em money," Justice had said, "'cause that good for nothin' Tommy gon' take it and drink it up."

"We just have to keep totin' milk and food over there to 'em, then," said Mint. "It's a wonder he don't take the food off his churren's plates and sell it. Reckon he would if he could, and Bess just stays right there with him, lettin' 'im treat her and the churren like dogs. Justice, it makes me so mad, it's all I can do to keep from layin' a two-by-four up 'side his head."

"I know, Mint," said Justice. "You ain't never seen no mess like Tommy. Miz Emma use to say all the time how your papa was just as sweet and kind as you. Never lifted a finger to her, never talked mean or nasty to her, just like you. . . . Everybody want their churren to have good as the parents have. I just wish Bess could've married somebody who'd be even half as good to her as you been to me. And she use to be so headstrong! Why you think she turned so meek and mealy mouth?"

"Cause she's treated like a slave," Mint responded. "There's all kinds of slav'ry. There's the slav'ry where a man treat his wife like he a slave owner and she a dangerous slave that he got to beat to keep her in line. He treat her like she a wild horse that he got to break. He beat her body so long and talk to her so mean and she feel like she ain't got nowhere to turn, and pretty soon he done beat her spirit down."

"Once he got her spirit down, why you think he keep beatin' 'er?" Justice asked.

"Cause she ain't the reason he beatin' her. Nothin' she done is the reason he beatin' her. He beatin' her 'cause he can. He beatin' her 'cause of hisself. He so fragmented, Justice, so broke into little pieces, he don't know who he is, and he fightin' like a dog under water to get some air. He so imperfect, Justice, he hates hisself and he's a coward, too, so he turns his self-hatred on his wife."

"When my papa kilt hisself," said Justice, "it was 'cause he couldn't face what he had done. He hated hisself so bad 'bout what he had done, he couldn't bear to live another day. He could've turned mean and stayed mean 'cause he hated hisself so much, but he took another way out. Some say it was a coward's way out."

"I would hate to get to the point where I would try to kill myself," Mint replied, "but I ain't never judged your papa. If I had gone crazy and I had hurt you like he hurt you, and I come to my senses and understood what I had done, I hope I would've just spent the rest of my life tryin' to make up for it and tryin' to earn your forgiveness and God's forgiveness. But if I was half crazy, I might not be able to see beyond my regret and sorrow and self-loathin', and I might hate myself so much I would do the worst thing I could possibly do to myself. I think that's what your papa done, and I understand that. He loved you. I look at you right now and I know I would rather die than hurt you. I love you too much. He would've rather died than hurt you, too, but he had already done it and couldn't take it back, so he died."

"You think he was a coward?" Justice asked.

"Not a bit," Mint answered. "I think he had lost his mind with grief. A lot of people kill theirself from grief by drinkin'. They just do it slow. Then there's other folks like Tommy who think the world owes 'em, and they take the best they can get of everything for theirself. They take from their own innocent churren to have more for theirself. Seem like they don't care 'bout hurtin' their wife and churren, but they wouldn't hurt theirself for money. It would take a lot for a man like Tommy to kill hisself. You want to see a coward, just look at Tommy Maben."

"For the life of me, I can't see why Bess stay with him," said Justice, "but I reckon she shame to come here even though we both told her not to be."

"Maybe she think she don't deserve no better'n him," said Mint. "Then again, maybe she loves him just 'cause he is so doggone no 'count. No 'count men don't have nary bit of trouble gettin' women to love 'em. You ever notice how a woman will just love a no 'count man to death?" he asked, smiling and raising his left eyebrow at Justice.

"Not this woman," said Justice, who rose from her chair and burrowed her bottom in his lap and began to prove her point.

* * *

When Bess and Tommy moved to her parents' place in November, she was pregnant with a baby who was due in June. In February, as she helped Tommy to control the fire that he had set to burn a head row of their cotton field, Bess was suddenly doubled over with excruciating pains to her lower abdomen and with a clawing inside her as if her womb were being ripped out. She felt the plug of mucous lodged between her uterus and her vagina leave her body in a rush of blood. Her knees upon the ground, her head bowed, she shut her eyes against the pain and the dark red spread of blood over the old pair of Tommy's work trousers that she wore.

When Tommy reached her, he grew alarmed.

"I'm awright, Tommy," she lied. "Gone put the fire out. I'm gon' just stay here while you kill the fire, then he'p me to the house."

"Helen, you and Tommy Lee go tell Mrs. Haskins I'm sick and can't get there tomorrow," she directed the older children once Tommy had helped her to get inside the house.

When the stillborn child came and Bess had cleaned herself, she went to bed, developed a high fever, and did not begin to recover for three weeks. Left on his own for the first time with five children, the oldest of whom was ten, Tommy was beside himself with fear that Bess would die. During her third week of illness, he brought Miz Agnes Dees to the house to provide Bess with healing attention.

"In 'dition to the miscarriage she done had, she done leaned on the wet ground and took cold through her knees and ain't gon' git well 'til summer done cooked the cold out'n her," the old woman declared when Tommy had explained how he had first noticed Bess kneeling in the field.

"He'p me up, Tommy," Bess said, disgusted at the poorly

disguised incapacity of Miz Dees to aid anyone advancing in any direction except towards death. "Then move this here bed to face the east. . . . Tommy Lee, you go outdoors and get some juniper leaves, and, Helen, you take 'em and make me some tea. And later make some ginseng tea. Switch 'em off and on for me to drink. And cut up a 'tater fine so it'll boil quick and mash it up and carry it in here for me to eat, get my strength back. Booker, you open up that window and let some air in here."

The room smelled of slop jar and illness and Bess was weak from loss of blood and lack of food, but Tommy was ecstatic that his wife would certainly live. When he left his family to return Miz Agnes Dees to her home, they did not see him again for four days.

During the month that Bess was bedridden, Mrs. Haskins found someone else to do her family's cooking and cleaning on a temporary basis. And after six weeks, when Bess could walk a distance and work for a decent stretch of time without sitting down, she found herself with full responsibility for the farm work which Tommy had let go. She did not have the time to resume work for the Haskins family, and that source of income was lost. On their second Christmas in their own home, Bess used the last of the flour to make a sweetbread which she "streaked" with some of Justice's blackberry preserves. At night when the children were sleeping, she had made corn-husk dolls for the girls and had whittled little wooden toys for the boys, and, without their father, the children had a nice Christmas.

Tommy had taken up with a fast, childless widow whose husband had been stabbed to death two years before over the pot in a game of poker at a good-time joint near the water. Living his new life, Tommy came home only occasionally and only to get things that he needed. On a balmy Sunday in May, apparently in need of proving his power over another human being, he came home, banished the children from the house, and raped his wife, leaving her with a fertilized egg that would become Peggy, their sixth surviving child, born in 1917. By mid July, Bess knew that she was pregnant, and she suspected that the thick white substance secreted from her vagina was a sign of gonorrhea. She began an aggressive routine of treatment using bloodroot, Seneca snakeroot, hops, blue cohosh, sweet flag, and rattlesnake weed. By the end of July, she had also learned that in less than a two-year period, Tommy had mortgaged their house and farm to the hilt and that it would be sold at auction at the beginning of September.

"Lord," she prayed. "I ain't got nowhere else to turn. I don't ask nothin' for myself. Just let me live and be able to raise these churren. That's all I want in this world."

She went to see Mr. Haskins about moving back to his place.

"Mr. Haskins, suh," she said, "I can do the work of a man. I can plow and pull tobacco and dig peanuts and gather corn 'longside a strong man. And my son, Tommy Lee, he a big boy now, a big he'p. And my daughter, Helen, she the oldest, she can do all the cookin' and carin' for the churren and housework, too. I can do the fieldwork, Mr. Haskins, if you can see fit to let me live in the house we used to live in and work the land."

In January, when Bess was eight months pregnant and becoming increasingly concerned about being able to have her baby and being ready almost immediately afterwards to prepare the land for planting, Tommy, thrown out of the widow's house in favor of a man with something to spend, reasoned with Bess that if he moved back home, he could get the land ready and the crops started while she recovered from childbirth. It was not so much that Bess gave Tommy a chance. In truth, she wanted to give Tommy Lee a chance because he was a little boy, only nine years old, and too inexperienced to start farming literally by himself. And she wanted to give Mr. Haskins a chance because he had taken a chance on her, not knowing that she was pregnant but wanting to help her and her children. And she wanted to give herself a chance not to break her body irreparably by discing up the land and by walking behind the mule while handling the heavy plow too soon after having the baby. She saw her body and its ability to work as her only valuable commodity, the only shield between her children and starvation. So she allowed Tommy back into her life.

26

Irretrievability

Death ain't nothing. I done seen him. Done wrassled with him. You can't tell me nothing about death.

from *Fences,* August Wilson, 1987

THE CHILDREN ALWAYS STRAGGLED home from school. Bess could see them coming in little clusters, their shirts and dresses disembodied blobs of color distinguishable in the distance far before you could make out their faces. They would turn off the road into their yard, dawdling, one now, the others maybe a few minutes later, yelling goodbyes to their school mates out on the main road. At the house they would hurry into their work clothes and "go in the field." There was chopping and planting in the spring; in the fall, grading and tying cured tobacco, picking cotton, digging sweet and white potatoes, gathering corn. During the weeks of digging peanuts in September or October, the children hardly went to school at all, spending their days shaking the dirt from the plowed up pea vines, stacking them to dry on "pea poles," and staggering home at night dirt-encrusted and sore. On most days one of the girls would quit work a little early to fry up corn bread or "flat bread" for the family's supper of boiled vegetables and meat left over from the noonday meal. When there were no leftovers, they would fry salted herring or side meat, sometimes ham, with gravy. Wasting almost nothing, they might stew the tough green tops of onions in gravy with a little lard, cracklings, or bacon fat, served with biscuits or flat bread. Throughout the day of fieldwork, Bess would make periodic trips to the house to see how the two smallest children were doing, and after school, if supper time was far off, one of the older children would make the trip in her stead. "Go 'head, Helen," Bess would say. "Your legs younger'n mine."

Wednesday, October 9, 1920, blazed into a beautiful, hot day. The sky waxed blue as sea water. Maples and sumacs at the wood's edge shone red and gold beyond dun-colored corn. The earth felt hot to Bess's bare feet, the grass, dry enough to spring fire. Rows upon rows of cotton billowed like clouds awaiting her quick fingers. She had picked over two hundred pounds already and would have over three hundred by the end of the day. Bess stood up and saw one of the children, Tommy Lee, running. He ran stoop shouldered, face down, neck extended, as if parting the air with his head, arms pumping, carrying nothing. Then she saw Booker, running, and behind him, Esther. No Helen, no Mary. "Lord, you have mercy, now," Bess said aloud. She let the strap of her heavy picking bag drop and stepped free of it. She began to walk from the field, toward the running children, wishing she had kept them home to do fieldwork. Esther, younger than Booker, was far outrun by him. Booker ran far behind the older boy, Tommy Lee. All of the children ran silently. Then, within hearing distance, Tommy Lee began yelling, "Mama, you got to come! Mary got hurt bad! Got run over back on the main road!"

"How far back, Tommy Lee?"

"Just this side of the store, Mama!"

"Where Helen at?"

"She there with Mary, Mama."

"You run over to the Coleman's place and get your papa. Go 'round near the corn crib and holler out loud. Say, 'Papa, Mary been hurt bad, suh! Got run over near the store, and Mama say you got to come, suh!' Don't wait for him, Tommy Lee. Come on back and get my cotton, stay with the churren. Tell Esther to mind them and get supper. I'm gon' carry Booker with me." She was already down the road from Tommy Lee, head turned toward him, but now she straightened up, meeting Booker.

"Mama, Mr. Monk Jones done run over Mary!" Booker shouted, running toward her.

"Go on back, Booker!" Bess said. "We got to hurry!" The little boy sucked air through his open mouth as he spun around on the dusty path and headed back the way he had come, passing Esther, who had begun sobbing loudly, before his mother caught up with him.

"Look after the churren and get supper, Esther," Bess said as she passed her daughter. She did not pause.

People had gathered. The white people had come out of their houses bordering the road by the store and had walked down to the accident. The schoolchildren had stopped and stayed. People had emptied out of the store. The few cars that had been heading somewhere had postponed their journeys. The crowd opened on the roadside to let Bess and Booker in. Helen, thirteen years old, tears streaming, knelt beside her sister's crushed body. Mary's face, bruised to the color of eggplant, was swollen, bloody. Her whole head was bloody, her hair thick with blood. A tire track ran down her face, trunk, and right leg. Her left leg and foot, unlike the rest of her flattened body, was twisted due west.

"I'm so sorry, Miss Bessie. I wouldn't of hurt that chile for the world. I'm so sorry! Lord, ha' mercy! Lord, ha' mercy!" Monk Jones, a deacon of Chesterton Baptist Church, stood between the crowd and his car, which had been lifted from the child's body by men and women, too, when it had finally stopped, its brakes completely gone. Splotches of blood marked the hot asphalt for maybe an eighth of a mile. Later, bystanders would speak of hordes of flies feeding on the bloody tarmac. Others would tell of finding a piece of paper, a tablet, a pencil. Some would speak of signs and warnings that they had not heeded—portentous dreams, vaporous and watery sightings, cocks crowing at the wrong times and in the wrong places, dogs' dismal howling—almost all undecipherable without the light of hindsight. Until her death at the age of eighty-seven, Helen would speak of the deep sadness that engulfed her every autumn.

"Hush cryin', Helen," Bess almost whispered. "Hush cryin'. You, too, Booker. You a big boy. You got to be a big boy, now. Y'all don't want to 'sturb your sister, now. Hush cryin'." She sat crossed legged on the dry grass and cradled Mary on her lap, rocking back and forth, and her "Hush cryin', now, hush cryin'," was a lullaby for her children, who would not sleep soundly for countless days and nights, and for Mary, who was beyond its reach.

* * *

The fights began after the burial. No longer beatings, they became contests with Bess defending, creative, devious, courageous. During the three days of "settin' up," Bess and Tommy spoke to each other only out of dire necessity.

"Where the money comin' from for the coffin and the preacher?" Tommy asked.

"Out my money for the cotton," Bess said. "They can wait to get paid 'til it's sold, since you done spent everything we would of got from the 'bacca on that ole nasty woman."

"Don't sass me," Tommy ordered. "You lose your mind, woman? I'm tryin' to figure things out!" He stood up from the table.

"I don't need you to figure nothin' out. I'm gon' see to buryin' my child. I'll take the churren to he'p me work. I'll bind the baby to my back. We'll finish the cotton here, and we'll pick day in and day out for anybody who'll hire us as long as the cotton lasts. And you won't touch a red cent for your ole trashy woman and your ole piece of car. You won't take nary other thing out these churren's moufs."

The children, finishing their breakfast, hung their heads, frightened, waiting to hear their father's open hand hit their mother's face. It was too early in the day for fists. They had witnessed the beatings when she had done nothing that they could see to precipitate them, and now she was wild. She seemed to want to make him angry.

"Papa was a mean man, very mean," Tommy Lee explained to Marty, his sister Esther's teenage daughter, in 1967, the day before Bess's funeral. "I remember he was not nice to Mama, would beat her, and I remember I wanted to fight 'im, but I was pretty small, and he would of snapped me like a twig and still beat Mama. And it would of hurt her worser if he had beat me 'cause of her. He didn't hardly ever hit us."

Marty happened to know that both Tommy Lee and Booker had beat their own wives and terrified their children for years, perpetuating their father's terrible legacy.

"Didn't have to hit us," snapped Helen. "Didn't stay home long enough to notice us, let alone hit us; didn't have time. And we was already scared half to death, worked half to death. What else could he get from us? And I 'clare I don't think Mama would of stood for it. She would of gone after him way 'fore she did."

"He didn't hit Mama that time 'cause he was so shocked at how unafraid she was," said Esther. "He had to feel some kinda bad, too, 'cause he didn't get down there where it happened that night before they had moved Mary, and Mama and everybody was gone. He didn't get down there at all that night unless he went much later to see if he could sense in the dark how everything had been in the daylight when it happened. He musta felt some kinda bad!"

"Should of felt bad," said Helen. "He was out there in the woods with that old white woman, car hidden in the bushes. He never heard Tommy Lee callin' 'im. Wasn't in the corn crib doing his mess with that ole woman like Mama thought. He had come home plenty of times before with little pieces of corn shucks all over 'im, when it wasn't nowhere near corn gatherin' time, like he thought Mama was blind and crazy. He didn't know anything about what had happened that day 'til he got home to eat, always fillin' his belly and only he'pin' Mama and us work when he felt like it. And Mama's strength that night was just herself and us churren. Tell me something, sugar," she said to Marty. "What you want to know 'bout him for, anyway? He wasn't a nice person."

"I remember he gave me a doll once," said Peggy, who was three at the time of Mary's death.

"Mama was Mama and Papa to me," said Myra, the baby of the family. "I don't remember him at all."

"Sometimes a man just loses control of hisself 'cause of a woman," Booker said. "I ain't sayin' it's right. I'm just sayin' that it can happen, and the man can't hardly he'p it. Men are different from women—weaker—and I tell you, Mama was strong. Had to be."

"She never let us straggle home one or two at a time after that," said Esther. "Always made us come home all together. Couldn't stand the thought that somethin' was wrong with the ones who didn't get home first. And wouldn't let us run home. Had to walk, all of us along together.

"You know, I always made you churren do the same thing," she said to Marty. "It seemed safer, seein' all of you comin' home from school at the same time."

27

Poison

You're asking to have your head split and the wind let out.

from *The Swamp Dwellers*, Wole Soyinka, 1958

IN 1920, the year that Mary died, the weather stayed warm and dry all through October and November. Tommy Lee and Helen, woven seamlessly into the rhythm of work, would never return to school. Money was needed. There would be no grave stone, of course, but Tommy made a wooden cross to mark Mary's grave, and Bess planted sweet william perennials over her mound. Digging, then picking, peanuts. Picking cotton. Gathering corn. Pulling fodder. Feeding livestock. Chopping wood. Digging and banking white and sweet potatoes. Killing hogs. Rendering lard. Making soap. Washing. Cleaning, smoking, and pickling herring. Cooking, cleaning, washing, and ironing for Mr. and Mrs. Haskins. Tommy's sporty clothes, his carousing, and his car required monetary as well as physical sacrifices from his family, and when he sustained a burn to his right hand from his car's cracked carburetor, he accused Bess, perhaps justifiably, of holding back her ability to help him, of refusing to "blow fire" from the hand that he needed for just about everything, out of her meanness, jealousy, and spite over another woman. Years before, he had seen her arrest the pain and blistering of what should have been a nasty burn when he had doused her naked arm with a ladle of boiling water from the wash pot.

"You ain't breathin' on it right, and you know it!" Tommy shouted. "You done sold your soul to the devil, and I'm gon' send your body to 'im in hell where you b'long!"

Tommy jerked his right hand from Bess's grasp, picked up the car crank in his left hand, and advanced toward Bess, who had begun backing up, never taking her eyes from Tommy's, straight to the hickory stump where so many chickens had lost their heads, so much wood had been readied for the flames. Reaching behind her, she grabbed and raised the sharpened axe, settling its handle in both hands in front of her, somewhat aloft and to her right. She flexed her arms a little, acclimating her hands anew to the feel of the axe handle. Like a baseball batter readying his muscles for a home run, she rocked on the bottoms of her slightly spread feet, left foot forward.

"Come on me," she urged softly. "Come on me, Tommy, and I'm gon' watch your body twitch and dance like a chicken at my feet while your head is over yonder, cleaved clean off by this here axe. I just sharpened it this mornin'. Come on me, and I'm gon' see your yaller blood soak in the cracks of this dry ground like piss from a herd of cows. Come on on me, Tommy, if you don't want your ole nasty woman to ever see you again in this here life, 'cause I guarantee you it's gon' be the last thing you gon' do."

"You must be crazy," said Tommy, trying to detect an instant when he could clobber her with the metal crank languishing in his left hand. He wouldn't kill her, just lay her out for a while, knock some sense back into her, teach her not to go up against him ever again, not to ever question him about his women. No woman had the right to mouth back at and fight her husband, and he would stop it, had to stop it, before she started to believe that she had some kind of power over him. She had gone way too far in that direction already, and Tommy was waiting for the split second during which he would teach her a lasting lesson. But Bess, alert as a hemmed in viper, afforded no instant for him to "lay her out."

"Done gone to your head, I reckon, all that mess folks talk 'bout you able to conjure and power placed on you 'cause your papa got kilt 'fore you was born. Well, he was evil. How could anything good come out of him? And you just like 'im; no better'n him. No wonder that Indian mama of yourn got clear of you. Who would want somethin' like you? She should of left you. I'm gon' leave you, too. Should of left a long time ago, you ole sausage lip Indian squaw! Think you can hurt me? You ain't got no power can hurt me. Never could, never will. You a fly to me. A gnat."

Tommy flexed the car crank in his left hand, trying to look relaxed, nonchalant, unafraid. His right hand, blistering now, seemed on fire with pain. His aim would not be sure, using his left hand, and one misstep in felling Bess would likely result in his dying a death worse than a hog's, his head practically severed among wood chips and old chicken feathers. He did not believe Bess was strong enough to take his head off completely with one or two swings. But what difference would it make, since one swing of the glistening axe would kill him dead enough?

"Say your piece," said Bess. "Anything that pops in whatever brains you got, you say it, 'cause they soon gon' be spilled like guts, and the dogs and chickens gon' eat 'em. I sho' ain't gon' clean 'em up, and I ain't gon' let the churren out here to clean 'em up. Ain't nobody gon' know you dead for a while. You come on over here, Tommy, and meet this blade. It's gon' be your chariot to the other side." Bess brandished the axe slightly, and Tommy began to wonder—to hope—that her arms were tiring.

"And you can take your time," said Bess, appearing to have read his mind, "'cause I got as long as you want. I can swing this axe for hours 'thout hardly gettin' tired. I done chopped wood all day, and right back at it the next mornin'. I sho' ain't gon' get tired waitin' on your one li'l ole neck, so take all the time you want and say your piece."

It occurred to Tommy that he saw in Bess a power, a mystery, that he recognized, that he had experienced in himself almost always when he beat her. He saw an insanity in her eyes that he had felt in himself when he hit her beside her head with a stick of stove wood, knocking her cold, and when he choked her with both hands until her eyes bulged and her face was almost purple. Once he had hit her in the lower back with his fist, and she had walked bent over for more than a week. He had fired his shotgun at her several times, sending her racing through the night to hide in thickets of waist-high dog fennel and burdock, creeping back in the house only when one of the children, usually Tommy Lee or Helen, called to her softly that he was asleep or gone. These actions had never failed momentarily to stir his blood, and now he saw in Bess a kinship to himself, a man he did not know, whose internal torment had been fed by cruelty and power. He wished that one of the children, cowering, he knew, inside the house under Helen's watch, would defy his standing order, backed by threat of a merciless beating, and "'sturb" his "dealin's" with their momma. His fire turned to ashes, the heat left to him was in his burned hand and in his face, seared by shame that his wife, who even now had never hit him, had, nonetheless, beaten him. Despair burned within him as he imagined, perhaps for the first time, the world through the children's eyes and saw their mute horror caused not only by him but now by their mother, also, and by the prospect of witnessing a second death within the family. His mind jumped to his own childhood and to the long-repressed memory of his father's last cruelty to his mother. "What is life?" he wondered, "and why do a colored man's sorrows and dreams get all mixed up and go sour in his belly and rise up through his gullet, chokin' him and hurtin' his fam'ly and fillin' his mouth with bitter vomit?"

"I don't want to hurt you, Bess," he said. He dropped the car crank on the ground and, turning his back to her, went into the kitchen, where he plunged his right hand into the bucket of drinking water.

28

Bequest

Gonna talk with the Prince of Peace,
Down by the riverside,
Gonna study war no more.

from "Down by the Riverside," Anonymous, 1927

IT WAS A DAY like no other day, but at 6:30 p.m. on Sunday, August 8, 1896, when Tommy, then a nine-year-old boy, heard his father's drunken herald announcing his homecoming after two days of swilling and whoring, the day had not begun to distinguish itself. Tommy would someday become the abusive husband of Bess and the father of their six children, but he did not know this, and now he heard his own father's hoarse, rumbling, drawn-out, menacing, sing-song "Oh-oh-oh, Glo-ry-y-y!" and he moved from the shade of the front porch to a spot in the still scalding sun on the side of the house where he would not be detected. An only child who had long ago learned to keep his own counsel and to avoid his father's wrath, he moved to a spot of safety from which he could see everything: his father emerging from the path through the woods into the clearing; his mother in the small kitchen, her thin arms long and bare in the close heat emanating from the open door of the wood stove. She had bent to shove in sticks of stove wood. The fire gulped oxygen from the open door, and Tommy could see its light strike her face, damp with perspiration. Her sleeveless tan dress, thin and faded from a thousand washings, stuck to her back and abdomen in sweat-drenched patches. "She look like a dirt road with mud holes after it rain," Tommy said to himself.

She was frying corn bread. The pot with cabbage, potatoes, and side meat left over from dinner sat on the stove, heating up for supper.

"She weak and dumb," Tommy thought. "She too weak to stand up to 'im, and she too dumb to run. She oughta hide 'til he gone to sleep. She know he got to sleep it off 'fore tomorrow mornin'.

"Run!" he said to her in his mind, willing his silent words through the window glass and into her head. "Leave that corn bread! Git out of there fast as you can git 'fore he hem you up in there!" Perhaps she was dumb, with a skull too thick for Tommy's unspoken words to penetrate, so her movements remained unhurried, her face placid.

She crossed from table to stove, carrying the bowl of corn bread batter, stirring and ladling it into the skillet of hot grease. "He come near you, hit 'im with that hot spider," Tommy pleaded wordlessly. But his pleas were like dust that settles upon the surfaces of things, permeating nothing, its hosts largely unaware of its presence.

Eleven years later when Tommy was eighteen, he would beat Bess almost unmercifully for frying chicken. He had slapped her before, the flat of his calloused hand meeting her jaw and pivoting her head a sharp forty-five degrees, for frying side meat. He had hollered at her before that for frying up a mess of sausage cakes one Sunday morning to go with his coffee, biscuits, and eggs. Bess was dumb, Tommy thought, so telling her something plain as day over and over wasn't going to do any good, and he had no intention of telling her anything over and over like she was a dim-witted child that he had to humor. Every time he had to repeat a simple instruction, he reasoned, he would make it memorable—more memorable than it had been the last time he had told her. So his admonitions were spiked with quick and incredible violence, and Bess learned. She learned not to fry meat, though Tommy loved fried foods and would devour them greedily when they were prepared by anyone, other than his own wife, anywhere, other than in his own kitchen.

Tommy's father qualified as a souse, but he was selective about when he drank. Monday mornings found him in the fields early—eyes bloodshot, breath and pores dispelling hog mash liquor, skin looking pickled—to work throughout the day at a furious pace. He was a "smart" man, and that may be why he was able to avoid getting run off the farms of white men who hired him and only subsequently observed his temper. But when he hit Jim Brevard's hundred-and-sixty-dollar mule in the head with a claw hammer, he was run off, the proceeds from his crops used to replace Mr. Brevard's property as well as to restore his feelings of triumph and superiority over "a crazy black nigger idiot."

But by and large, Tommy's father was tolerated because Monday through Friday he was a mule himself, though with the consistent proclivities of a camel or a rattlesnake or both. Every Friday night, his participation in the world's work completed for the week, he would clean himself up and head for the bootlegger's, the gambling den, and the whorehouse. As a teenager he had earned the name Bullet because he was mean and deadly and because his fucking was over so fast a whore could serve him and take his money in less than half the time she had to give to another customer. Everyone called him Bullet, even his own wife, but nobody reminded him that derisive strumpets had spread much of the news that had spawned his name, and he, himself, had chosen to forget the story. No one reminded him because doing so would have hurt his ego, and he would have hurt the fool who had reminded him. A furious man who approached life furiously, he never came close to discovering the deepest meaning of human existence. He was too consumed with hurt to love anybody.

"Oh-oh-oh, Glo-ry-y-y!" Bullet's anguished howl erupted from a verboten well of pain and recriminations as his drunken tread crossed the front porch and his brogans stumped haltingly through the open hallway to the kitchen door. He loomed unsteadily in the doorway, the tails of his chambray shirt hanging outside his pants, his shoes and pant legs wet and caked with mud from every mud hole between his home and his previous destination. From his hiding place outside the kitchen window, Tommy observed his mother, whose frightened eyes were fixed on his father's face. She did not see the rest of him, only the demon who took possession of his body in the form of drink and cloaked his mind in madness. She had learned that you cannot reason with madness, that it is accountable to no one and to nothing. It spoke to her now through Bullet's mouth, a viscid pit beneath his wooly beard that stretched upwards into sideburns and joined his burr-like, matted hair. His cotton cap, discolored by the sweat and grime of daily enterprise, clung precariously to the back of his head. Accept, as a point of argument, that a living body is the habitat of a soul striving in love toward oneness with God. Does madness trump love?

"Where my meal, you ugly hog?"

"Food right here," she said, hurrying to the cupboard for a plate. "Got you a nice, hot supper ready." Under its coating of glistening sweat, her light skin, made paler still by chronic illness and fear, seemed almost translucent. To her son, she looked eerily insubstantial.

"Where it at? Ain't ready if it ain't on the table. How many times you 'spects me to have to tell you that, you gotdamn dumb dog?" He staggered into the hot kitchen. "I'm gon' learn you good this time to have my vittles on the table when I git home."

"It's ready, Bullet," she pleaded, backing out of his reach toward the stove, plate in one hand, the large spoon that she had used to mix the corn bread in the other. "I'm gon' take up your food now. If I had it on the table, it woulda got cold by now."

She remembered, and Tommy remembered, the last beating that she had taken for having Bullet's food on the table when he walked in the door. She had heard him coming and had served his plate, but he had beat her because, he said, she had let his vittles sit there and get "cold as Jan'ary," like he was "some gotdamn farm animal that don't eat cookin'." Tommy remembered all this as he watched his father close in on his mother. He did not feel the sun beating upon his bare head and torso as he stood shirtless at the window, his heart breaking for his mother whom he could not help but love, and whom he felt helpless to protect.

"I'm gon' learn you to git my vittles offen the stove and onto the table in my plate like I'm's a man," Bullet said. Then he was lifting her up and sitting her upon the hot stove, her thin dress disintegrating immediately beneath her, her buttocks and thighs, the backs of her legs and heels frying against the fiery iron of the stove's top and side. Bullet held her to the stove, and the smell of his mother's burning flesh met Tommy's face and his nose and his open mouth as he ran wailing into the kitchen. His screams merging with those of his mother, he shoved his drunken father aside and tore his mother from the cookstove, leaving a horrible layer of her flesh behind. He tried to stretch her out, face down, on the kitchen floor, but her knees and legs would not straighten, her muscles shocked into paralysis, her raw tissue quivering and beading with blood. Her body formed a slope from her behind, raised into the air, her head down between her arms that stretched forward, to her fists on the floor. With her knees bent as if she were still sitting upon the stove, she rocked slightly forward and back, begging for water. Tommy emptied the contents of the water bucket that stood in the kitchen over his mother's lower portion before rushing to the well where he would draw more. How many trips did he make to the well? The kitchen did not flood because the spaces between the floorboards let the water run out into the dryness underneath the house. And in the evening, when God sent the relentless storm, Tommy pulled his mother onto a quilt, and he dragged her on this makeshift conveyance to the porch where the driving rain could reach her and could war against the flames that raged within her flesh.

In the morning, his belly full of the cold dinner that had scorched unattended on the stove before the fire died down, Bullet stepped gingerly over his wife's inert form on his way outside to relieve himself and then to feed the livestock. He went out the front door and stepped across his wife on the front porch to avoid the huge puddle that always formed around the back steps during a hard rain. Tommy, lying in the hallway with his head almost abutting his mother's, arose and brought her a glass of water, a ritual that he had repeated over and over throughout the night. But now she seemed to be sleeping soundly, so he headed up the road to fetch the healer, Miz Emma Sutton, in hopes that she could ease his mother's pain. As he walked into the storm, he chewed a piece of the corn bread that his mother had fried before her final trial, and he imagined that the sun would soon come out and embrace him like a loving father.

29

Discovery

I played Lazarus too long, stayed under the table and never got nothin' but the crumbs. I want to eat the rest of the while that I'm here. So then I got to get out from under the table. If the meat on top of the table, then you got to stand up where it is.

from *I Dream a World* by Brian Lanker,
words of Cora Lee Johnson, 1989

"WHY'D MAMA STAY with Papa all them years?" asked Myra. "It just seem like doomin' herself to a life of misery to me."

"Well, she had all of us," offered Peggy. "It was hard 'long then—still is—for a woman to raise a bunch of churren on a farm without a man to he'p out with all that heavy work."

"The longer she stayed with 'im, the more churren she had," countered Myra. "I think she could've made it a lot easier if she'd left 'im right after they came back home, when she only had Helen, and Tommy Lee was on the way."

"Even if she had left 'im," said Tommy Lee, "she could've married somebody else and kept on havin' churren, and that husband might not've been any better'n Papa. There's a whole lot of wrong people out there to marry. Look at us. Esther the only one had a good marriage right from the start. Helen, you on your second marriage. Myra, you divorced. Peggy, you separated. Booker, you been divorced twice. And the only reason Janet still with me is 'cause I quit beatin' her. I'm nicer to her now."

"Should've been nice to her in the first place," said Helen. "I don't know what get into men folks, thinkin' they got the right to beat somebody. That's why I divorced Harry, you know, and if Dave had hit me again, I would have left him, too."

"Helen, how'd you get Dave to stop hittin' you?" Myra asked. "Seem like somebody ought to find out how to make a man stop beatin' his wife, and they ought to tell everybody else. Now, it's gon' have to be a woman to do that. If a man know, he sure ain't gon' tell nobody."

"I didn't feel like runnin' no more," said Helen, "and I didn't feel like takin' no more beatin's. And I thought about it after that last time he hit me. I asked myself why I had the bad luck to wind up with two husbands who beat me. I asked myself what I had been doin'—and kept on doin'—that would make a man think he ought to beat me. Now, I didn't think all men was like that, 'cause Grandpa was the nicest man you ever saw. He loved Grandma and Mama and all of us churren that was born 'fore he died. And you know what I decided? I decided that if Dave or any man ever beat me again, he was gon' earn the privilege. I remembered what Mama done that made Papa stop beatin' her. She let 'im know that if he hit her, she was gon' kill 'im. . . . So, the very next time Dave went out and got drunk and come in the kitchen talkin' 'bout he gon' beat me, I didn't act scared or look scared. I pulled out the butcher knife, and I looked 'im right in his old red, beady eyes, and I walked a little closer to 'im, and I told 'im if he thought he could beat me, he could go 'head and try, but he better think about it long and hard 'cause I was gon' slice his fat stomach open and let the air out of it, and he was gon' be able to see his feet for once."

"Why'd he b'lieve you," asked Booker, "since you hadn't ever cut him before?"

"I hadn't ever got a butcher knife out after him before, either," Helen answered. "I hadn't ever looked like I won't scared to kill 'im before. He could see in my eyes that I was not playin'. And you know what else I told 'im? I said, 'You so much as touch me wrong, and if I can't get you then, I bet you better not ever go sleep 'round here again, 'cause I'm gon' bash your big ole empty head in with one of these here cast-iron skillets flatter'n the flat side of a flat iron." Everyone howled with laughter.

"How long ago was that?" asked Esther.

"'Bout thirty-three years," Helen replied, and everyone laughed again. "After that was when he started to get religion, and now he's a preacher. I bet there's a whole lot of preachers out there who heard the call 'cause of a iron skillet or a ice pick or a pot of boilin' water."

"I wish somethin' had happened to change Joe," said Peggy. "Of course, I'm thinkin' 'bout divorcin' him. He ain't never hit me, but the things he say and the way he make me feel! He so jealous, and he always tryin' to make me feel bad 'bout myself. He don't ever compliment me, but the minute some other man say, 'You lookin' mighty nice, Mrs. Wright,' I have to hear his mouth for a month at least talkin' 'bout how fast I am. And anything good happen to me, he try to pull me down. When I got that job at Belk-Tyler's, all y'all tellin' me how proud y'all are of me, and Joe sayin' they just put a nigger in there to get other niggers goin' in there to spend their money. I said, 'Joe, black folks been goin' in Belk's since it opened, I reckon, and they gon' keep on goin' in there, whether I work there or not. Where else they gon' go, 'lessen you gon' open up a department store?' Well, that shut 'im up, 'cause he ain't gon' do nothin' but talk. I get tired of folks like that. They don't never lift you up none."

"Papa was like that," said Esther. "Mama was just as pretty

as Helen. Papa use to go 'round with all kinds of old ugly women. He thought he was a sport, but Mama was much better lookin' than he was. I don't think he wanted her to know how pretty she was. I remember he called her 'sausage lips' one time."

"I called Clara some hard names, too," said Booker, referring to his first wife. "But none of y'all can sit here and tell me she ain't a clinker."

"Why'd you marry her if you thought she was so ugly?" Myra asked.

"I was drunk. She and her whole family kept me drunk for three days. First thing I knew, I was married, and T-Bone was on the way. And Clara kept ownin' churren, and I kept beatin' a fit on her, tryin' to get her to leave me. But it seemed like she didn't hardly have no self-respect. I can't stand folks like that. Never could. Finally, she got the message that I was sho 'nuff gon' kill her, and she left."

"Why were you even messin' with her if she was so ugly to you and you didn't even like her? I ain't never messed with no ugly woman," said Tommy Lee.

"'Cause I was stupid," Booker answered. "I wouldn't do it again. Mama use to say, 'Don't mess with nobody you wouldn't marry,' and she was right. Come to think of it, why'd you marry Louis, Myra? He near 'bout as ugly as Clara."

"I really loved him," said Myra. "He's just a beautiful person inside, kind as he can be. And I just don't think lovin' somebody can be all about how they look, long as they neat and clean. If Louis had quit drinkin', I'd be married to 'im right now. But he was too weak, couldn't do without that bottle, as y'all know, so I had to throw him out. When he lost the fourth job 'cause of whiskey, I had to get rid of him. He won't good for the churren. I ain't gon' let no man mess my churren up."

"I don't blame you, Myra," said Esther. "And even though it took her a long time to get there, that's one of the things I admire the most about Mama. I b'lieve she got rid of Papa 'cause he was so bad for the whole family. I ain't never known her to court nobody after Papa left, but I know men tried. She was a hard-workin' woman, and she just devoted her whole life, every day of it 'til we got grown, to raisin' us. I really do think that she decided that pleasure for herself in this world didn't matter. I believe she wanted to give us as good a life and as normal a life as she could, and no cost to herself could be too great. Of course, we had already been messed up some by seein' and hearin' all the beatin's she took from Papa. What I do is I try to keep any of that from seepin' out of me and gettin' to my husband and churren."

"How do you do that, Esther?" asked Peggy.

"Well, I got a good husband, which is very important," Esther replied. "Charlie is so nice to me. He don't ever try to make me feel bad, and he loves our churren. We just work together to try to have somethin'. We try to look out for the churren's future by makin' sure they get a good education. But y'all know what? One of the main things is I don't think the world owes me a thing. Never have. Whatever I didn't get when I was comin' up—whether it's love from Papa or toys or clothes or food—whatever I didn't have, I just didn't have it, and that's that. I ain't gon' dwell on it, and I sho ain't gon' take it out on my churren. They innocent. Charlie innocent, too. He ain't responsible one iota for anything that happened to me or didn't happen to me when I was comin' up. I don't want to live the way we used to have to live. I don't want my churren scared the way we was scared. I don't want none of that in my house 'cause it ain't got no place in my life now. It's just part of the past.

"And I 'clare I ain't gon' let no man beat me. I'm too good for that. I'm good as any man, and I teach my churren they good as anybody and better than nobody. And any love and attention I ever wanted when we was comin' up that I didn't get, if nobody gives it to me now, I give it to myself. I b'lieve in lovin' myself and tellin' myself I look good and I'm a good person. I can do that anytime I feel like it without takin' anything away from anybody. If I got to feel low for somebody else to feel good, then that somebody's got a problem that don't rightly have anything to do with me. I give myself compliments and love anytime I need them. 'Course, I don't have to do it too often 'cause Charlie and the churren tell me all the time."

"Everything Papa done that messed us up won't nothin' but the devil," said Tommy Lee, "and folks is the ones that got to stop the devil. Long as folks don't stop him, he gon' keep goin' from one generation right on down the line to the great-great-great grandchurren and even further'n that. We suffered from the evil the devil done through Papa, and who knows how long ago that all got started. Now, Esther stopped it in her family; just look at every one of her churren. I shoulda tried to stop it in my family way 'fore I did. But I was busy bein' selfish, thinkin' 'bout myself and what I thought somebody owed me 'fore I die, tryin' to make the world pay up, I reckon. Like Esther said, Mama was thinkin' 'bout us way more'n she thought about herself even though our life was so hard. And maybe that's why she stayed with Papa long as she did and also why she finally got the nerve to stand up to 'im and to get rid of 'im. I b'lieve everything she done was to try to give us a better chance."

"I hate to say this and she ain't even hardly cold yet," said Helen, "but Mama needed to think about somebody besides herself. I remember from the time I was really little, she use to always say Grandma didn't want her. But Grandma and Grandpa both was so good to her and to all of us. And when Papa was at his worst, Mama would still find time to complain about Grandma. And I use to think she ought to get over whatever she was mad with Grandma 'bout, specially with all the bad things that was goin' on in our lives 'cause of Papa. Grandma and Grandpa's was 'bout the only safe place we could go when Papa was around, and it sometime seemed like Mama didn't want us to have that, didn't want us to love Grandma.

"I know I got to work out the bad feelin's I got 'bout Papa. When you carryin' 'round dislike for somebody a long time, it's a real burden. It eats at you. I know after Papa and Mama split up for good and he come back that one time and asked us to forgive him, I know that won't enough. Part of the job is ours; we the ones got to do the forgivin.' Carryin' 'round all that resentment in your heart gets heavy. Now, love ain't like that; love is light, and that's why I hope and pray Mama realized that way 'fore she died.

"I remember the time Papa come home and put us outdoors, and he had Mama trapped in the house. . . ." She paused and looked at Peggy. "And I ain't never been scareder in my whole life, and for days afterwards I couldn't sleep. And then we learned Papa had lost Grandpa and Grandma's land, and we had to hurry up and find someplace to move . . . and thank God Mr. Haskins took us on as sharecroppers. Mama said Miz Haskins made him do it, said that woman was near 'bout a saint. Y'all watch. She'll be at the funeral tomorrow, and Mr. Haskins, too, if he's not doin' too poorly. I wouldn't be the least bit surprised if their churren showed up. The Haskins family loved Mama.

"I used to try to bargain with the Lord when Mama would be goin' on and on and on feelin' sorry for herself 'cause her real mama didn't want her, sayin' the same old things she always said 'bout Grandma done this to her and Grandma done that to her. I use to say to the Lord, 'Lord, just make Papa be half as nice to this family as Grandma been to Mama, and I'll serve you the rest of my life. I won't never mistreat another of your creatures long as I live.' Now, y'all know my prayer won't answered, but I've tried my best to hold up my end of the bargain even though I admit I've failed over and over again. I keep on tryin' 'cause that was my bargain all by myself. God didn't really enter into it. He didn't have anything to do with it. He don't take bribes. That's what we do. He don't need to improve."

30

Light

Sundays too my father got up early
and put his clothes on in the blueblack cold,
then with cracked hands that ached
from labor in the weekday weather made
banked fires blaze.

      from "Those Winter Sundays," Robert Hayden, 1966

IN THE EARLY MORNING, before the spangled stars had given way, before the sun's ruddy fingers had streaked the darkness with their brighter hues, Charlie stepped outside his back door and headed for the woodpile. A heavy frost, uncharacteristic for so late in April, had formed during the night and lay like dustings of sugar over the yard and fields. Stiffened under their icy coating, the blades of grass where Charlie walked crunched under his feet. The sound that they made—feet, frost, and grass—was like the pleasant crackling in Charlie's ears, from inside his mouth, when he chewed roasted peanuts, their slightly acrid bouquet filling his nose. Perhaps it was the imagined smell of roasted peanuts that first drew Charlie's nose to the actual smell of tobacco, and his eyes followed.

  At the edge of the driveway, on the side of the culvert that divided Charlie's front yard from the public's right-of-way, a man wearing a heavy overcoat and a fedora stood smoking. Charlie knew the man was smoking a cigar, not a cigarette or a pipe, because its neon tip, glowering in the darkness, was far too wide for a cigarette, and its shape was all wrong for a pipe. As fast as these thoughts came to him, Charlie straightened his body to a fully upright position, retaining the load of wood in his left arm and grabbing the axe with his right hand. Immediately he felt that the man was no one that he knew, and then, almost as quickly, that the man was no threat to Charlie or his family.

"You, there!" Charlie called out. "You lookin' for someone?"

"No, sir," the man answered. "I'm just admiring the view. Sun's going to rise up right out of the sound in a short while. The colors on the horizon are just starting to change. Gonna be prettier than silk flags."

"'Spect you right about that. . . . You lost? You visitin' folks 'round here I can he'p you find?" In the breaking grayness of dawn, Charlie could see and hear that the man was white and educated, and his clothes marked him as well-to-do.

"Thank you," the man answered, "but I believe I'm fine. My car's just a few feet up the road. I thought I'd watch the sun rise over the water, rather than over the treetops, which I don't think you can do in a lot of places around here. I figure the view's about perfect from your yard. Hope my car didn't wake you and your family."

"Not at all," said Charlie.

"You have a nice day," the man said. "It'll be a pretty one."

"Much obliged, and the same to you."

The stranger started to move toward the road.

"No need to leave, sir. Have a seat on the porch, if you like, and enjoy your sunrise. My wife'll have coffee ready shortly, breakfast, too. You welcome to come in and have some."

"I certainly thank you, but in a few minutes I'll be getting along to the Haskins place. They're family of mine."

"Nobody 'round here' got better family than the Haskins," said Charlie. "They're 'bout the best there is, black or white."

"Kind of you to say that," answered the stranger. "I'll make sure to tell them what you've said." Then he moved off toward his car, the much anticipated sunrise apparently forgotten. Charlie dropped the axe that he had been holding, and when he reached the door to the back porch, he heard the whine of the ignition as the man started his car and pulled off.

* * *

Hours after morning had broken, the house teemed with family, some of whom had come a great distance and needed room to change into their funeral clothes. The single bathroom seemed to sputter and groan from over usage, so Charlie and Esther's children filled basins at the kitchen sink and hid in corners of their bedrooms to wash and dress themselves. Having bathed prior to daylight, long before the subdued hum of company had begun to curl like smoke against the rafters, Esther and Charlie were fully dressed for the service. They moved through the crowd offering a brunch of boiled eggs, sliced ham, sharp cheddar cheese, pear preserves, sausage links, fried white and sweet potatoes, light bread, tea, and Kool-Aid, prepared by Esther that morning and laid out in the dining room with Charlie's help. The light repast was appetizing and delicious, though as cold as Bess's body, already enroute from the colored funeral parlor in Chesterton to the house, its last stop before the church.

"You think anybody'll want to eat this stuff cold?" Esther had asked Charlie as they'd hurried to complete the preparations.

"This kinda food s'posed to be served cold," Charlie had responded.

The hungry had helped themselves, and some had been thoughtful enough to wash and dry their dishes that would certainly be needed for dinner following the funeral. Already the kitchen and back porch were stacked with foods prepared by friends and neighbors, identified by names scribbled on masking tape stuck to bowls and platters, for the post-funeral meal. Cakes, pies, cobblers, yeast rolls, potato salad, collards, cabbage, string beans, fried chicken, baked ham, roast tenderloin, roast beef, deviled eggs, pickled beets, pickled watermelon rind, and more—all to sit for a few hours without refrigeration. Then their tin-foil and plastic-wrap covers would be removed, and they would be laid out to satisfy the living in honor of the dead.

"Dinner's gon' be cold, too," Charlie had reminded Esther mischievously, "and some of them women bringin' food can't even cook. But that won't stop folks from eatin' near 'bout everything that's set out. Now, me, I ain't eatin' nothin' but what you cooked if I have to go in the kitchen and get it out the pot. You the best cook I ever met, thousand times better'n my own mama. Thousand times better'n yours, too!"

"Hush up, Charlie," said Esther. "You just sayin' that to humor me, and you know you not s'posed to speak ill of the dead."

"I'm just tellin' the truth," Charlie said, smiling at his wife. "The truth's the light. The dead know that. And for them that didn't know it in life, it's the first thing they learn when they get to the other side. If you don't b'lieve me, just ask anyone who's crossed over Jordan and come back."

"What haints you been talkin' to, Charlie?" Esther asked, smiling.

"Plenty," said Charlie. "See, they get mighty lonesome sleepin' by theirself. Pay 'em a little attention, and even the quiet ones'll talk more'n a preacher. You can't shut 'em up. They're noisier than a bottle tree tryin' to catch spirits in a March wind!"

"And how many spirits you ever caught, Charlie?"

"I thought I was 'bout to snag one first thing this mornin' when I went out to get wood for the stove and fireplace."

Esther smirked at Charlie and rolled her eyes in faked exasperation.

"Now, all jokin' aside, Esther, there *was* a man out there in the front yard, a dressed-up white fellow, just smokin' a big ole cigar."

"Why was he in our yard, Charlie?" Esther was clearly agitated now. "What'd he want? Only time white folks ever come up here just lookin' was years ago when that old poor white trash woman Papa courted come up here in a car with three men, and I was in the kitchen, and I saw her and recognized her through the kitchen window. I hadn't seen her since I was a child and she used to hang 'round our house with Papa all the time when Mama was off workin' like a dog. Remember, I told you to tell that trash to get out my yard. I don't think I can stand nothin' like that on the day we buryin' Mama."

Charlie took her in his arms. "Ain't nothin' like that, Esther," he said. "There's nothin' trashy 'bout the man was out there this morning. He's some kin to the Haskins family. He said he just stopped to see the sun rise. Thought it'd be mighty pretty from our yard. Maybe he ain't never seen the sun rising from the Haskins place where it's spectacular, and the shoreline seem like it goes on for miles and miles. He was very polite, very friendly, and after we spoke and all, he got in his car and left."

Charlie did not mention that the man had been facing the house, not the sound—which meant that his back was to the east where the sun would surely rise—and he'd been so lost in thought that he'd seemed shocked and embarrassed when Charlie first noticed him and called out a greeting in the early dawn.

31

Revelations

Does man love Art? Man visits Art, but squirms.
Art hurts. Art urges voyages—
and it is easier to stay at home. . . .

from "Negro Hero," Gwendolyn Brooks, 1967

ON THE DAY after Bess's funeral, her children gathered at Esther's house to carry out the simple task of dividing among themselves their mother's earthly possessions. Having been buried barefoot and in a corpse's lacy dress-front, Bess had left three everyday cotton frocks. For church and other dressy occasions, she had a gray gabardine skirt, two blouses, one light blue and the other a creamy yellow, and a light brown tweed wool suit. She had left a tan cardigan, really a man's sweater, and a lightweight, unlined dark gray winter coat. She had a pair of black string-up dress shoes with thick, two-inch heels. Her everyday shoes were brown oxfords. She owned two plain Sunday hats, one in gray felt for winter, the other in beige straw for summer. Her everyday straw hat had begun to unravel from its brim's edge after a decade's battle against sun and rain. Her few articles of underwear and nightgowns were threadbare, and her cotton stockings had been darned and re-darned at the toe and heel.

"Mama, why don't you let me get you a few things? You deserve a few nice things, hard as you done worked all your life," Esther would say.

"I got plenty," Bess would reply. "Now, you go wastin' money buyin' fripp'ry for me, all it's gon' do is lay here in its store wrappin', pushin' me to my grave so the next person can hurry up and use it. We don' need more'n we need."

Bess had left a pocketbook—black patent with a tortoise-shell clasp—a pair of white cotton gloves, and four white cotton handkerchiefs with tiny flowers embroidered in one corner. There was not one piece of jewelry or other decorative adornment among her possessions, not one watch, ring, bracelet, necklace, brooch, pin, or earring. Helen, chosen by Bess during her latter years to take care of her money, gave an accounting of her mother's financial position after deducting for funeral expenses. Bess had left eighty-four dollars and twenty-two cents, a little more than two cents shy of one dollar for every year that she had lived.

"Looks like we all get 'bout twelve dollars apiece," said Peggy.

"Looks like we don't get anything!" Helen contradicted her. "Those few dollars Mama left should stay right here with Esther and Charlie. Mama lived here all these years and never paid a penny. Every time she flushed a toilet or ate a meal, it cost Esther and Charlie, and they ain't never complained. Any of you thinkin' 'bout claimin' that twelve dollars should be prepared to show that you gave twelve dollars to Mama's upkeep over her last years. I myself gave nothin', offered nothin', and have rights to nothin' 'ceptin' *things* that she left."

"You right, Helen," said Booker. "And don't think for a minute you gon' get me to wear any of Mama's clothes. Bet Tommy Lee'd look good in her Sunday shoes, though, if them flat bottomed boats of his wasn't so big." A white man sitting in a corner of the dining room laughed louder than anyone else present, and only then did Bess's children notice him.

"Sorry I startled you," he said. "I've been sitting here awhile—ever so kindly let in by your husband to wait for you all to get here," he told Esther, "and I felt so comfortable I must have dozed off 'til right then. I can't tell you all how sorry I am for your loss. My name's Solomon Lowrey. Family and friends call me Solly." He stood and moved from one of Bess's children to the next, shaking their hands and correctly naming each of them, as they murmured, visibly puzzled over his presence, "Nice to meet you," "Welcome," "Glad you're here," and the like.

"I'm from Lumberton," he continued, "and if Esther will allow me to use the phone to call my sister Mabel Haskins, she'll come right over and help me present some gifts I've brought along."

"Mrs. Haskins your sister?" someone murmured.

"You welcome to the phone, Mr. Lowrey," Esther said. "It's right on the table there, by the door. . . . Did you first meet Charlie yesterday morning?"

"I'm the one," said Solly. "He caught me doing a little sky gazing just before sunrise. I got up here from Lumberton a bit quicker than I thought I would, and I decided I'd kill some time rather than show up at Mabel's that early."

"I remember seeing you at the funeral," said Tommy Lee. "We 'preciate you for attendin'."

"I wouldn't have missed it for the world," said Solly, smiling. "I'll be right back."

Bess's children were dazed. They felt uncertain, expectant. What gifts did this man have for them, and why? Their eyes swept each others' faces.

"Mama always said her mama was a full-blooded Indian from the Lumberton area," Helen said softly, tentatively. "But he ain't no Indian. Mrs. Haskins neither. Maybe they know somethin' of Mama's Indian folks."

They all heard Solly's brief telephone exchange: "Mabel, it's time." Then he was back in the room, and they did not pursue Helen's whispered musings.

"Now, I hope I'm not making you too nervous," Solly said reassuringly. "You just lost your mother, but I believe she would be gladdened by the contents of these valises." He gestured toward two wide leather portfolios placed against the wall where he had been sitting in the dining room. For the first time, Bess's children noticed the cases, clearly handmade with great skill from leather as soft as doe skin, decorated with renderings of birds and animals, their necks festooned in beaded halters, their eyes like flashing jewels reflecting waning light.

"The gifts that Mabel and I bring today are part spiritual, part material, and all from the heart. What we receive in return will be beyond value to us and to all our kin. These gifts to you were made over a period of decades. And in a minute, when Mabel gets here, I'm going to open them up, and the valises and all that's in them are yours, if you want them."

When Mabel Haskins was a part of their circle, Solly laid out the contents of the valises, fifty-seven portraits of Bess, each labeled with her name and age from the time that she was sixty-two years old, reaching back until she was a child of four or five. "Bess at 62 yrs.," the caption under the first one read.

"That's Mama!" Myra exclaimed when Solly had taken out the first portrait and laid it on the dining table. Bess's children cried, laughed, and hugged each other as they traced the regression of their mother's years. Ecstatic as brand-new parents witnessing the mystery of easy childbirth, they spoke of how Bess had looked just like them or their own children. They exclaimed over her beauty, her shapeliness, the softness of her face, her warm smile, and her kind eyes.

"We never saw that ease and gentleness in Mama," said Tommy Lee, choking back tears.

"Who was it that saw this peaceful spirit? Who saw this happiness, this love in her face?" Peggy asked.

"The story is long," answered Solly, "and its events took place long ago. Mabel and I will tell you the story as our father Samuel told it to me. Will it be true? We know that some of it will be, but as for the rest, we cannot judge, for facts are often false and fiction true. Also, neither of us was there except for the part at the very end. We can swear, however, that our father was honorable and truthful as the day is long."

"We do swear it," said Mabel, "of our father and of our mother, too."

Then Solly held them spellbound as he related Samuel's story in Samuel's own words:

* * *

Your mother and I were born and raised here in Lumberton, as you know already. When I was a young man, I began to take notice of your mother's gifts from the Great Spirit and of her kindly ways, and so I persuaded her to marry me, and I asked her father for his permission. He agreed, but before doing so he said:

"How will you take care of my youngest daughter? She is closer to my heart than all of the others because she is the last and there can be no more after her. As your own father has done, I have cared for my family by farming the land, hunting game, and fishing the river and streams. But the forests are still struggling from Sherman's fiery march to the sea, and nowadays it can be hard for a young man to find a place to farm. I know you are smart, hard-working—but sometimes a man needs more than his will. How can I know that you will be able to provide for my daughter?"

"All that you say is true," I replied, "and I have thought your words

and have answered your questions. When Mary and I are married, I will go to Georgia where the woods are thick with aged pines whose veins are rich with turpentine. I will take Mary with me, and we will make a fair living from our wages in the turpentine forests and from the old ways of living upon the bounty of the land. In some of the darkest hours of our history, our people have relied upon the ancient skills and knowledge, and they have served us well."

"So I shall lose my youngest daughter to Georgia forever?" the old man asked. "Georgia is a distant place."

"In a few years, less than ten, closer to five, we shall return ready to resume our happy lives among our people. Our children will play about your knees and will profit from the love and wisdom of our elders."

In time, the old man gave his blessing, and Mary and I were married as we had planned. On the morning that we were to leave for Georgia, our belongings protected in leather knapsacks, two on each of our horses and two on the spare mare that we took with us, the sky split in equal halves and deluge after deluge of water poured from the gorge that formed between the clouds. We watched for two hours as the swamp waters rose and the path from your grandparents' home to the main road was practically submerged in water. We saw a snapping turtle that was trudging slowly from the cow pasture beside the road, suddenly swept up by the angry waters rushing into the roadside ditch. We saw the turtle climb upon a floating tree branch in the roadway and ride that limb like a brave upon a stallion.

"No leaving yet," said my father, and it was well past the noonday meal, a royal repast laid out by my mother, before the rent in the sky was sewn shut and the clouds thinned and moved to let the sun through. When we left, a rainbow arched the clearing, and the land drank the flood as if it had been thirsty and the rains had rained just enough.

We traveled by day, camped by night, and our journey gave us joy in seeing the country and being together as man and wife. It was as if the rainbow that we had seen over the farmland had stayed around our shoulders.

When we were finally in Georgia, we went for work at the turpentine camp near Altoona. You could smell the thick smell of pitch as you approached the turpentine still, and you could hear the farther off voices of workers singing. I could hardly wait to begin tapping the longleaf pines, attaching the buckets to catch the sluggish sap, and carting the filled wooden barrels to the still. I was eager to start earning money, and the sounds of the camp were full of life and promise.

Mary and I had accepted food and lodging at the camp as part of our wages, knowing that we could get ahead much faster without the expense of renting a place in Altoona. Women worked in the turpentine camps, and Mary was to work alongside me, but we had just completed a long trip on horseback, and I thought she should get some rest that first day. So Mary cleaned up our tiny cabin before lying down to sleep a little.

I started work at two o'clock. Knock-off time was six o'clock. I had told Mary to rest all afternoon and start off fresh the next morning, but she had insisted that she'd come and find me in time to get in at least two hours of work. When she didn't come to join me after a couple of hours, and she still didn't come, I was happy thinking that she had fallen fast asleep and was getting much-needed recuperation time from our journey. When the knock-off whistle blew at six o'clock, I hurried to our cabin to wash up and fetch Mary. Supper would be served to the crew at 6:30.

There were no real windows in the cabin, just a window-sized opening in the side wall with a little shutter that could be latched shut. The door to the cabin was closed, and when I opened it, it was stifling hot and almost pitch black inside, the window shutter also being closed. I heard whimpering like a hurt animal might make, coming from a corner of the cabin, and the hair stood up on the back of my neck. "Mary," I said. "Mary," and I blinked as my eyes adjusted to the dimness in the cabin. She was naked, and her face and body bore bruises where she had been beaten. And she had been defiled. "Who did this?" I said. When we had first arrived, she had fetched a bucket of water to our cabin for our use, and I made a bath of it for her, and I tried to wash the evil from her body and spirit.

Then I went quickly out of our cabin and joined the turpentiners in the chow line. I was looking for the garrulous, squat and ape-like black man who had brought a barrel of sap to the still when we were checking in. My hatred enabled me to eat the beans, corn bread, cabbage, and side meat served as my portion of food. I slaked my thirst with water after the salty meat, and I sat and observed as the man they called Joe African finished his meal and washed his own cup, plate, and utensils in the cauldron of hot, soapy water provided for that purpose. I observed him as he went to his cabin and fetched a juice harp and sat on a tree stump by his cabin door and began to play with little skill. And I noted his cabin in my mind and went into my own and held my wife before helping her to quietly repack our knapsacks. We did not lie upon the soiled bed but threw upon the floor a cowhide from among our possessions and lay together there.

"We have provisions from our journey," I said to Mary. "Won't you eat?"

She had no stomach for food, and I fetched fresh water and mixed a potion for her to drink, and then she slept.

When the earth had spun across the line from west to east, when the noises of snoring throats rivaled the chug of frogs from woods and low lands, I took the knife kept sharp for skinning hogs and deer, and I moved like a shadow to the cabin of the one who had hurt my wife. With one small thud, I forced open the door held by a wooden button, and I was upon him, my left hand holding his mouth and nose shut, my legs straddling his chest and arms, and he could not free himself. He fought hard to free himself, but he could not breathe. Before all the air went out of him, I lay the sharp side of the blade upon his neck so he would know that his time had come, and I hewed it to the neck bone, and heard the gush of blood and air escape his body and taint the atmosphere. I went to the river and cleansed myself, and then I returned to my cabin and awakened Mary. Like shadows we led our horses from the campsite, and we traveled far from that place of sorrow.

We traveled and worked, worked and then traveled, never staying very long in one place, always on the lookout for lawmen on our trail. In the first months after we left the turpentine camp, Mary found that she was going to have a child, but she did not know whether the child was ours or whether it had been spawned during the rape. We knew the child was innocent, whether mine or not, *and Mary was not willing to do away with it because it might be ours. So we waited, and we reckoned to kill the child when it was born if it was not mine.*

Our working many different jobs in many different places and constantly running from the law had brought us back to North Carolina, to the northeastern region. We marked the place near the Albemarle Sound where Mary would deliver, and after its first breath, if the baby was the rapist's, the waves would embrace it and rock it to eternal sleep. But when the little girl was born, we could not tell whether she carried the rapist's blood or my own, so we nourished her. We grew attached to her even though, soon enough, it became clear from her dark skin and grizzled hair that she had sprung from the rapist's seed. She had Mary's beautiful gray eyes, as do you and Mabel.

When Mary knew that she was carrying you, your half-sister was almost four years old. Then we planned our return to this land, to our people amongst whom you and your sister would be born and raised. We had grown weary of hiding in swamps and in outposts among strangers, and we wanted to return home. And I say to you, my son, and to God Almighty, I now understand that the rape of your mother, the murder of her attacker, the birth and the giving away of the rapist's child when she was four years old may be nothing more than a single dewdrop on desert sand compared with all the events spanning all the human lives that have ever been. But what had happened to us loomed in our sleeping and waking hours like a scythe held aloft, ready to drop upon us at any turn. So we gave the child away to a good home, and we returned to our people, resurrecting ourselves in our own past image. I have tried to live an upstanding life. I thank God that I was allowed to live free, as I believe I deserved to live free. But how sure would my freedom have been if a judge or jury had decided my fate?

Will you decide that man should punish me for what I have freely confessed to you that I have done? If you are hell-bent on catching a murderer when you don't know the facts, shouldn't you also look within the house and heart of your own father, whose true confession of murder you surely have heard? Are you sure that Hitchy murdered Annie Mae? If Hitchy did return to this area, couldn't Acey have encountered him in the woods, discovered the truth about

Hitchy's affair with Annie Mae, and, overtaken by jealousy and rage, killed Annie Mae for her sin? Isn't it possible that Acey killed Hitchy, too, and that Hitchy lies rotting in a shallow grave somewhere in these woods right now? It's true that Hitchy could have committed the horrible crime of murdering Annie Mae without redeemable provocation. He could be running right now from the law and from justice, if he is guilty. But he can't run from himself, son. He can't run from his mind and heart and spirit any more than he can run from the devil. If he unjustifiably killed one of God's children, how could he separate himself from such evil? I'm telling you that if he is guilty, he will not escape. The devil's got a faster steed than he does. If he owes the devil, I guarantee you he's going to pay.

* * *

"In her heart," Mabel said, "our mother never gave up the daughter whom she gave away. And every year she created one of these portraits showing how she imagined her daughter had grown and changed over the previous year. She drew the last portrait in 1952 when her sight was failing. Of course, none of these likenesses is based on the way Bess actually looked at the time Mama made them, but only on a memory of how she looked as a little child and on vivid dreams of how the years would have changed her. Solly and I have spent most of our lives without knowledge that we had a half-sister, while here she was—someone I saw all the time, someone for whom I deeply cared. We are grateful for Mama's sake that her memory and her regret over losing her first child became an outpouring of creative restitution, an absolute outpouring of restitution and love. Our parents raised a black girl named Annie Mae, the one our father was talking about with Solly, and she too was lost to us many, many years ago through a senseless, unsolved murder."

"We're all sorry for your loss," said Tommy Lee.

"You all sure don't look no ways Indian," Booker murmured.

"Many among our tribe look as white as we do," Solly explained. "Remember reading about the Lost Colony? We believe that our people are the descendants of the English settlers from the Lost Colony of Roanoke and the Hatteras Indians who rescued them way back in the fifteen hundreds. Some people still think the so-called Lost Colony just disappeared, but we've been hidden in plain sight all along. Now, it has been proved that we descended from the English. Our bloodline has been traced all the way back to Great Britain, and many of our last names are English, too."

"There's a town near here," said Myra, "where all the colored folks look like they white. They say it's always been so. But everybody in the town knows who's colored and who's white. If the blacks want to pass for white, they have to leave and go someplace where don't nobody know them. If the whites wanted to pass for colored, they probably would be run out of town. I don't think we ought to ever tell folks 'bout this. Folks down here get confused easy. They wouldn't say anything much to us, but they might to you all," she added, looking at Mabel.

"That's why we ain't never gon' tell anybody other than the fam'ly 'bout this," said Helen, looking at her siblings. "It ain't nobody's business, 'cept ours."

"Everybody know we mixed already," said Tommy Lee. "Everybody known all along that Papa mixed, and everybody known that Mama part Indian, too. There's so many black folks mixed that it don't seem to hurt 'em. In many places, light skin black folks might even get 'long better'n dark skin ones. Ain't nothin' new 'bout our fam'ly situation regardin' race. But we don't have no call to go tellin' folks Mrs. Haskins is Indian. It won't help nobody."

"Y'all are right," said Booker. "These white folks 'round here mostly think they a hundred percent white. They might not take too kindly to knowin' Mrs. Haskins is Indian, and she and her churren and grandchurren got to live here."

Both Mabel and Solly were smiling a little, deeply appreciative of the strategies being set forth by Bess's children to protect the racial identity of their newly discovered relatives.

"Who you are is a state of mind," said Mabel. "Sometimes, if you're committed to your own values and principles, you can live as yourself. My life is a testament to that, as are the lives of my children. But I have not worn a sign saying 'I am an Indian' any more than Bess wore such a sign, and people have judged me on my looks more than on my heart, mind, and actions. That is why Bess was lost to my mother, and to my father, too, because they feared that our people would have judged Bess—would have judged them all—on Bess's appearance. I think they may have been wrong about that because people *can* let go of prejudice and hatred. From way before we were married, my husband has known of my Indian heritage. And since the day three weeks ago when Solly and I found these portraits in the attic of the barn where Mama painted and I recognized Bess, we have known who our sister was. While Solly and I agonized over the best way to approach Bess with proof of our kinship, she slipped through our fingers like water! My husband's arms are open to us all as ours are open to you, as we hope yours will be open to us, and as the ancestors' arms are always open to all of us, whatever race we call ourselves. You tell them, Solly, what you saw."

Solly stared above their heads at an undefined point on the far wall. "On the morning that I came to mark Bess's passing," he said quietly, almost as if talking to himself, "I was able to pick this house as where she had lived because what looked like thousands of our ancestors were here, even at daybreak, on that early morning." Solly shifted his gaze to the faces of his audience, whose eyes were riveted upon him. He continued speaking with both certainty and incredulity. "They stood in remembrance and reverence from the house, to the yard, to the highway, and along the fields and woods from here clear to the church where Bess would be buried. Later, they stood thousands deep and bore witness at her grave. Surely they had been present at her passing over and had welcomed her with open arms. I am certain that my mother, as well as my father, was first among the ancestors to usher her to her grave. I saw them clear as day standing at the front of this house on the morning of Bess's funeral. I saw them with my own eyes, and they saw me and acknowledged me, and they called me by my name."